Beyond
The
Maze

Beyond
The
Maze

Chris Tate

authorHOUSE®

AuthorHouse™
1663 Liberty Drive
Bloomington, IN 47403
www.authorhouse.com
Phone: 1-800-839-8640

Published by AuthorHouse   12/03/2012

ISBN: 978-1-4772-4998-7 (sc)
ISBN: 978-1-4772-4999-4 (e)

*Dedicated to
Michael,
Robert, and Meghan.*

CONTENTS

CHAPTER ONE

Their new surroundings

Peter and Jake were sitting in the back of their fathers car trying to think of the best way to occupy their minds, as it was a lot further away to their new home in the countryside than they originally thought. It was that far away that they were beginning to wonder if they would ever see any of their friends again, but the thought of another six weeks holiday before they joined their new school in Little Thornton cheered them up greatly, and they were both ready to explore their new surroundings every spare hour of each day.

Peter and Jake were twelve year old twins, and the fact that they were identical twins added to their mischievousness and wicked sense of humour. Many times had they played tricks on their teachers and friends by swapping their clothing halfway through the day, or attending each others lessons that one of them didn't like. This was one of the reasons why they seemed to spend most of their school hours in the headmasters office, writing lines like . . . .

I must not tease the teacher . . . .
I must not pretend to be my brother . . . .
I must not sit my brothers exams for him . . . .

Another one of their favourite tricks was to confuse whatever nanny they had at the time, and as a result, they never did have the same nanny for any great length of time.

Jake used to convince the nanny that it *'mustn't have been him'* she had told *'Don't do that'* and that it *'must have been Peter'* she had told, or vice versa, depending whoever it was getting a telling off at the time. This would often have their nanny close to tears at the end of some days with all the jokes and pranks that they loved to play, and as soon as the boys father would return home, nanny would leave as soon as possible.

Peter and Jake were identical in most ways, except a few that could not be noticed only by looking at them. Peter was a little quieter and slightly more intelligent than Jake, and Jake was a little rougher around the edges, always being the first to back chat anyone who'd confront them, or to be the one who would sort a problem out in the playground at school, whether it was himself or his brother that was being teased.

The journey seemed to be taking forever, and Peter was thinking of ways to relieve the boredom. He tapped Jake on the knee as he had an idea on how to while away the time on their already too long journey.

'I spy with my little eye,' said Peter.

'Boring'. said Jake with a two note tune.

'Come on Jake, it'll give us something to do'.

'Oh ok then'. Jake huffed.

'I spy with my little eye . . . ,' said Peter as he looked around for something that he thought Jake would never guess the answer to. 'something beginning with . . . . B!'

Jake looked out of the window, inside the car and out of the window again.

'Barn?'. said Jake.

'No'. said Peter.

'Badger?'

'No!'

'Brakes?' said their father, and Jake rolled his eyes, followed by a loud tut.

'Do you know how to play 'I spy' dad?' asked Jake, 'It's got to be something we can see, silly!' and he continued to look around for anything else he could see beginning with the letter B.

'It's very easy this one Jake! said Peter, who was trying his best to wind his brother up.

'I know,' shouted an excited Jake, 'Balloon?' he said as he looked through the sunroof of the car.

'Correct! Now it's your turn.' Peter said, and he was already looking out of the window for objects he could use on his next turn.

'I spy . . . with my little eye . . .' Jake said while still thinking hard, 'something beginning with . . . . S!'

Jake was really pleased with himself as he thought that Peter would never guess what he had just seen out of the window, and within five seconds Peter had his first guess.

'Silo?'

'Tut', Jake tutted, 'yes! How did you guess so quickly?' Jake folded his arms in protest and accused Peter of cheating.

'Can I have a go?' asked their father.

'Ok', said Jake, 'but no hard ones, we're only twelve don't forget.'

'Ok then, here goes, are you ready?' he said smiling.

'Hurry up daddy.' said Peter, as he couldn't wait to try and guess what it was that his father had just seen.

'I spy, with my little eye . . . . something beginning with . . . . O.N.H.'

'O.N.H?' said a confused Peter. 'Come on daddy, even I know there are no words in the English dictionary that begin with O.N.H! You'll have to think of something different than that!'

'Do you give in?' asked their father.

'We give in.' they both said together.

'Our new home!' he said with a grin, and he turned right into a tree lined dirt track that led to the largest and oldest looking house Peter and Jake had ever set their eyes upon.

'Is that our new home daddy?' asked Peter.

'Certainly is!' his father said proudly.

'But it's huge daddy.' Peter said with his eyes as wide as the smile he was wearing.

'Does that mean we can now have a room each then dad? Please?' Jake pleaded.

For as long as he could remember, he and Peter had always shared a bedroom, and he thought it was about time they were given a bit more privacy, 'After all we're nearly teenagers now.' he said, trying his best to sound a lot older.

'Let's get ourselves inside first Jake, then we can talk about it after I've shown you around the place eh?' their father suggested, and he parked the car in front of the huge oak door that stood proudly at the front of the house.

Peter was out of the car first, and his eyes didn't know where to look first. The look of excitement told his father that he was very happy with what he'd seen so far, and when Jake joined him, they were already planning their first adventure around the grounds.

'How big is the garden at the back of the house daddy?' asked Peter.

'Three acres.' his father answered with a smile.

'Three acres?' asked Jake in amazement, but didn't really know what three acres actually looked like.

'Yes, so after we have a good look around the house and a bite to eat, we'll spend some time walking around the grounds. What do you say?'

'Yeeey!' they both shouted, and they raced toward the huge front door to see who could get to the large cast iron knocker first.

'I won!' said Jake, and after a tribal victory dance grabbed the knocker with both hands. He tried to lift it high enough to make a good sound when he'd let it go, but before he could let go, Peter had found a small rope hanging at the side of the door and he pulled it.

DONG . . .

The eerie sound of the old chime made them realize how big and empty the old house was, and it gave the boys goose bumps.

'It won't sound so empty when the furniture van arrives boys.' their father said as he noticed the expressions on their faces. 'Oh, talk of the devil!' he said, and they all turned around to see a large white van carefully steering through the trees on the narrow dirt track that was just wide enough for the wheels to fit on. 'Tell you what boys, why don't you two go around the back of the house and do a bit of exploring while I give the removal men a hand. Now meet me back here in forty five minutes ok? And don't wonder outside the grounds, do you hear?'

'But I haven't got a watch daddy, how are we supposed to know when our time is up?' asked Peter.

'Here,' said father as he took his wrist watch off. 'You can use this one. I put my old one on today as I knew I'd be helping the men to move the furniture in.

Peter put his fathers watch on, but realized it was far too big for his small wrists. So instead, he slid the watch all the way up his arm and past his elbow until it was tight enough not to rattle around. Jake was a bit jealous of the fact that Peter was given the watch and not himself, but that feeling didn't last long, as his favourite word was echoing around inside his head.

'Hurry Peter,' shouted Jake, 'let's explore, come on, hurry.'

'Now be careful you two!' shouted their father as Peter and Jake ran to the gate at the side of what looked like an old washhouse that was obviously adjoined to the house at a much later date.

It seemed to take forever to reach the back of their new house, and they couldn't believe how big it was. As they took the last turn they stopped dead in their tracks with their mouths open in awe.

The gardens sloped down to a larger area that was as flat as a snooker table, with lots of plants and hedges in a symmetrical pattern, and it was Peter who first realized what it was they were staring at.

'It's amazing.' said Jake.

'It's not,' said Peter, 'It's a maze!'

They looked at each other, they looked at the maze, then at each other once more, and they ran as fast as they could to what looked like the only gap through the ten foot high hedge that stood before them.

'Do you think we should give it a try?' asked Peter looking at his father's watch and wishing he had took note of the time he was given it.

'I don't know,' said Jake, wondering if they had enough time before they had to meet up with their father,

'We'd better not, just in case we get lost!' Peter suggested and they stood there for a few minutes longer imagining what the maze hid within it's high walls, lefts and rights and dead ends, and even more about what lay beyond the exit on the other side.

'Tomorrow!' said Jake, 'Tomorrow we get up early, get dressed and make a pack lunch in case we get lost. Then we'll have the best days exploring we've ever had. What do you say Peter?'

'Yes!' Peter agreed, 'Tomorrow we find out what is at the other end. Oh, and I'll bring my compass just in case!'

For the next half an hour, the boys raced around the rest of the gardens playing a game of tag, and at the same time were into every nook and cranny they had come across. Jake couldn't believe that their own back garden was even bigger than the school field they used to play football on before they moved to Little Thornton, and as he climbed an old statue of what he thought looked like a pixie of some sort, he looked around the area where they stood. Peter was soon busy climbing another statue that wasn't too far away from Jake, and as he looked at the back of their house, he noticed a small window that looked like it hadn't been washed on the inside or out for a very long time. It was sticking out from the attic, and it gave Peter an idea.

'Jake.' Peter shouted, 'look!'

Jake turned, and in doing so, nearly lost his footing on the pixie's knee that was sticking out as if it was running.

'What?' Jake asked, as he couldn't see what it was what Peter was pointing at.

'Can you see that little window on the top of the house?' he asked. and Jake had to reposition himself further to see.

'Yes, what about it?'

'If we can find that room where the window is, we can get a better look at the maze!' he said, and he didn't know why he had expected Jake to know what he had in mind.

'So what!' said Jake who hadn't caught on, and Peter wondered if he had inherited more of his fathers brain cells than his brother had.

'Well,' Peter carried on, 'we can make a drawing of the maze from there and be able to work out the correct route so we don't get lost when we go in there tomorrow!'

'Yes I know that!' shouted Jake, 'That's what I was going to say!' and Peter shook his head in disbelief.

Jake had always wished that he was as smart as his brother, and he wondered if it was because Peter was a whole seven minutes older than he was. He hated the fact that *he* was the youngest, and that was why he tried to make up for it in other ways, like being tougher, and sticking up for his older brother in the playground when it was necessary.

Peter looked at the watch he had strapped to his upper arm and thought that it must have been time to return to the front of the house to meet their father by now.

'Hey Jake, time to explore the house!' said Peter, as he knew that if he used the word explore, Jake would be rushing to be the first there, and not dilly dally like he often did.

Peter climbed down the statue to race Jake back to the house, and as he glanced back at the statue he was admiring the view from, he stopped and stared at it for a short while. Jake noticed that the race was off and joined Peter to see what Peter was looking at.

'What's up Peter?' asked Jake.

'I always imagined mum would look like that!' he said, and Jake turned to look at the statue to see if it was at all like *he* imagined what mum would have looked like. But Jake had to change the subject quickly, as to him, mother was a topic that would upset him if he thought about her for too long.

'Very pretty Peter,' said Jake. 'but we've got to get back. Come on!' he said, and gave Peter a friendly thump on the arm in order to bring his attention back to the race to meet their father.

The large oak door to the hallway was open and they could see their father carrying a cardboard box up the staircase, and having to stop every few steps in order to catch his breath. Peter and Jake saw that there were other small boxes at the bottom of the stairs that were waiting to be taken up and they each placed one under each arm. They were soon standing by their father and giggling at him for being so tired and sweaty, and they asked him which two bedrooms were theirs.

'We haven't talked about that yet boys,' he said, 'let's just concentrate on getting all of our belongings into the house first eh?'

Jake was the first as usual to tut loud enough for his father to hear and then followed him up to the first floor landing where some of the removal men were getting confused about what items went where.

There was one particular removal man that Peter and Jake thought was far too old to be doing that sort of strenuous job, as he was sitting on the edge of one of the many boxes with a handkerchief in one hand mopping the beads of sweat that were trickling from his brow. He was very breathless, but they noticed that every now and then he would look at his surroundings, almost with fondness, as if he were reminiscing of a time he had spent their as a child long ago.

Peter dropped one of the small boxes he was carrying and was relieved when there was no breaking sound coming from within.

'Oops a daisy!' said the old man still wiping his brow. 'Not broken I hope?'

'I don't think so.' said Peter who was unsure about talking to people he hadn't met before, and he opened the box to check. 'Just books.' he said to the old man who was smiling at him.

'Oh good.' he said. 'I love a good read myself. You know, I used to stay in this very house when I was a child, and back then there were lots of books to choose from. Some more interesting than others I might mention.'

The boys father couldn't help overhear this old man who was talking to one of his boys, and he stared at him until he caught his attention. The old man got up from the box and placed his handkerchief in his pocket and noticed that the boys father was looking at him with his index finger over his two lips. He smiled and nodded as if he knew why and he continued as best he could with the rest of the boxes that needed sorting into the right rooms.

'See you later.' he whispered to the boys as he passed, 'You're going to have so much fun here!' he said, and he held on to the bannister as he slowly descended the stairs.

'Who's that daddy?' asked Peter.

'I don't know, he's just one of the removal men, why?'

'He said he used to stay here when he was a boy!'

'I didn't hear him say that. All I heard him say was that you were going to have lots of fun here! Now hurry up and put these boxes away and I'll make us some dinner. Are you both hungry?' their father asked in an attempt to change the subject.

'Just a little.' said Peter.

'I'd rather do some more exploring dad!' said Jake.

'Later Jake, later. Come on, I'll make us some sandwiches and a large glass of pop to tide us over.'

Another loud tut came from Jake that his father ignored and they followed him down to the kitchen, to which Peter and Jake thought had looked like their old kitchen at school.

Peter had noticed that Jake was in deep thought as he wasn't complaining as much as he would have in the past if he was told he couldn't do what he wanted.

'What's the matter Jake? What are you thinking about?

Jake looked back at Peter, then to see if their father was looking the other way and whispered . . .

'I heard that man say he used to stay here when he was a child, and I'm sure dad heard him as well!'

'I heard him say that too, but why would daddy lie about that? Do you think there is something he doesn't want us to know or to find out?' asked Peter who had a look of great interest painted over his face.

'I don't know, but I'm going to find out.' said Jake with determination, and he made an excuse to his father about leaving something in the back seat of the car.

'Jake!' Peter tried to call him back, 'You didn't leave anything in the back of the car!'

'I know!' he whispered, and winked his eye.

'Jake!' shouted Peter once more, but he was gone.

Jake stood near the front of the house watching the removal men getting the last of the items out of the big white van, and he was trying to grab the old man's attention. Jake was trying to look deep into the back of the van, and he noticed that the old man that Peter had been talking to was the only one around, then thought about what he should ask him first.

'Erm, excuse me mister.' said Jake.

'Please,' said the old man, 'just call me Monte.' and he smiled at him.

'Excuse me Mr Monte, did I hear you say to my brother that you used to stay here when you were a boy?'

Monte looked around to see if the boys father was anywhere in sight, and when he realized that he wasn't, he walked over to Jake and whispered to him.

'Fear not young man, er what's your name?'

'Jake.'

'Oh, fear not Jake, for this is a place of magic and happiness. This old place hasn't always been a home, for when I was younger, this place was a summer school, and my friends and I had many a good summer in this old house and it's gardens! . . . . Until one day when we . . .'

Jake wondered why the old man had stopped talking, and wasn't very happy that he had stopped just when it was becoming more interesting. Then he turned to see his father standing at the old oak door, and he was giving the old man a strange look.

'Come on Jake, your sandwiches are ready.' he said, and the old man once again went about his business, not returning any eye contact with their father.

Jake was a little uneasy about the fact that his father didn't ask him about what they had been saying, and decided that he wouldn't say anything until he was asked.

Jake was happy that there were a few sandwiches waiting for him, as the excitement about the move and all the exploring they were about to undertake in the maze had given him an appetite he had never experienced, and it wasn't long before he was asking for more.

CHAPTER TWO

Who's Monte?

Their father, after a lot of arm twisting, finally agreed that the boys needed more of their own space now that they were nearly teenagers, and so he gave them adjoining rooms situated at the rear of the house. This pleased Peter and Jake so much, that they even agreed to go to their rooms earlier that night and go to bed. But going to bed early that night was not on their list of things to do. Both rooms had a good view of the gardens at the rear, and of the maze that lay a little further yonder, but Peter knew that if he could somehow get into the room in the attic, then he would have a birds eye view of the maze and be able to make a good drawing of it. From that, both himself and Jake could make a map. A map that was going to help them get to the other side of the maze and what lies yonder.

'I wonder if daddy would show us the room in the attic tomorrow!' said Peter as Jake was entering his room.

'Why? I thought you could just draw the maze from here. We've got a good view, and we can also see that there is nothing further after the maze.'

'I need to be higher up to see it properly Jake. Over there, look!' Peter pointed to the center of the maze where he could see a clearing. 'I wonder what that is in the middle.'

'I can't see anything!' said Jake with a mouthful of his snack.

'Exactly!' said Peter. 'That's why we need to be in the attic. The angle is too low to get the birds eye view we need to be able to draw it properly.'

'Suppose so.' said Jake, 'Anyway, I've came to tell you what Monte told me earlier on!'

'Who's Monte?' asked Peter.

'He's the old man who was nearly passing out earlier.' Jake reminded him.

'Oh yes, I forgot to ask you about him. So what did he tell you then?'

'Listen to this!' said an excited Jake. 'He told me that this place used to be a summer school, and that he used to stay here as a boy. He said that this place was a place of magic!'

'Magic?' asked Peter.

'Yes, magic! Then it was just getting interesting when dad turned up, and he never said anything after that.'

'I wonder why!' said Peter. 'Daddy *must* be hiding something from us. If this 'Monte' stopped talking when daddy turned up, he must have known that he shouldn't have been telling you what he was going to say.'

'I wonder what was so bad. What kind of summer school was this place, then?' asked Jake.

'I don't know.' admitted Peter, 'But I bet you all the money in the world that all the answers lie in the room in the attic!'

'Yeah.' said Jake with a smile that said 'Another adventure.'

Just then, Peters bedroom door opened and in walked their father. He saw that the boys were together in the same room and laughed to himself.

'All the time you boys have been going on about wanting you own rooms, and I find you both in the same room already? Come on, it's getting late and I thought we'd get up early in the morning and have a good look around the house. There are still a lot of rooms I haven't seen yet, and we have to decide on which room is the best to give to your new nanny.'

'Another one?' asked Jake with the pain in his little voice obvious.

'Yes another one!' said his father. 'If you two weren't playing your tricks and upsetting the nannies all the time, you'd have had the same one all along.'

'But do we really need one daddy? asked Peter, 'After all, it *is* the summer holidays!'

'All the more reason for why we need another one Peter. I have a lot of things I need to do and I'm going to be out of town most days. I suppose you're going to cook all your own meals? Or wash all you own clothes? And do all the housework? their father said, knowing that the thought of them doing all the chores themselves would help them to see reason.

'I think you're right dad,' Jake agreed. 'But I hope you get us a younger one this time, the last one smelled of soap!'

Their father giggled a little and assured them both that they'd get on very well with the next nanny as she was a lot younger than even himself.

'Oh good!' said Peter, 'When are we meeting her then daddy?'

'She'll be here at noon tomorrow, so I want you both to be up bright and early and in the bath. We have to find her a room before she arrives and I know how much you two love your adventures, so we're going to look at every room in the house.'

Peter realized that his father said 'every room' in the house, and hoped it included the room in the attic.

'Daddy?' asked Peter, 'How do we get into the room in the attic? We can't seem to find any stairs that lead us up to that room!'

'Why do you want to go up there? I don't think there is anything up there.' he said, but the boys noticed a look in his face that he was hiding something else, and it made them believe that when they finally see the room, it might give them more clues to the history of the house.

'So how would anyone get up there then?' asked Jake who didn't want it to be the end of the subject.

'Er . . . I don't know.' their father lied. 'We'll look tomorrow. I promise!'

Jake gave a small cheer, but then thought that 'If their father was willing to take them up there, there mustn't be anything to hide up there! Still, we'd be able to get the drawing done that would map the correct directions through the maze.' and went through to his own room to go to bed.

When their father retired to what he called 'his new study,' Peter went through the rest of the unopened boxes looking for his drawing paper and pencils. He wanted to have everything ready so there was no time wasted in the morning before their tour of the house.

'Goodnight boys,' their father shouted from the bottom of the stairs.

'Goodnight daddy.' shouted Peter.

'Goodnight dad.' shouted Jake.

CHAPTER THREE

Looking around

The sun shone brightly from the east and woke up Peter as there were no curtains in that room yet, and he looked at his fathers watch, that he still had from the day before. It was only seven thirty, and he couldn't yet hear any movement in the room next door. That didn't surprise him at all as Jake always found it hard to get out of bed in the mornings. He quickly found his slippers and ran through the door that joined his room and Jakes together then jumped up and down on the bottom of Jakes bed.

'Rise and shine lazy bones.' Peter shouted.

Jake kicked wildly at the sheets and threw his pillow at Peter, which was closely followed by his socks. Jake was always in a bad mood in the mornings, especially if he was woken before his alarm clock had sounded, but Peter knew exactly how to change the mood he was in by suggesting something that he knew he loved doing.

'Come on Jake,' Peter said, 'It's time to explore the house!'

Jake sat upright and stared at Peter with only one eye open.

'The attic!' he said, and from that point on, there was a race going on to see who could make it to the bathroom first.

'I won!' said Jake, and after a tribal victory dance, jumped into the large tub and pulled the shower curtain around himself.

The large chrome tap handles on the wall at the end of the bath tub were much larger than the ones he was used to, and it looked like they hadn't been turned on for a long time. With both hands, Jake tried his hardest to turn the cold tap anticlockwise, but it seemed to be welded shut. After a few more tries, he managed to turn it enough so it was free, but all he could hear was air rushing through the pipes, with small splashes of water spurting through the shower head at intervals. He then tried the hot tap handle and it seemed to be already free, but still nothing. Jake was about to give up when the shower burst into life, and he couldn't get out of the way quick enough. The shower covered his entire body with freezing cold murky brown water, which Jake thought that it smelled like something you would only find in a sewer.

Peter was standing at the wash basin trying to turn on the taps, and when he heard Jake yell, he turned to see his brother hanging off the shower curtain being ten times filthier than he was when he went in. It was the funniest thing Peter had seen in a long time, and he couldn't stop laughing at his brothers little mishap. He laughed and laughed until he saw that his brother was becoming angry with him, and he threw him a towel to clean himself up.

Jake was starting to look more normal when they heard their father walk past the bathroom door.

'Be sure to use the bath boys, as the shower isn't working properly yet!' he said, and that started Peter giggling again, which Jake was not too pleased about, and trying to change the subject, Peter asked Jake what *he* thought they might find in the attic, and expecting to hear something ridiculous, Peter was quite impressed when he listened to what it was that Jake had to say.

'I think that . . . when this was a summer school a long time ago, I think it was a school for bad children. There's probably things in the attic that proves what really went on, like tools they used to torture the really bad ones with, and old documents that prove it, and . . .'

Jakes imagination was going into overdrive, and Peter had to stop him to bring him back into the real world.

'Calm down Jake,' said Peter. 'What makes you think they would be tortured or anything like that? I thought that Monte told us that we'd have fun living here!'

'Yes but, why are people trying to hide things from us? It can't all of been good if there is anything to hide!'

'I suppose you're right Jake, what *is* there to hide?'

'We'll find out soon enough!' said Jake, 'Have you remembered your paper and pencils?'

'Yes, I put all my things in a bag last night to save time this morning.'

'Good, let's go down to the kitchen, I need some breakfast before I do anything else.'

Peter and Jake got dressed and off to the kitchen they went with a number of items they thought they'd need for the exploration of the house.

Peter had his bag, and inside was his drawing book, his pencils, eraser, and a ruler. Jake had his torch, his tape measure, and an old screwdriver he found on the ground outside. He didn't know if it would come in handy for anything, but he wanted to carry as many things as Peter was carrying.

They sat at the large table in the kitchen with their father and filled their bowls to the brim with cereal, and they shared the rest of the milk between themselves. Jake always had a large breakfast when he new they were about to go on an adventure, as he had learned from his mistakes in the past. Being stuck down a well all day without any breakfast or lunch, was not one of the best experiences he had ever had. So from then on, he always had the kind of breakfast that could last him all day if need be.

'Ok boys,' their father said as he picked up the empty bowls off the kitchen table, 'I think we should start from the bottom and work our way up! What do you two think?'

'I thought we were already at the bottom dad!' said Jake, a little confused.

'No no Jake, did I not tell you about the cellar?' he said in a creepy voice and held his hands up as if there were long claws on the ends of them.

'A cellar?' Jake cried, 'This just gets better every day!' he said, and he was already at the kitchen door waiting for his father and Peter to catch up.

Father led them to a part of the house they had not seen before, and he had with him a large bunch of keys that looked as old as the house.

They walked through what looked like an old greenhouse that was attached to the rear of the building, except this greenhouse was full of plant pots that only contained weeds and old dried out flowers. All the plant pots seemed to be attached to one another by a matrix of spiders cobwebs, and although Jake was the tougher of the two, he couldn't hide the shudder that shook his entire body as his hand brushed against a dead spider lying on its back on the top of a work bench.

'Here we are!' said their father as he searched through the bunch of keys hanging from his belt. 'This looks like the one!' he said, and after he unlocked the door to the cellar, he tied a tag onto the key and wrote 'Cellar door' onto it.

It was almost pitch black in the cellar as the lights had not worked for a very long time, and Jake was over the moon that his torch had come in very handy.

'Well done Jake.' said his father, 'Good idea of yours to bring your torch!' and Jake grinned from ear to ear. He was so used to Peter getting all of the attention that he'd almost forgotten what it was like to do something that wasn't naughty.

The torch was switched on and their eyes followed the circle of light as it swayed from left to right and up and down. It didn't look like there was much worth saving in the cellar apart from a couple of unopened bottles of whiskey, until Peters keen eye caught something that was worth a second look.

'Go back daddy, I saw something.' said Peter, pointlessly waving his finger in the dark to the direction of where he had spotted something.

'Where?' their father asked,

'Left, left, left, right a bit, up, stop!'

Father held the beam of light from the torch on what looked like a small statue, and Jake crept towards it as he couldn't see where he was placing his steps. The statue was of a small pixie that was situated on the very edge of a shelf, and it was in a position of climbing up onto the ledge with both its hands and one foot on the shelf, and with the other foot dangling off the side.

'Dad, can you reach it? I want a closer look.' said Jake who was standing on his tiptoes by this time.

Very carefully, his father reached for the small statue, and before handing it over to Jake, he shone the torch onto every part of it by turning it around in his hand.

'Fascinating!' he said, 'I think we should get this into the daylight and take a closer look.'

'Let me hold it dad.' said Jake, 'I promise I'll be very careful.'

Father gave the statue to Jake, and on the way back to the staircase he picked up the two bottles of whiskey.

'Oh daddy,' said Peter, 'you're not going to drink those are you?'

'Peter my boy,' said his father, 'A fine malt is like a fine woman!'

'What do you mean dad?' asked a curious Jake.

'The more mature the better. You'll understand more when you're a little older Jake.' he said with a smile that told Jake his father was looking forward to sampling the age of the old single malt.

'Does it smell like soap then dad?' asked Jake while remembering the last nanny they had.

Father shook his head and laughed as they all climbed the staircase and closed the cellar door behind them.

'Put that key in your pocket Peter, we've got a lot to get through today.' he said, and looked through the bunch of keys for the next place of interest. 'Now then,' he said, 'on with the tour!'

As they walked through the greenhouse, Jake remembered the dead spider, and he stayed far away from the workbench where he knew it lay.

They walked along the passageway that led to the kitchen then on to the large dining room, and when the boys entered that room, they thought that Monte must have been telling the truth when he said that the house used to be a summer school.

'The tables and chairs are definitely not the sort that a family would buy,' thought Peter, 'even if they *did* have twenty children!'

Peter even noticed some chewing gum that was stuck to one of the chair legs, and he looked around further to see if there was any more evidence to prove that Monte was in fact telling the truth.

'Look Peter.' Jake whispered loudly as he walked towards the side of a set of drawers, 'It's another little statue!' and he knelt down to slide his arm around the back of the draw unit that sat in the alcove.

'Wait!' shouted Peter, 'Let me have a look before you move it.' and Jake waited for his older brother to come over as he was curious to why he had stopped him from picking it up.

'Why?' asked Jake.

'Nothing!' he said, and Peter took the torch out of Jakes hand and knelt down next to Jake to see exactly what position the statue was in.

'This one's also in a weird position!' said Peter.

'What do you mean?' asked Jake.

'Remember the last one we found?'

'Yes?' he asked, still not knowing what his brother was going on about.

'Well, this one is also in a position that goes with it's surroundings!'

'That's what I was going to say!' Jake huffed, and again Peter shook his head in disbelief.

The statue was of another pixie, but this time the position the pixie was in was that of someone crawling on all fours, as if it were trying to get to somewhere and not have enough room to get through.

'Funny this statue would be in a position like that!' said Peter, and again Jake had an expression that told Peter that he didn't have a clue to what he was talking about.

'Put this one with the other one will you Jake.?' asked Peter, and Jake was more than happy with the request.

Jake now had two statues that his brother found interesting, and Jake was happy to be able to display them in his new bedroom. 'At least' he thought, 'whenever Peter was in *his* bedroom, there would be more to talk about than . . . 'What joke shall we play next?' or 'what's the next nanny going to be like?' But the day was proving to be better than they ever imagined, as when their father took them through to the next room, they wondered why they never heard about this room before.

This room was a library full of books and games, and it also had some old records, like what their father used to play at the old house.

'There's an old gramophone!' their father shouted from the other end of the room, 'I've never seen one of those for years!'

Father plugged it in and hoped for the best, and he was delighted to find that the nearly fifty year old music center was still in fine working order.

'I think I'll have a look through these old records later on tonight!' he said with one eye on a bottle of age old single malt.

'Daddy?' asked Peter, 'Isn't it time we looked for a room for our new nanny? She'll be here soon and we haven't been upstairs yet!'

'Good point Peter, we'd better get a move on.'

Off they went up the staircase, with father in front of Peter, who was in front of Jake, who's mind was more on the statues he was holding than going to look at some boring old bedrooms.

'I wonder if there are any more of these statues around Peter.' asked Jake, 'I could start a collection if there are!' he said, and he told Peter he'd be back soon as he was going to put them in his bedroom for now.

'Now this room seems to be nice enough doesn't it? Father said, 'The carpet is clean, and the decoration isn't all that old, yes, I think this room will do nicely.'

Peter was glad the room was at the front of the house and not the back. He'd just 'hate it' he thought, if the nanny was keeping an eye on them from her own room as well. 'Now that daddy's found a room for the nanny, maybe it's time to go and find a way into the attic!' Peter thought, and he asked his father if he had forgotten all about that room.

Just then, Jake came running into the room as he heard Peter mention the attic.

'Can we see the room now dad? Please, you did promise didn't you?' asked Jake while jumping on the spot.

'Yes, I did, didn't I!' father admitted, and the boys could tell there was regret in his voice.

'What is it daddy? Why don't you want us to go up there? Are you hiding something, what is it daddy?' asked Peter, and he went over to his father and held his hand.

'Are you scared of heights dad?' asked Jake, and his father smiled at him, and he told them both a story that he should have told them a long time ago.

Peter and Jake did their best to get comfortable, but somehow knew father was going to bring up the subject that they disliked the most. That subject was about the time when mother went missing. They were only eighteen months old at the time so their 'memories' of their mother were left more to their imaginations rather than actual memories, but Peter and Jake had a picture in their own minds of what their mother was like. They knew from photographs that she was slim, dark haired, very pretty, a few years younger than father, but the rest was a mystery to them. Was she fun? Was she liked? Did father love her? And most of all, they wondered if she loved them, and if she didn't, was this the reason for why she went 'missing'. The boys never did tell their father about their thoughts on the subject as the subject never came up that often. But when it did, they both knew the conversation would end with father either getting upset, or they would never see him for days on end as he would retire to his study until the 'next book' he was writing had been finished.

Father took in a deep breath and let it out slowly. The boys then knew what subject was about to be brought up, but they didn't know why.

'Ok boys,' he said, 'the fact is . . . . we have all stayed in this house before!'

Peter and Jake looked at each other but didn't say anything.

'Well, you two were for too young to remember, but when you were about eighteen months old, we all spent a week here on a short summer break. You see . . . . after this place was a summer school, part of it was run by an old couple as a guest house for a while, and with the place having a bit of history, your mother thought it would have been a bit of fun to check it out, and . . . .'

'What do you mean daddy? A bit of history!' Peter interrupted as he was becoming very interested.

Father drew another deep breath and hoped he was doing the right thing by telling the boys something that they may be too young to understand, but after a little thought, he carried on.

'Now don't get any silly ideas or anything like that ok? But . . . .'

'What?' said Jake excitedly, and he hoped father was going to say one of his favourite words.

'Sorry Jake, no ghosts!' his father said as he knew how his small mind worked.

'Tut!' Peter and his father heard coming from Jake who was still interested all the same.

'What you *should* be asking Jake, is . . .' his father said.

'What dad? Spit it out!' Jake was near uncontrollable at this point, so father hesitated no more.

'The place was closed down by the police due to an ongoing investigation into the disappearance of a lot of the boys who stayed here one summer!'

'Wow!' said Peter. 'You mean this was once a crime scene?'

'Were they tied up, beaten and tortured, then murdered on the grounds dad?' asked Jake, and his father wore a shocked expression as the words Jake used rang in his ears.

'No Jake! Why on earth would you think such an awful thing like that?' he asked.

'Well,' Jake said still thinking hard. 'It must have been pretty bad to have closed the place!'

Peter was proud of his slightly younger brother for saying exactly the same thing as he was thinking himself.

'He's right daddy!' said Peter, which put a huge grin on Jakes face. 'To close the place down must have meant that something really bad happened, and if mummy knew there was a history to the place, then it must have been in the papers or something!'

Their father smiled. He smiled at the fact that they were as bright as their mother was, and he wished that their mother was here to witness their brightness, but he knew deep down there was no chance of that! Wherever she may be, or whoever she may be with, he felt he was no longer in her thoughts. Without ever telling the boys, he hoped she was satisfied with what she had done to them all.

'You're right!' said father, 'It was in the papers, and it was on the news. But because it was a school for let's say . . . . boys and girls who were too young to go to prison . . . . the authorities assumed they must have just taken off somewhere, and to tell you the truth, I don't think the authorities were all that bothered about finding some of the countries worst behaved children!'

'Out of sight, out of mind!' said Peter.

'Something like that son yes!'

'But that doesn't explain why mum thought it would be a 'bit of fun' to stay here! said Jake, and father tried his best to think of a way to tell the next bit of the complicated story.

'You're right Jake,' he said. 'from this point on I don't quite understand it myself!'

'Why daddy?' asked Peter.

Father was silent for a moment until he tried to remember exactly what had happened on the night that he last saw their mother, as it was in fact in the very room that Peter and Jake were dying to see.

'I don't know if you have seen the maze at the back of the house yet boys, but . . .'

Peter and Jake were silent again, but neither of them took their eyes of their father, even though they could feel the eyes of their brother's needing to look into their own, as they wanted to know more about the maze and what may lie within. Peter thought 'the maze must have the answers to a lot of their questions,' and he needed to see the room in the attic more than ever now to find what the maze may be hiding.

'Mummy became more and more obsessed with the maze that I couldn't take her mind off it! All she ever wanted to do that week was to get to the other side, or should I say the center!'

Peter's mind was racing as he remembered only yesterday that it was the center of the maze that had grabbed his attention more than finding the exit, and he wondered if *he* was going to become as obsessed as mummy was before she went missing.

'So what's at the center then dad?' asked Jake, and he looked at Peter knowing it was a question that *he* wanted answering too.

'I don't know!' he said, 'but I think your mother knew. It was in the very room you are both wanting to see where I saw her last, and she was excited about something, something that she wouldn't tell me about!'

'You mean it was the week that we stayed in this house when mummy went missing?' asked Peter.

Father looked to the floor and whispered 'Yes.'

Jake looked at Peter and Peter looked at Jake, and they both knew that it would be the wrong time to ask father to see the room.

'We'll ask tomorrow!' Peter whispered to Jake, and Jake agreed.

DONG . . . . ! Went the front doorbell and they knew it was time to meet their new nanny. Jake raced down the stairs but was almost immediately called back by his father.

'Wait there Jake,' he said, 'we'll all open the door together, that would be nicer!'

Jake couldn't wait to see her, so while he was waiting for the others to catch up, he opened the letter box very quietly and peeped through. He saw a young woman who he thought looked as old as his mother did in the photographs, but with long blonde hair and a summer frock. 'Very nice' thought Jake, and he felt someone tap him on the shoulder. It was Peter, and it startled Jake just enough to make him lose grip if the letter box. It made a loud 'clunk' sound as it fell shut, then father opened the door and smiled at the person who would be looking after his two boys from now on.

'Miss Montgomery I presume?' asked father.

'Yes!' she smiled, 'And you must be Mr Stokes?'

'That's me,' he said, and extended his hand towards her for them to shake and meet properly. 'but I insist you call me Brian!'

'Brian it is then.' she agreed, 'Then I insist you call me Helen!'

'Helen it is then. Please come in. Would you like a cup of tea or something while we chat? That way you can get to know the boys a bit better.'

'Yes please Mr Stokes, sorry, er Brian.' she said, and left her suitcase near the front door.

'Please excuse the mess Helen, as we only moved in yesterday ourselves.' said father feeling a little embarrassed, as he didn't want her to think that they were as messy as that all of the time.

'Oh I understand, It'll be some time before you properly settled in a house this size.' said Helen, which reminded her of one of the questions she was meaning to ask but was a little nervous about asking it, and she thought she'd ask a few other questions to lead onto what she really wanted to know.

Father and the new nanny sat at the large kitchen table with their cups of tea and the boys sat with their pop. they all thought the atmosphere was a bit awkward as nobody knew what to say at first, then father tried to ease the tension slightly.

'So Helen,' he said, 'you must have lots of questions you want to ask so, fire away.'

'Just a few Brian, er . . . I was wondering . . .'

'Yes?' Father smiled.

'I was wondering if you had any plans on renting out any part of the house, or make it a guest house like it once was? Or are you just making it a family home?'

He knew what she was getting at, as Helen had a slight look of panic about her, and he reassured her that only half the rooms would actually be used.

'I know it's a large house, but don't worry Helen, I'm sure your workload won't get too hectic, It's mainly looking after the boys when I'm out and about.'

Helen felt a sense of relief inside as she knew she would have found it difficult to manage the boys and the whole house on her own.

'Hello, I'm Peter by the way, and this is my younger brother Jake!' said Peter, and he gave his father a nasty look for not introducing them properly.

'Yes, I'm Jake, but me and my brother are the same age!' said Jake, who was tired of being reminded that he was the youngest.

'Seven minutes Jake!' Peter smiled an exaggerated smile.

Father held his finger up at them and the boys stopped niggling each other instantly, and Helen was glad to see the boys were capable of doing what they were told.

'Hi there!' smiled Helen, 'And which one is it that likes to peep through letter boxes eh?'

Jake wore a nice pink colour to his cheeks which gave him away, and Peter giggled.

'I know we are going to get along just fine!' she said, 'I've got lots of things to do during the summer holidays, so get ready for some fun eh Peter, Jake?'

Deep down they both hoped it wasn't going to get in the way of the exploring they had planned, but they were happy because she did look like fun, and wasn't an old school mistress type nanny that smelled of soap like the last one.

'Forgive me for asking Brian,' she said and looked around the huge kitchen, 'but it does seem to be a rather large house for just the three of you, is there a Mrs Stokes?'

As soon as she asked that question she wished she hadn't. She couldn't believe that question had just came out without thinking about it first, and she apologised before she received an answer.

'It's ok, I don't mind you asking,' Brian said, and he began to explain the situation about the boys mother, being glad he had spoke to the boys first.

Helen sat fascinated at what Brian was telling her, as she had heard stories about the maze from her grandfather when she was a child. She listened to what Brian had to say but kept the stories she had heard to herself as she started to sense unhappiness in the voice of her new employer, so she thought it best to change the subject altogether.

'Would it be possible to see the room I will be staying in please? I'd like to unpack if that's ok with you?'

'Sure sure.' he said, 'Just follow me.'

'Thank you.' Helen replied and picked up her suitcase as they passed the front door.

'Let me get that for you!' said Brian, and he smiled at her, trying to hide the fact that the suitcase was a lot heavier than it looked. He had to make an excuse to stop halfway up the stairs as his lungs felt like they were going to collapse, so he pointed out an old picture hanging on the wall and asked if she would like to hang it on the wall in her room.

Helen politely smiled and told him that she had a few of her own to hang if he didn't mind.

'No not at all!' he said, and carried on struggling with the case to her room.

Helen Montgomery walked into her room and had a quick glance around.

'This will do nicely Brian, thank you.' she said as she tested the springs in the single bed by lightly bouncing on the edge where she sat.

'Anything you need, just let me know. I'll be in the kitchen, ok?'

'Thank you, I will.' she said and unzipped the suitcase to start unpacking.

CHAPTER FOUR

Helen and the statues

The boys were finishing off their lunch at the kitchen table when their father came down from Helen's new bedroom. He seemed to be in a very good mood, and the boys were happy that 'the subject' didn't seem to have had a massive effect on him like it had done in the past.

Jake was itching to go exploring, but he didn't want to do it with their father. He always liked it when father *did* go with himself and Peter, but this time he just wanted to do it with his brother. He thought that because father was in such a good mood, maybe he will let them go exploring in the house on their own this time, and he had to ask. Jake didn't want to go in the gardens until Peter had drawn a good enough map of the maze as the temptation to try it out would be too great, and he knew they would end up getting lost.

'Dad?' asked Jake.

'Yes son, what is it?'

'Can me and Peter go in that room with all the games in? We'd like to check it out.'

'Yes, I don't see why not!' he said, much to the liking of the boys, so they took their empty plates over to the sink and ran them under the tap.

'Thanks daddy.' said Peter, and he picked up his bag, hung it over his shoulder, and slightly quicker than a walk they headed for the games room. When they reached the door of the kitchen, Peter suggested calling in on Helen to see if she needed anything, and without saying 'GO', or counting 'one, two, three', they raced as fast as they could up the staircase.

'I won!' said Jake with his arms high up in the air and doing his usual tribal victory dance.

'Only just though!' said Peter as they walked over to the door of their new nannies room, and they noticed that it was slightly open, so they peered inside.

Helen was on her knees doing something that the boys couldn't quite see, as the cupboard door was in the way. She was reaching far into the the bottom of the cupboard, and they were curious about what she was doing.

'Er hum!' Peter deliberately coughed to attract her attention.

'Ooooh! . . . Hello you two, you gave me such a fright, and I nearly dropped this little fellow!' she said as she took out what she had found at the bottom of the cupboard.

'It's another one!' shouted Jake. 'Let me see Helen, please.'

'Where exactly was it Helen?' asked Peter as he got closer. 'Can you show me?'

'Yes sure, come closer.' and Helen pointed to the very back of the bottom shelf and far into the corner.

'Weird!' said Peter.

'What's weird?' asked Helen.

'We've found another two of these statues around the house, and every time they're in a funny position!'

said Jake pleased that he had another to add to the collection.

'What he means Helen is . . . .' said Peter, 'We found one on a shelf in the cellar, and the statue is in a position of climbing up onto it. The second was under a drawer unit in the games room, and the position we found that one in was a crawling position. Now . . . This one you say was tucked away as far into the corner at the bottom of the cupboard.'

'Yes, and?' she asked, becoming more interested the more she heard.

'Look at the position it's in!'

Helen studied the statue and she saw that this little pixie was crouched down with its knees tucked into its chest.

'It's as if it was hiding!' she said, and the boys agreed with her immediately.

'Can I put it with the other two I found Helen, please?'

Helen studied the small statue a little while longer. She looked at it closely, and the boys thought that she had recognised it or something because it looked like she had seen it before.

'What's the matter Helen?' asked Peter, and she said nothing . . . At first.

'Jake?'

'Yes Helen?' he asked curiously.

'I want you to take this and keep it with the other two you have found. Listen Jake . . .' she said very seriously, 'You must put them somewhere very safe, and keep them away from any harm. Do you understand? This could be very important!'

'Sure,' he said. 'I've got just the place! But why?' he asked, as he was hoping to put them on display on his shelf.

'Are they valuable?' Peter asked.

'Very!' said Helen. 'But not in the way you are thinking!'

Peter was now more confused than Jake which didn't happen very often, and he needed to know more. 'If they weren't that sort of valuable, then what could she possibly mean?' he wondered.

Helen Montgomery walked along to Jakes room with him to make sure the 'safe place' he said he had for the statues was actually safe enough.

'Here it is Helen.' said Jake as he pulled a wooden box from underneath his bed that held all his best toys.

Peter watched him pick up his box and empty the contents onto his bed as if they were no longer his favourite toys, and gave the box to Helen.

'Is this good enough?' he asked. 'I've got a lock for it as well!' he added.

'This is perfect!' she said. 'Or it will be as soon as I put some padding in the bottom of it.'

'Padding in the bottom of it?' thought Peter, 'I wander what she thinks they are if they 'are not that sort of valuable'.

Helen put one of her towels in the bottom of the wooden box and carefully placed the three statues inside. Peter and Jake looked at each other in amazement. Jake thought she was 'as nutty as a fruitcake' and Peter, he just wondered why she was treating the statues as if they were little humans, and he was about to ask Helen if *she* was hiding anything from them, when Helen closed Jakes door and whispered . . .

'I shouldn't be doing this, especially on my first day as your nanny but . . .'

She motioned them to come closer as if she was about to to tell them the biggest secret in the whole wide world. Peter cautiously moved toward her, and Jake was more excited than he was when he first set eyes on the maze.

Helen, Peter and Jake sat on the floor around the wooden box that contained the 'valuable' statues, and the boys gave their nanny all of their attention.

'Now then boys,' she said. 'You've got to make the biggest, most truest promise you have ever given. Can you both do that?'

'Sure can!' said Peter.

'Scouts honour!' said Jake.

'You're not in the scouts!' said Peter.

'So! I wanted to be though!' Jake argued.

Helen interrupted their bickering and told them to listen hard, and they both sat upright as if teacher was in front of them.

'Ok.' she said, 'You father is going into town soon, so when he drives off, come and see me and I'll tell you all the stories that my granddad told me when I was a child.'

'Can't you tell us now?' asked an impatient Jake.

'No, your father wouldn't like it if he knew I told you these stories. They might not even be true!' said Helen, 'But these do look like the little statues my granddad told me about when I was a young girl, and . . .' Helen stopped what she was saying as she heard a faint voice in the distance saying that he'd 'be back by teatime, and don't take any nonsense off the boys. Goodbye!' said the boys father.

'Great!' whispered Jake a little too loud, 'Oh . . . goodbye dad.' he shouted.

'Bye daddy.' shouted Peter.

Helen sat there with her fingers over her lips until she heard Brian drive to the end of the dirt track.

'And?' asked Peter who was dying to hear what she was going to say next.

Helen got herself comfortable and tried to recall the stories from her childhood.

'My granddad used to stay here when he was younger because he was very badly behaved. You see . . . . This place used to be a . . . .'

'Summer school for naughty children!' Jake finished her sentence.

'Don't interrupt Jake, that's very rude!' said Peter. 'I'm sorry Helen, but we know what the house used to be, and that there were a lot of children going missing. That's why it was closed down. Is that what *you* were told?'

'Yes, but do you know what happened to them?' she asked.

'No! What happened Helen?' Tell us!' asked Jake, who was leaning that far forward he nearly tipped over onto the box.

'The maze!' was Helens answer, and the boys were more confused than ever.

'What about the maze?' asked Peter. 'Were they just lost? But daddy said they searched for months!'

'They never got lost Peter, it was what they found in the maze!'

'Is there something that beats up bullies and gets rid of them in the center of the maze Helen?' asked Jake, and he was hoping he was completely wrong.

'No no Jake, no bullies.' she reassured him. 'What they found was a place where they never wanted to leave. A magical place where there is no more trouble, where there are no more teachers, of the kind that you know anyway! Everything is free, and there's no such thing as money or horrible tasting medicine. But there are two things that whoever goes to live there should think long and hard about!'

'What's that then?' Peter and Jake asked together.

'Firstly, you never grow old, and you never die.'

'Well that's not too bad!' I'm sure I could live with that!' said Peter.

'Secondly,' said Helen, 'If you ever try to leave, you only have an hour before you turn to stone!'

The boys were silent, and even thought they didn't believe all of what Helen was telling them, they looked over the edge of the box at the little statues, and imagined them as real little people that story books called pixies.

'Helen?' asked Jake, 'I don't really mind if you want to keep these in your bedroom you know, if you think they'd be safer that is.'

Helen smiled at the boy who sat in front of her, and she knew that he was too tough to admit that he now found them a bit creepy.

'I'll put them in my room Jake, but promise me this boys . . . If you happen to come across any more of these statues, be very careful with them and bring them to me. Promise?'

'Promise.' said Peter, and crossed his heart two or three times.

'Scouts honour, if I was in the scouts!' said Jake.

'So how did your granddad find out about all of this Helen, did *he* not go to this place that they found? And if not, why? asked Peter.

'He was about to! But one night, when he saw one of the teachers chasing what he thought was a mouse, before his very eyes, this 'thing' that was being chased all of a sudden froze, and turned into solid stone. My granddad said that it was one of the little pixies from the place they found, and his friend picked it up and hid it from all the other boys.'

'So does that mean that if you decide to live in this place, it makes you the same size as the pixies?' asked Peter, who wondered what it would be like to be able to sneak about unnoticed.

'I don't know, and neither did my granddad know. He said he didn't want to find out!'

'So how much of this do *you* believe Helen?' asked Jake, 'Or are you just making the stories more believable because it's your job as a nanny?'

Peter giggled at first, but then realized what a good question it actually was, so he waited to see what answer she would give.

'I believed them all when I was a small girl, who wouldn't? But as I grew up, I realized that they were all silly stories.'

'So that's what you believe now then?' asked Jake, and he looked disappointedly at Peter.

'Not necessarily Jake, you see, after a while I learned that there really *was* a maze at the back of this house, and this house actually did used to be a home for 'bad children'. And now that I'm looking at these statues of little pixies, I don't know what to believe!' she said, and she stopped herself from picking one of the pixies out of the box.

'I wonder.' said Peter.

'Wonder what?' asked Jake.

'If there is any way of bringing these pixies back to life, I mean if they're able to turn to stone, maybe there's a way to turn them back into pixies!'

'I think you'd have to find where they came from to find that out!' said Helen, and Peter thought he knew exactly where that was.

'The clearing in the middle of the maze! It's got to be there, I just know it.'

'That's what I was going to say!' Jake said, and it was his turn to ask Helen if *she* could make the best promise. 'Helen? Can you make the best promise ever if we tell *you* something?'

'Too right I can Jake!'

'Ok then.' he started, 'Me and Peter need to get into the room in the attic, as there will be the best view of the maze from there!'

'And why do you need to see it Jake?' asked Helen.

'So Peter can draw it! That way we can work out the correct route before we even try it. Impossible to get lost!' Jake said pleased with himself.

'Very clever! And er . . . What is it you want me to do Jake?' she asked.

'Could you find out how to get up there, and if we need a key, could you get it for us?' Jake put on what he thought was his cutest smile, and he kept on wearing it until Helen answered.

'Now you both know I can't do that, I'd lose my job for sure!' said Helen, and the boys showed their disappointment by remaining silent. 'But,' she said, 'I know someone who can tell me how to get up there!'

Jakes eyes widened and the grin that was appearing under his nose copied the grin that was on Peters face.

'Your granddad?' asked Peter.

'Is he still alive?' asked Jake.

'Yes my granddad, and he's still alive! He's still working as a matter of fact! But he is finding it more difficult as the years go by.'

'It's Monte, isn't it Helen? The removal man?' asked Peter after putting two and two together.

'I was going to say that!' said Jake, and gave a loud tut.

'You've both met him then?' asked a shocked Helen.

'Yes! He was the one who told us about the house being a summer school, and that he stayed here a few times!'

'*And,* he said that this place was magical!' added Peter.

'Well I can't remember him telling me that part!' she tried to recall, but she then had an idea that she knew the boys wouldn't say no to. 'Why don't we go and ask him, now?' she asked, and looked at her watch to see how much time they had before father returned.

'Please, please let's go Helen, let's go now Helen.' Jake said excitedly, and Peter was already at the bedroom door waiting impatiently.

'Ok then, but you must remember that this is our little secret. If your father finds out, I'll lose my job for certain!' she said, and the boys eagerly nodded their heads in agreement. 'Let me get the keys and I'll see you at the front door in five minutes ok?'

'Ok, five minutes.' said Peter as he struggled to see the dial on the watch that was at the top of his arm.

Peter and Jake were standing at the front door eagerly awaiting their new nanny, who they had decided was the best nanny they had ever had, and they agreed that under no circumstances should their father find out that they went to see the old removal man.

'So . . .' said Jake as he thought hard, 'Monte . . . must be short for Montgomery!' he said with a smile.

'UREKA!' shouted Peter in a sarcastic tone, and Jake gave Peter a nasty look for joking about his lack of intelligence.

'Stop making fun of me Peter.' said Jake, 'You know you're older than me, it's not fair!'

'Jake, listen!' said Peter, 'We are twins . . . I am you . . . You are me . . . We are the same! If I make fun of you, I'm making fun of myself! And I wouldn't do that, would I?' explained Peter.

Peter always had a way of putting things a way that Jake could understand, and he always succeeded in making him feel better.

'Suppose so.' said Jake looking down with his hands in his pockets, which made him look sorry for his little outburst, then becoming excited all over again as he saw Helen locking the old oak door behind her.

CHAPTER FIVE

Visiting Monte

Helen opened her handbag and searched for the keys to the home she had shared with her granddad, and after unlocking the door, she shouted 'granddad' a couple of times so he knew who it was that was entering his home. Monte wasn't just the oldest relative she had, but also the only living relative she had, and she dreaded the day she would hear the worst news she'd ever want to hear. As when granddad passed away, she'd be truly alone as only herself and her fond memories of the man who brought her up would only exist.

'Is that you Helen?' he shouted from the kitchen.

'It's me granddad, and I've brought a couple of guests who would like to say hello. Is that ok?'

'That's fine love, I'll be through in a minute.' he shouted, and they heard the breathlessness of of an old man they had met before as he entered the living room where they had sat down.

'Hi granddad.' said Helen.

'Hello love, and who do we have . . . . Well, I didn't ever think I'd see you two in *my* house!' he said, 'Unless,' he went on, 'you've came to ask me twenty questions about the old house?'

'Yeah!' said Jake, 'We want to know everything, about the place you found, and the pixies!'

'Oh, and how to get into the room in the attic!' Peter remembered to ask him.

'I was going to say that!' said Jake.

'They want to know more about the maze granddad, and what's inside.' Helen told him, and Monte sat in his big armchair rocking back and forth with his fingers rummaging through the whiskers on his chin.

'The room in the attic eh? Hmm! Now let me think.' he said, and the boys were on the edge of their seats waiting for their answers. 'Tell me.' said Monte, 'Why all the interest in the room in the attic?'

'We want a better view of the maze so I can make a drawing of it!' Peter told him.

'But why would you want to draw it?' Monte asked.

'So we can work out the correct route to take before we go in there and get lost!' said Jake.

'Very smart boys, but I'm afraid drawing the maze wouldn't actually do you any good!' said Monte, and the boys were confused.

'What? Why?' asked Jake who was bitterly disappointed that their plan wasn't going to work.

'Because my dear boys, the entrance of the maze is also the exit!'

'What do you mean?' asked Jake who thought that Monte was winding them up. 'Is it a trick maze or something?'

'Basically Jake, It is Jake isn't it?'

'Yes.'

'Basically Jake,' he continued, 'the pixies planted the maze themselves years ago so people would get lost inside of it!'

'But why would they want to do that Monte?' asked Peter.

'So they can have their fun! They love to play tricks on people. And when they've finished having their fun, they help them find their way out again. They love to do that as well!'

'Why? I don't understand! And what happens to the people who chose to stay there? Do these pixies live in the maze Monte?' asked Peter.

'No, not really!' said Monte, 'But the entrance to where they do live is in the maze, somewhere! Can't exactly remember where, but I've seen it.'

'I don't understand.' said Jake. 'Do they live underground then?'

'Hmmm . . . No! They live in what you call another dimension Jake. Do you know what a dimension is?' Monte asked him, but knew he was going to have to explain.

'Er, No! said Jake, and he looked at Peter to see if *he* knew what Monte was talking about.

'They're only twelve granddad!' Helen reminded him.

'We're nearly teenagers!' Jake reminded Helen.

'Ok then, nearly teenagers, I'm sorry Jake.

'How will we know when we see it Monte?' asked Peter, who had seen an old film on the TV that had something to do with dimensions.

'All you have to do Peter, is look for a little green gate!'

'A little green gate?' asked Jake, 'Is their world on the other side of this gate?' he asked excitedly.

'Yes! Well, no not really. You see Jake, you have to go through the gate to enter their world. You can go round it, or even see over the top of it, but you can't enter until you find the key to go through it!' Monte told them, 'Only then can you experience the forth dimension which their land sits!'

'But what happens to the people who chose to live there? Do they end up shrinking to their size or what?' asked Jake, who was contemplating the idea of going through when they found it.

'Don't know for sure, I never did see any of my classmates come back through as a pixie I don't think! Come to think of it, one of my friends went in and out for days, and *he* always looked normal! I think that only the pixies that originally come from there come into this world in their original size. Does that make any sense?' he asked.

'None of it makes any sense to me!' said Jake.

'Me neither!' said Helen, but Peter was in a world of his own, as if he were already working out ways of entering their world and making it back safely.

He knew he still needed a map, even if it were only to find his way around once he got in there. The next thing he needed to do was to find the key! 'Was it on the bunch his father had on him that morning?' he thought, 'And how do I get a hold of them to find out?' He knew there were more clues to be found, and he thought that the clues he was looking for must have been in the room called 'the attic'.

'Monte?' asked Peter. 'Is there or has there ever been a staircase to the room in the attic?'

'Yes, of course!' he laughed, How do you think that room was ever used?'

Peter felt a bit silly, but soon realized he wasn't being silly, as there were no obvious ways of getting up there!

'But we've looked high and low, and we can't seem to see any stairs!'

'But have you seen the secret stairs? he said, and the look on his face told the boys that a secret was about to be unveiled.

'Secret stairs?' asked Jake, as another one of his favourite words whizzed around in his imagination. 'Why were there secret stairs Monte?'

'Well . . . Not so much secret, more like unused and probably decorated over. I don't know what it will look like now, it's been a long time since I was in the room where the entrance was!'

'My mother and father stayed in the attic room about ten years ago, so there must be an entrance you can still see!' said Jake.

'The main entrance to that room is actually in the main bedroom, so if you find that, your laughing!' said Monte, 'But you'll have to be tall to use that door!'

'That's fathers room!' Peter realized, 'So that's why he always keeps that room locked.'

'But I walked past fathers room yesterday,' said Jake, 'and I know there wasn't a staircase in there. I would have seen it, surely.'

'No Jake.' said Monte, 'The stairs come down from the ceiling with the help of a pull string.'

'A pull string?' Jake repeated.

'Yes! When you pull the cord, the staircase slides down from a sort of loft hatch. They're very steep mind, you have to come back down backwards. That was the room that my friend stayed in, and if I remember correctly, he used to hide his diary under one of the floorboards in the attic before he went missing!'

'What was in the diary Monte? Were there any clues to where the gate was?' asked Jake.

'I don't know, but I do know that he used to write about all the adventures he had with the pixies in that book!'

'I'd love to find that!' said Peter, 'Imagine, a story book about real live little people in their own little world!'

'Their own little world called Pixity, I think!' added Monte.

'Pixity?' asked Peter.

'Pig city?' asked Jake, and Helen tried to hide her smile.

'P . . . I . . . X . . . I . . . T . . . Y!' said Monte.

'Oh!' and Jake turned his head to hide the pink flush.

'Fascinating.' said Peter, 'I wonder what they're like!'

'Pixies, Peter, are a good race mostly, very kind and helpful. The only problem with becoming part of their life full time, is that when you join them, they don't like it when you try to leave!'

'Do you have to join?' asked Peter.

'No, but the temptation to join their way of life is great. And once you do take their vows, pixie size or not, you'll turn to stone if you do not return within the hour!'

'So,' said Jake, 'If you try to leave their world for good, and you're not back within the hour, the next thing you know is . . . You're stone cold dead!'

'Oh, I don't know about dead Jake, but definitely stone! And by the way, my friend told me that one of our hours is the same as one of their days! I don't know how that works, but there you go!'

'I can't get my head around all of this!' said Jake.

'Neither can I!' said Peter.

Although Helen was fascinated by everything her granddad was telling them, she wanted to get the boys back to the house, as there were a few thing that needed to be done before the boys father would return from his meeting. Helen told the boys to thank her granddad and she ushered them towards the front door.

'Can we visit again Monte?' asked Jake, as he had one of the best afternoons ever, listening to the stories of the old house and what Monte and his friends had got up to when they were younger. Jake didn't know why, but somehow he knew that this old man wasn't telling any lies. 'Even if they weren't true,' he thought, 'this man believed he was telling the truth, and there must be some reason for why he thought the stories were true.

Helen, Peter and Jake sat at the kitchen table in the old house, and they each held a cup of hot cocoa. They were talking about all the stories that Monte had been telling them that afternoon. Helen seemed to be more interested as the time went by, and what she said next made the boys know they weren't going to get any sleep that night.

'We'll know for sure tomorrow!' she said, and the boys were wide eyed and staring at her.

'How?' they asked.

'Because Peter and Jake Stokes, if it's the last thing we do, we're going up there!'

CHAPTER SIX

The diary in the attic

'Daddy? You're going to be late for your appointment!' shouted Peter as he stood at the bottom of the staircase.

'I'm coming! Can you get my hat for me please Peter? I think it might rain later today!'

'Already got it, and your scarf!'

Father came down the stairs still tying his tie, and mumbling to himself. He was making sure he had everything he'd need for his appointment with his publisher.

'Got my briefcase, my book, my wallet, my car keys . . .'

'Sandwiches and a flask of tea?' asked Helen, and gave him an extra bag.

'Ooooh, thank you Helen,' said Brian, 'I don't know what I'd do without you all! Very efficient bunch you are! And if I didn't know any better, I'd be thinking you are all trying to get rid of me this morning!'

'Your umbrella dad!' said Jake as he joined them at the front door.

'Thanks Jake,' father said, 'and don't you boys be any trouble for Helen, do you hear?'

'We won't.' they almost said together, and they stood to watch their father start the car and drive down the dirt track and through the trees.

As soon as the car was out of sight, Peter and Jake heard a sound of something rattling behind them, then they noticed what Helen had in her hands.

'It's daddy's keys!' shouted Peter.

'How did you manage to find them Helen?' asked Jake.

'I saw him hide them after you both had gone to bed last night!'

'Where?' asked Jake.

'I'm sorry Jake, but you know I can't tell!'

Jake did the biggest tut noise he had ever tried to make, and he rolled his eyes, making sure Helen could see.

'I thought you were on our side Helen! Why won't you tell us?' Jake asked.

'Because my dear little Jake, this is my way of making sure you don't go exploring around the house without me knowing about it! It is *my* job after all to make sure that you two are properly looked after, isn't it?'

'Suppose so!' said Jake.

'It's not all that bad Jake!' said Peter, 'Helen can come with us. Can't you Helen?'

'That's right Peter. Do you think *I'd* want to miss out on any adventure or exploration?' she said, which made Jake smile a smile he could not hide.

'You're just a big child, you are!' said Jake, and he allowed Helen to ruffle his hair without him moaning about it.

'No I'm not!' Helen joked, But I'll race you to the top of the stairs to prove it!'

The sound of their hard shoes hitting each step of the carpet free staircase echoed around the house, and it was Jake who reached the top first.

'I won!' said Jake, and while the ritual of his victory dance was in motion, he didn't notice that Helen and Peter were standing at the door of his fathers room.

'Wait for me!' he moaned, and hurried along the passage way to catch up.

The three of them stood and looked at the door that was slightly ajar. None of them knew what to do next as they thought that it might have been deliberately left like that.

'It might be booby trapped!' suggested Jake. 'See if there's a string attached to the handle Peter, or a bag of flour on top of the door!'

'I can't see anything Jake,' he said, 'In any case, father was in a rush this morning, so he's probably just forgot to lock it this time!'

'The simplest answer is usually the right answer Peter!' said Helen, and she pushed the door open.

'I won't tell if you won't!' said Peter, and he looked at them with a straight face to show he was serious, and both Helen and Jake nodded in agreement.

The room was just like all the other rooms, and the air smelled a bit damp. There was no bed in the room to even suggest that father had been sleeping in there, but there were a few unopened boxes that were left over from the move. Then Helen noticed something that was hanging from the ceiling. It was the pull string that granddad was telling them about.

'Stand aside boys.' said Helen as she went to grab the pull string, but stopped as she heard Peter shout . . .

'I've found another one!' he yelled with excitement.

In one of the alcoves was an old bedside unit with no cupboard door and a drawer handle that hung at an angle.

'Look at the position it's in!' said Jake as he knelt down beside it. 'It looks like it was about to jump!'

'You're right Jake!' said Peter. 'Why don't you go and put it with the others in your box, and we'll see if there are any more.'

'Great!' said Jake. 'I'm getting quite a collection now!' and he carefully picked up the little statue, but then noticed that there was something very different about this one from the others. 'Guess what everyone!' he said.

'What Jake?' asked Helen.

'This one's a girl pixie! You can tell, look Helen.'

Helen took the pixie from Jake and had a closer look.

'Your right Jake, but trust you to notice those!' she said, and Jakes face warmed up again.

Slightly faster than a walk, Jake went along the corridor to his bedroom and opened the box that held the other statues. He placed the forth pixie carefully along side the others and closed the lid. As Jake walked back along the corridor towards his fathers room, he heard a strange noise, and he wondered what it was. He entered the room where he had left Helen and Peter just a few moments ago, but there was no sign of them.

'Where are you?' he shouted.

'Up here!' he faintly heard Peter say, and when Jake turned around, he nearly walked into some ladders that came down from the ceiling.

'Tut! You never wait for me!' he moaned, and he climbed the ladders to the room in the attic.

Helen was looking out of the window at the maze that she had heard so much about when she was a child, and it 'didn't seem real' she thought.

'After all these years,' she said, 'and there it is! Come and look boys, you'll be able to do a good drawing from here Peter!' she said, but Peter just stayed where he was. Helen went over to him to see what was wrong.

'Peter? Are you ok?' she asked him, then she noticed what it was he was staring at.

Next to their fathers bed was a photograph of their mother that he had never seen before. He wanted to pick it up, but he was too scared in case he put it back in the wrong position and father would know.

'Is that your mummy?' Helen asked softly.

'Yes, I wish I could remember her.' he said.

'If you could remember her Peter, It would have been a lot harder to get over her disappearance though, eh?' and Peter had never thought of it that way before, and he smiled at Helen to say thank you.

'Come on Peter.' said Jake, 'Get your drawing book out, I don't want to spend too much time in here as dad will go mad if he finds out!'

Peter rested his paper on the window sill and started to draw the lines of the hedges of the maze that he now had a much better view of. He could now see further into the center of the maze, and the small clearing he had noticed earlier had what looked like a table with some benches around it. 'Must be for people who get lost and need a rest.' he thought, and it wasn't long before he had a good enough drawing to work out the correct route to the center of the maze.

While Jake was waiting for Peter to finish his drawing, he was pacing up and down the room, moaning about how long it was taking, then he gave Peter and Helen such a fright as he stood on a floorboard that gave an eerie creaking noise.

'Jake! You gave me such a fright!' said Helen.

'Sorry, it was just one of the floorboards creaking!' he said, but as soon as he said it, he was moving the rug that lay over the top of it and looking for the board that creaked.

'Jake! What are you doing?' asked Helen.

'Remember what your granddad said about his friends diary?' he asked her, and both Peter and Helen rushed over to see if another of Monte's stories were true.

'Look Peter!' said Jake, 'All the floor boards are nailed down apart from this one, look!'

Peter saw that Jake was right. All the floorboards were in deed nailed down, but the one in question was screwed down instead.

'That's got to be so it's easier to get in and out!' said Jake, and he pulled the old screw driver out of his pocket. 'There's a piece of luck!' he said as the driver was a perfect fit, and he began to remove the screws.

'Only one more.' said Jake, and slowly the screw twisted out of the place it had been for countless years.

Jake put the screw driver to the side and went into his other pocket where he kept his penknife. After squeezing the blade through a gap in the boards, he was able to lever one ends of the floorboard high enough for Peter to take hold, and he slowly lifted the board out of its place.

'Nothing?' Jake asked.

'Wait Jake,' said Peter, 'It might be pushed under!' and he put his arm far in between the joists to see if there was anything *he* could feel, but Peter pulled his arm out and was as disappointed as Jake was.

'Let *me* have a go!' said Helen who wasn't going to be beaten. 'I've got longer arms, so we might get lucky!'

Helen got onto her knees and lay on her side in order to get her arm as deep as she possibly could. She could feel something, and with the very ends of her fingertips, she managed to get a grip tight enough to slide out whatever it was she had a hold of.

'There we go!' said Helen as she dusted off the ancient cobwebs that covered the old book. 'Now be very careful, it's very old!' she said and handed it over to Jake.

'Let Peter have a look at it first Helen!' said Jake, as there were too many bits of old cobweb still on the cover for his liking.

Peter placed the old book on the floor in front of them and read the cover.

'*Marcus Bullman's secret diary. keep out!*'

Peter read, and turned to the first page. As he did, a tiny little spider scampered from between the pages into Jakes direction, and it made him jump off the floor.

'Aaargh!' shouted Jake, and the large shudder that went through his entire body was obvious to Peter and Helen, and they couldn't stop giggling at Jake which made him both angry and embarrassed at the same time.

'Come and sit down Jake, it's gone now.' said Peter, and he started to read out the first entry in the decades old diary.

Monday 4th August 1952.

Was sure I seen another rat in my room this morning. Told caretaker but he doesn't want to know. Think he still hates me for the water balloon I got him with yesterday. Busy setting a trap to catch one of those dirty vermin and put it in Maisy's knicker draw. Me and Monte going to try maze again tomorrow.

They all sat with their mouths open and urged Peter to read on. Helen couldn't believe that her granddad was mentioned in this old diary, and that all the stories he had told her as a child must have been true.

Tuesday 5th August 1952.

You wouldn't believe it! I was woken in the middle of the night as something set off the trap I had set up. Just as I was about to hit it with a brick, it shouted 'please don't kill me, I'll be your friend'. I'm twelve, and I have never seen a person as small as that!

I was going to keep him, but he kept arguing that he didn't have much time left. Then before my very eyes, he turned into a statue. Nobody, apart from Monte believes me, and everyone thinks I'm mad. Going to catch me another one!

'This is the best read ever!' said Peter.

'I'll tell you what,' said Helen as the floor was now hurting her knees, 'put the diary in your bag Peter, and Jake? Can you carefully put the floor board back in its place?'

Yes!' he said, and he took the four screws out of his pocket.

'Good! Now, have you finished your drawing Peter?'

'Yes.' he said.

'Excellent! Now as soon as Jake fixes the floor and puts the rug back, make sure everything is in its correct place before we leave. We don't want your father seeing anything that shouldn't be here!'

Jake put the rug back over the floorboard and headed for the ladders. They were a lot steeper as he looked down and asked Helen to go first. She did so, and Jake followed her before she had a chance to get to the bottom. When they were all safely down, Helen lifted the ladders from the bottom step and pushed upwards. They seemed to go back automatically, as if they were on a spring of some sort, and they closed tightly shut. They also left the door slightly open as it was when they had found it and headed down to the kitchen for some lunch.

'All this exploring has given me such an appetite!' said Helen, and she asked the boys what they would like to eat.

'I'll have an omelette!' said Jake.

'And what about you, Peter? Would you like an omelette too?' asked Helen, but Peter didn't answer. He was studying the drawing he had made of the maze, and he saw something that didn't add up.

'I thought your granddad said that the exit was the same as the entrance!' he said with a puzzled look.

'That's what he said, why?' asked Helen.

'Well, I drew exactly what I saw, and this maze has an exit on the other side!'

'Let me have a look Peter.' said Helen, and she took the drawing from Peter and sat at the table with Jake. She studied it for a short while before announcing that she had found her way to the clearing in the center of the maze.

'But what about getting to the other side?' asked Peter.

'I don't know yet, let me look at it a bit longer.' she said, and Jake was becoming impatient as his tummy was starting to rumble. 'Just a moment Jake, I haven't forgotten about your omelette!'

Ten minutes later, Jake was munching his way through a packet of crisps he had helped himself to, when Helen gave the map back to Peter and declared that it was impossible to get to the other side.

'Impossible?' asked Peter. 'How?'

'No matter which way you turn, you either come to a dead end, or go round in a circle! Then you end up exactly where you started. I can't work it out!'

'There must be a way!' said Peter, and he got the diary out of his bag to read the next entry. Jake came over and sat next to him with a couple of biscuits, and he stopped munching while he read.

Wednesday 6th August 1952.

No luck with the trap last night, and me and Monte got lost in the maze again. It took us ages this time to get out, but we did find a strange little green gate at one of the dead ends! It didn't seem to lead anywhere and we didn't have the key to open it anyway. I wonder if it has anything to do with the little person I found yesterday. If I catch one tonight, I'll ask.

'So there *is* a little green gate in the maze!' said Jake. 'We've got to go in there soon Helen, we have to! Peter?' asked Jake, 'Read the next page in the diary, because if this Marcus caught another pixie, he might have told him where to find the key!'

'Good thinking Jake, I never thought of that!' said Peter, and Jake was really pleased with his good idea, but he didn't see Peter wink at Helen.

He opened the diary at the next entry, but there was nothing written for the seventh of August. He turned the page again and saw there was more writing than usual for the eighth.

Friday 8th August 1952.

Caught a little pixie the other night!

But this time we had a chat. It turns out he was looking for his friend that went missing, but I told him he was the first I saw. Had to, felt terrible for what happened to the other one. This one started saying he didn't have much time left, so me and Monte followed it to the maze where he said he lived with a lot of others like him. We watched as he opened the gate, and it closed behind him before we got a chance to look through. He didn't come out the other side! Very strange! But then we got really lost and it was pitch black. Good job it was a warm night as we didn't find our way out until the sun rose. When we got back to our rooms, Brannigan was standing there with his trouser belt in his hands. Monte got ten, and I got six! Monte got ten because he told him it didn't hurt. Grounded for three days, and probably can't sit down for the same time.

'What a horrible place this must have been. Young boys being whipped? I've never heard of such a thing.' said Helen, and she shed a small tear for the way her granddad had been treat all them years ago.

'Look.' said Jake as he leant over the table for a closer look. 'That must be a drawing of the second pixie he caught!' and they all took turns looking at the picture Marcus drew.

'Is that his name? Look!' said Helen, and Peter read the name out loud.

'Trickster. That's a funny name!' he said, 'I wonder why they called him that.'

'Maybe because he was always playing tricks on others! said Jake. 'If I ever meet him, I think we'll get on really well!'

'Get on really well with who Jake?' their father asked as he entered the kitchen and went straight to where the kettle was.

'Er . . . no-one! Just someone Helen was telling us about, that's all.' said Jake, and he quickly changed the subject. 'How was your meeting dad?'

'Very good actually!' he said as he took a bottle of cheap bubbly wine out of a carrier bag he brought home with him. 'In fact so good, that I'm going to celebrate tonight by taking you all out for a lovely meal!'

'Did they like your new story daddy?' asked Peter as he slid the diary and the drawing of the maze into his bag.

'Yes, they loved it! They've asked me to start writing the sequel, and asked for it by Christmas!'

'Oh that's wonderful news Brian.' said Helen. 'May I have a copy of your latest book to read? I love children's books, they remind me of when mother used to read to me in bed, and . . .' Helen had to stop there. 'I'm sorry, I wasn't thinking.' she said and looked over at Peter and Jake who were sitting quietly at the table. 'Please forgive me boys, my mouth opens before I think sometimes.'

After a little thought, Jake went over to Helen and sat next to her.

'It's ok Helen,' he said, 'we can't remember anything about mummy so it's difficult to get upset about some one we didn't know!'

Father smiled at Helen, and he was so pleased that they found a nanny they liked. Never before had he seen

Jake sit next to his nanny like that, and he pictured in his mind that Helen was their mother for a moment, but she wasn't. No-one could replace their mother, even if he hadn't known the reasons for why she left. He knew deep down Olivia was still alive, he could feel it, and stranger than that, he could feel her presence more than ever since he bought the house in which he laid his eyes on her last.

Helen smiled at Jake and ruffled his hair again, but this time Jake couldn't help have a little bit of a moan.

'I wish you wouldn't do that!' he said, but couldn't completely hide the slight grin he was wearing.

'So where are you taking us then daddy?' asked Peter. 'Can we have a Chinese meal tonight please?'

'Well let's ask Helen shall we?' said father, and before he could ask, Helen was already nodding her head with delight as the only Chinese meals she had ever tasted were delivered to her front door on a Friday night.

CHAPTER SEVEN

Their first riddle

For the next few days, father was in the house most of the time as he had started work on the sequel to his latest book. This didn't please the boys much as the weather was 'not of the exploring kind' and they spent most of their time colouring in and doing jigsaws. But they were looking forward to Monday, as Helen had told them that their father was spending the whole day in London signing his books. The weather for the next few days was looking good and the boys had already written a list of things they might need if they got lost in the maze. Peter decided that he should keep the list hidden with the diary and the map as he was after all the oldest between the two of them. Jake didn't mind much though, to him it was more responsibility than he could care for.

Helen was in the games room going through all the books that were stacked on the shelves, and she came across one or two that she recognised as a child. She put them to one side to read later, and carried on picking the books up one by one, giving them a quick wipe with a damp cloth, and placing them back on the shelf in order of their size.

'Oh good,' thought Helen, 'the last shelf!'

She cleared the shelf of all books and gave it a wipe down with the cloth. The largest book in the pile on the floor was picked up and placed on the shelf until there were no books left, but as she picked up the last one, a folded piece of paper that was tucked away neatly between the pages fell to the floor. When she picked it up, she realized that it was covered in handwriting, very small handwriting!

Helen glanced through the book in which the paper fell from. She saw that it was full of pictures of elves and pixies, little fairies playing in the sunshine and walking in the countryside. She looked at the cover again to read the title of the book, but the writing had worn down that badly she couldn't read what it had said. Then Helen looked closer, and in the distance on the drawing, she could see a long hedge with a little green gate in the corner. Pixies were going in and out, and they looked like they were dancing and playing games. Helen wondered if the drawing was a scene from the very garden that was behind the house and didn't put that book back on the shelf, as this was probably the 'most important find yet!' she thought, and it was put in her pocket to show Peter and Jake at a later time.

After very carefully unfolding the piece of paper she had found and laying it on the table, Helen had found the writing to small to understand and decided that she would have to show the boys what she had found. At the top of the stairs, Helen called for Peter and Jake to come to the games room, and to bring with them a magnifying glass.

Seconds later, Helen heard what she thought was a stampede of wild horses, but this stampede of wild horses were running along the corridor to the games room.

'What do you need this for Helen?' asked Jake who was pulling the magnifying glass from his pocket.

'Close the door behind you will you please Peter?' asked Helen, as Peter had once more been beaten to the games room door in a race.

'Sure!' he said, a bit out of breath.

'What have you got?' asked Jake, 'Just looks like a piece of paper to me!'

'That's exactly what it is!' said Helen teasing him a little.

'Do you need glasses?' he asked in a way that showed he would have disapproved.

'No Jake, but I believe that what I am looking at was actually written by one of the pixies!'

'What?' Jake whispered loudly, 'Let me see.'

Helen showed him the paper without giving it to him, then took the magnifier in her left hand and began to read.

'It looks like a poem, or maybe a riddle of some sort!' she said, and laid it back on the table for everyone to see. 'Peter, I need you to write this down as I read it out. Can you do that?'

'Yes, just wait until I get my paper and pencil out of my bag.' he said excitedly as he loved puzzles and rhymes. 'And Jake? I need you to listen very carefully, and tell me if you have any idea of what this riddle might mean, ok?'

'I certainly can!' he said, and he felt good, 'like an important part of the team' he thought.

'Ready boys? Here goes!'

> *One two three, they seek for a key,*
> *to enter a world which is happy and free.*
> *It's not left, it's not right,*
> *not in day, nor in night,*
> *somewhere else instead, you shall see.*

'Did you get all of that Peter?' asked Helen, as it was important not to miss out any of the riddle.

'Yes, got it! he said, proud of his quick writing skills.

'Ok then, second verse coming up!'

> *Too large for a town, too small for a city,*
> *as soon as one sees it,*
> *you'll admit that it's pretty.*
> *We can also acquire*
> *anything you desire*
> *in our magical land of Pixity.*

'Pixity!' That's the place Monte told us about.' said Jake, 'Are there any more verses Helen? There maybe more clues!'

'There are Jake, but it's becoming more difficult to read.' she said whilst rubbing her eyes.

> *The entrance is easy unless you are really*
> *hiding a feeling that's hidden*
> *if your intentions are cruel,*
> *then it's back to school,*
> *and I believe the word is forbidden.*

> *Remember these lines,*
> *as there has been times*

when a newcomers time has flown.
When they visit their past,
an hour doesn't last
as long as a statue of stone.

Yet the entrance may seem
a weird shade of green,
all fancy and fashionably chiselled.
To open the lock, an object it's not,
but a tune that is cunningly whistled.

After Helen had finished reading the very small print on the paper, there were a few moments of silence. In that silence were the thoughts of three people who were repeating over and over the words they had just heard, and it was Jake who had what he thought was one of the first answers to the riddle.

'Is there anything else written on that piece of paper Helen? Any more writing of any kind?'

'No.' she said as she quickly glanced over the dusty old paper that was nearly twice her own age,

'Are you sure?'

Yes I'm sure. Why?' Helen asked, but as she turned the paper over, she noticed there were some musical notes written on the other side. 'There's only these notes of music, that's all!'

Jake smiled widely as he knew he had figured out a major part of the riddle, and he ran back to his bedroom to get out his old electronic keyboard he received as a birthday present from his father a few years back.

'Where's he gone to?' asked Peter, as he was reading through what Helen had read out a minute earlier.

'I don't know, but I think he's worked out part of the puzzle judging by the smile on his face!' said Helen, and Jake came running back through to the games room more excited than ever.

'Why have you brought that?' asked Peter with his eyes rolling in disbelief.

'Because Mr know it all, the musical notes on the back of the paper is the key!' he said, and his whole body was strutting its stuff without knowing it.

'The key to what?' asked Peter.

'The key to the little green gate!'

'I don't understand!' said Helen. 'What do you mean?'

'To open the lock, an object it's not.' he repeated. 'What does that tell you?'

'That it's not a key?' asked Peter.

'Correct! And the next line is? Peter, if you don't mind.'

'*but a tune that is cunningly whistled!*' said Peter, who was waiting anxiously for the reply off his younger brother.

'I don't think it's an actual key that opens the lock, but if you whistle this tune that's written on the back of this paper, I think the gate will open automatically!'

'Jake?' said Helen, 'You're a genius! How in the world did you work that out?' she asked, and Jake never felt so good in his life.

He knew that what he had just worked out was something that his brother would have been proud of, and he bathed in the moment.

Peter looked over to Helen and he was smiling. He was smiling because he was proud of his brother, his younger brother, his younger brother who needed a confidence boost like this to show he was as bright as anyone else.

Jake was busy doing his tribal ritual dance and Peter was going over some of the lines in the riddle again. The more he read it, and thought about these little people missing their loved ones that had never returned, the more he thought about his own mother, and he thought he'd love to be able to reunite them all if he could only make his way into their world.

'Can I have that piece of paper now please Helen?' asked Jake as he plugged his keyboard into the socket on the wall.

'I didn't know you could read music Jake!' said Helen.

'Father made me take piano lessons about a year ago, because I wouldn't join the choir like Peter did, but I didn't stick it for long. Or should I say the piano teacher didn't stick it for long!'

'I wonder why!' Helen joked, and Jake wore a cheeky grin that told her enough to stop wondering.

He looked at the music and tried his best to remember what each note was called.

'Ok,' said Jake, 'the first note on this stave is A!'

'A what?' asked Peter.

'No silly, I mean the note is A!'

'Oh sorry, carry on.' he said, and felt a little embarrassed.

'The second is one note higher so that's B. The third is the same as the first, so that's A again. The fourth note had Jake running through to his bedroom looking for his old music theory book as he had completely forgot what the note under the bottom line was called.

'Here we are!' he said, 'The note underneath the bottom line is a D! The first line is . . . let me see, an E! The last two are the same as each other and they're on the second line which is a . . . G! Done it!' shouted Jake, and he wrote all the letters of the notes on a separate piece of paper and Gave it to Peter.

Peter looked at it and smiled.

'Not bad eh Peter?' said Jake, but was confused when Peter burst into a fit of giggles. 'What?' he asked, 'What's so funny? All the letters are right, I checked them against my theory book, look!'

Jake handed the book over to Peter in the hope that he would stop laughing at him, but when Jake read out the letters he himself had written, he realized that it wasn't himself that Peter was laughing at.

'A.B.A.D.E.G.G. he read then he looked again. 'Haha,' he laughed. 'A bad egg!' And both Peter and Jake giggled like two babies, and Helen wanted to know what they were laughing at.

'What's so funny?' she asked.

'A bad egg!' Peter laughed, and Jake held his hand over his mouth and nose to add to the joke.

'Oh you haven't!' said Helen, and she left the room before what she thought was going to be a bad odour reached her vicinity.

The boys were in a state of uncontrollable hysterics after Helen left the room, and they heard her faint voice from the bottom of the stairs.

'I'm not coming back up until its gone!' she shouted.

'It's safe Helen, we were only joking, promise!' said Peter, as he couldn't be bothered to explain to her what had really happened, and he heard her footsteps climbing the staircase.

Jake was practising the seven note melody that was written on the old piece of paper, and when Helen finally entered the games room, apart from smelling the surrounding air, she commented on the tune she heard that was filling the room.

'That's nice Jake! Did you write that one yourself? Or is it one you had learnt at piano lessons?' she asked, then hummed the catchy tune on her way over to Peter, who was going over the lines of the riddle again.

'No.' said Jake, 'That, is the tune that is written on the back of the paper you found!'

'You mean that's the tune you have to whistle to open the gate?' she asked.

'Yes! Do you like It?'

'I love it! Don't you think you should record it somehow, just in case we find the gate and you can't remember the melody?'

'Good idea Helen!' said Peter, 'I'll go and get my tape recorder.' he said, and he ran to his bedroom to open the last unopened box it must have been in.

'Actually, I think it's a good idea too!' said Jake.

'Oh, and why is that Jake?' asked Helen curiously.

'Well, I can't whistle! That would have made me look a bit silly wouldn't it!'

'Just a little Jake, Just a little!'

Peter came back in the room with his recorder and used the remaining socket next to where Jake had plugged in his keyboard into.

'Have a few more practices Jake, then we'll go for a take.' Peter suggested, and Jake agreed as it had been over a year since he last played.

After a few tries, Jake said he was ready to go for a take, and Peter held the small opening where the microphone was near to the speaker on the keyboard.

'Ok, after three!' said Peter. 'One, two, three,' and then Peter pointed to Jake to silently say . . . 'Go!'

Jake played the tune without fault, and Peter waited a second or two after he had finished to stop recording.

'Good!' said Peter, 'But I'd better rewind the tape to make sure it has recorded properly! Stay there just in case Jake.'

The tune had been recorded clearly, and Peter put the tape player on his list of things that he mustn't forget on Monday.

'Oh, and batteries!' he remembered.

CHAPTER EIGHT

Off to Pixity

Helen entered Peters room and placed a bowl of cereal and a glass of milk on the unit next to his bed.

'Wake up sleepy head, it's time!' she said.

'Time? Time for what?' asked Peter as he rubbed the sleep from his eyes.

'It's Monday morning Peter, and your father has just left to catch the train for London!'

'London?' he asked, and he realized that the big day had finally arrived.

'Yes Peter, now eat your breakfast and get yourself dressed while I wake up your brother.

Helen opened the door that joined Peter and Jakes room and was just about to shout 'wake up' when she saw that Jake was already up, dressed, and sitting at the bottom of his bed.

'I see *you* haven't forgotten what day it is Jake!' and handed him his bowl of cereal and glass of milk.

'Me? Forget? Huh, no chance!' he said.

'Good, now make sure you both have everything you need, and I'll see you both in the kitchen in twenty minutes!' and she left to make them all a large pack lunch.

There wasn't a cloud in the sky as Peter and Jake showed Helen the way through the gardens to the entrance of the maze, and they were going through their list, making sure they had everything they thought they'd need.

'Sandwiches?' said Peter.

'Check!' said Jake.

'Pop?'

'Check!'

'Tape player, compass, map, daddy's watch and extra batteries?'

'Check, check, check, check and check!' said Jake as they passed the larger statues near the entrance.

'Here we are!' said Jake as he handed over the map to Peter.

Peter unfolded the map and lined his drawing up so it was facing the same direction as the maze.

'Pass me the compass Jake.' he said, and when Jake passed it over, he placed the compass on top of the map. 'Ok,' he said, 'to head for the clearing in the center, we have to head south!

'Listen up you two.' said Helen, and they stopped right where they were. 'Now nobody take a turn without telling the others ok? We don't want anyone getting lost on their own, so may I suggest that we all stick together and never split up!'

'Check!' said Peter.

'Tut, ok then.' said Jake who didn't want to hang around waiting for the others.

'Good!' said Helen, as she realized that they all should have had a copy of the map. 'Don't want to go back one short do we?'

'You mean like a pixie?' asked Jake, and both Peter and Helen didn't know if Jake was being serious or making a joke.

'You know what I mean Jake!' said Helen.

Peter led the way as he followed the line that was in red ink put on by Helen when she had worked out the correct route to the clearing and the sun was warming the air nicely as it rose in the sky, and Helen was beginning to regret not bringing an umbrella for there was a lack of shade as the sun rose.

Jake was always ahead at the next turning waiting for the others to hurry as he wanted to be the one who would find the little green gate that led to the magical land they had all heard about, and he sighed as Helen called him back.

'Not too far Jake!' said Helen. 'Remember what we agreed? No splitting up!' and Jake gave a large tut that both Peter and Helen could hear from thirty foot back.

'I bet if we straightened this line out, we would have been back at our old house by now!' said Peter, who was feeling the strain in his small legs.

'Only a few more turns!' said Helen as she looked at the map that he was turning every time they had made a turn themselves to keep it facing south.

'Second turning right!' Peter said, and he turned the map anticlockwise as they turned right.

'Here's the clearing!' shouted Jake, 'I've found it!' and the others could see a tribal ritual dance being performed on a stone table by an excited Jake.

The area at the center of the maze also had old park benches around the stone table in the middle, and there wasn't anywhere where Helen could sit in the shade. She took the large bottle of lemonade out of the bag and poured it into three plastic cups.

'Thirsty anyone?' she asked, and the boys ran over to her and gulped down their drinks. 'Slow down you two.' she said, 'We've got to make it last, and it's going to get hotter before it gets cooler!'

'What kind of sandwiches did you bring Helen? I'm starving!' said Jake, and he was pleased that Helen had remembered what his favourite kind were.

'Cheese and tomato for you Peter. and for you Jake, I've made some peanut butter and Marmite!'

'Yeeey!' shouted Jake, and Helen gave a shudder as she remembered the smell as she was making them.

Peter and Jake were tucking into their sandwiches while Helen read the copy of the riddle that Peter had written out.

'I wonder,' she said, 'what if the gate is so small that I can't fit through!'

'I'm sure you can Helen,' said Jake, 'If others have, then you can, especially with you being nice and slim!'

'Why thank you Jake.' she said, and Jake blushed. 'But I think at least one of us should stay on the outside of the gate in case there is some kind of problem!'

Jake was silent, hoping that his name wasn't brought forward, and although Peter had agreed with Helen, he too was hoping it wasn't going to be himself.

'Let's just see if we find it first!' said Peter, 'I'll mark whatever way we take off the map as we go along in order to make sure we don't check the same hedge over and over!'

'Good idea!' said Jake, 'I say we go . . . this way!'

'Why not!' said Helen, and she picked up her bag, happy to find some a little shade behind the many hedges that lay ahead.

Jake was now walking along with the others at their side studying every corner and dead end they came across, looking for any signs of any activity like footprints and snapped twigs, although, he thought, they'd be very small footprints.

They walked for another ten minutes or so when Jake heard someone giggle.

'What are you laughing at Peter?' he asked, and Peter looked at him as if he didn't know what he was talking about.

'I didn't laugh!' he said.

'It wasn't me either!' said Helen, and Jake gave them the kind of look that said he didn't believe them.

'There it is again!' said Jake, but this time he knew that it wasn't either Helen or Peter as he was looking in their direction when he heard it.

'I heard it too!' admitted Helen, and as she turned to see behind herself, in the very corner of her eye she saw something move and go quickly out of sight. 'What was that?' she asked, and the excitement from the two boys made them run back to where Helen was to see if they could see what it was that Helen thought she had seen.

'What did it look like Helen?' asked Jake, 'Was it one of the pixies?'

'I don't know, it was small enough though!' she said.

'Lets go this way instead.' said Peter, and they all changed their direction to try and find what it was they had heard.

'It must have been a pixie!' said Jake, 'rats and other little animals don't giggle!'

87

The others knew that Jake was right and their hearts beat louder and faster as they hoped to catch a glimpse of their first pixie. Their pace quickened as they heard the leaves of the hedges rustling ahead of them. They followed the trail of little noises until they became completely lost, as with all the excitement, Peter had not been marking off the route they had already taken. The sun was now high in the sky as it must have been nearing midday, and with the sun high in the sky, it was harder for Peter to get a sense of direction.

Peter got the compass from his pocket and watched the dial closely.

'What's going on?' he asked, and the others went to him to see why he was staring at the compass.

The pointer wasn't doing what it should, all it was doing was spinning uncontrollably and not giving any clues to where south, or any other direction actually was.

'That's it then!' said Peter.

'What does it mean?' asked Jake with a worried expression.

'It means that I cant' tell at all what direction we are facing until the sun starts to go down! When there's no shadow, and the compass isn't working, we don't know exactly where we are!'

'That's just great!' said Jake, 'But now that we're here, we might as well keep looking for the gate! There's no point in turning back now is there?'

'I suppose not!' said Helen, and they stood silent for a few moments to see if they could hear any more giggling or anything else that sounded out of place.

Peter looked behind himself and seen something that worried him greatly, and he felt he had to ask the others something in case he thought he was imagining things.

'Helen?' We *did* just come this way, didn't we? I mean, facing this direction?'

'Yes, I think we did, why?' she asked.

'Well, the way we came is now a dead end! I mean, if we walk back that way, we'll just come to a hedge in every direction. This doesn't make any sense!'

As the others looked to see if Peter was right, they all heard another giggle, but a little louder this time. They all turned as quickly as they could, and there, in the corner, stood a little man. His height was guessed at about twelve inches by Peter, who noticed straight away that he was about the same height as the little statues they had found dotted around the house. He didn't move at first, he just stood there smiling at them, as if he were wanting them to follow him.

'I knew I should have brought my fishing net!' said Jake as he stared at the pixie that stood before him, and he slowly edged his way to the pixies direction.

'Don't Jake, you might frighten him!' said Helen.

'I wonder if he speaks English.' said Jake.

'I should think so! It *was* a pixie who wrote the riddle that helped us to find this place!' said Peter in a tone that didn't go down too well with Jake.

Helen moved towards the little man with her hand held out in a fashion that she thought looked to be in a friendly way.

'Hello!' she said softly, 'I am Helen, and they are Peter and Jake. We seem to have got ourselves a bit lost. Can yo help us?'

They all held their breath, waiting to see if he would at least say something back to them, but what they heard was not speech. The pixie whistled a seven note melody, and before they knew what to do next, from the side of the hedge, in the far corner of what looked like a dead end, opened a little green gate that was about two feet tall. The little man ran through the open gate and it slammed shut behind him.

'Did you see that?' said Jake as he jumped up and down on the spot pointing to the dead end before them.

'Yes I did!' shouted Peter.

Helen stood silent, not knowing what to do next. She heard the boys call her to follow, but their voices went in one ear and out the other. She wondered if *every* story her granddad told her was true, especially the one about her own parents going 'missing' in this very maze. Were they in the world that was not their own? Were they in fact still alive and lived behind the gate? she knew she had to tell the boys the truth and why she had applied for the job as their nanny, but she had kept that secret for far too long and it was too late to tell them now. To tell the boys that she thought she knew what had happened to their own mother so soon would be cruel, as she didn't want to build their hopes up until she had a better idea of what was exactly behind the little green gate.

Helen remembered what her granddad had said about the time in their world not being the same as their own, and she looked at her watch. 'If it is midday in our world, then we'll at least have four or five days in their world before we have to get back in time for Brian returning home' she thought, and she told the boys not to do anything until she had caught up.

'Hurry Helen,' said an impatient Jake, 'don't you want to see what's behind?'

'Yes, of course I do, But let's talk about what exactly we're going to do first!' she said as her heart beat faster than she could ever remember.

'Why?' asked Peter. 'What about?'

'Well . . .' was all that came out as she didn't quite know what to say.

'Well what Helen? We'll soon find out, come on.' said Jake as he took the tape player out of Peters bag.

'Ok, let's do it!' Helen finally said before she changed her mind.

'Cool!' said Peter, 'You're the best nanny ever!' and Helen felt awful for keeping everything she hadn't told them from them, and she made herself promise that she would make it up to them some day.

Jake made sure the tape was rewound all the way back to the beginning, and he looked at Peter and Helen before he pressed the play button.

'Ok, here we go!' he said, and with his free hand he pressed the play button.

The tune that Jake played on his keyboard was loud and clear, and when the seven note melody had stopped, they waited and watched.

'Nothing is happening!' Jake said disappointedly.

'Rewind the tape Jake, and play it again.' Peter suggested.

Jake did as he was told and once again they waited for the little green gate to open.

'Still nothing!' said Helen. 'Are you sure they were the right notes Jake?'

'Yes I'm sure!' Jake snapped.

'Ok ok, I'm sorry for doubting you Jake.' she said, 'But wait, what if the tune actually had to be whistled! Maybe that's where we're going wrong!'

'But I told you that I couldn't whistle Helen!' said Jake, and he folded his arms and gave a big 'tut'.

'Let me try.' said Peter. 'I've heard the tune enough times to whistle it correctly.'

'Ok then Peter, give it your best shot.' said Helen, and they all waited once more to see if the gate would finally open.

Peter had a few practices in his head before whistling the tune, and when he finally whistled the tune correct, the gate made an unlocking sound and slowly opened.

'You did it!' said Jake, and he popped his head around the door to look inside.

'What can you see?' asked Peter who was eagerly waiting his turn.

'I can see a path, it goes all the way down to a field that's got some strange looking flowers in it!'

'Can you see anything else Jake?' asked Helen. 'Do you see any pixies yet?'

'Not yet, but I'm going in to find one!' he said, and before the others could do anything about it, Jake was already inside.

'We had better go in after him Helen,' said Peter, 'as we'd lose him for sure.'

Helen agreed, and after Peter went through the gate, Helen was on her hands and knees struggling through the tiny opening.

Helen wasn't quite all the way through when she saw that Peter and Jake had shrunk to the size of a pixie. She panicked, and was considering turning back, but as she looked behind herself she noticed that her legs were five times the size of the rest of her body, and she then knew she had to go all the way in.

Helen stood with Peter and Jake, and the first obvious difference she noticed was that she was the same size as they were. They looked at each other in amazement and the next thing they heard was the gate slamming shut behind them.

'You're the same size as me Helen!' said Jake with a smile.

'I know, fascinating! It's as if all the pixies are the same size as each other in Pixity. No-one smaller or taller than the other!'

They all jumped with fright as they were all of a sudden greeted by what they thought was an ordinary human, as they were forgetting that they themselves were now a mere pixie size.

'Greetings.' he said with a smile, 'And welcome to Pixity. I see by the melody you used at the gate that you have come from the summer school, correct?'

'Er yes,' said Peter, 'but it isn't a summer school any more!'

'Oh?' said the pixie, as if it was a question.

'No, it's our new home now. We've just moved in a few days ago.' said Jake, as he didn't want Peter doing all the talking.

'Well that explains why we haven't had any visitors from there for a long time doesn't it!' he said.

'I'm Peter by the way, this is my brother Jake and our nanny Helen.' he said, as he hated it when people didn't introduce themselves properly. 'And you are?'

'I my friend, am the one the others call Trickster. I live near here so I am usually the one who answers the gate when we hear a melody that is authentic!'

'Trickster?' Jake whispered to Peter, 'Isn't he the one who Marcus wrote about in his diary?'

'It must be! I can't imagine there being two tricksters can you?' asked Peter, but he was interrupted by the pixie who told them that it was rude to whisper, and that it wasn't allowed in this land.

'But saying you are knew to this land, I shall oversee it.' he smiled.

Jake felt like giving him a sarcastic 'thank you' and an especially large 'tut' but thought he'd better not as Helen was giving him a stern look.

'Tell me Trickster, do you know someone called Marcus Bullman?' asked Helen and she was surprised she had even remembered the name.

'Marcus Bullman?' repeated Trickster with surprise, 'Why, Marcus and I are best buddies! He doesn't live too far from here, would you like to go and visit?'

Helen couldn't believe what she had just heard, and she wished that her granddad was well enough to have came along with her.

'Yes, I'd love to!' said Helen, but didn't know what she'd say to him once they met.

'Do you know Marcus? I think it will be a long time since you seen him last, he's one of our long timers. He joined us back in fifty two I think!'

'Er no, I haven't met him before,' said Helen thinking that he wasn't very good at mathematics, 'but he knew my granddad very well. They were at summer school together!'

'Then it is strange your grandfather isn't here also!' said Trickster, which confused Helen. 'Not many who have visited have not wanted to stay for good! We pride ourselves on catering for the every need of visitors, as we wish to grow to a size that is good for our economy. Each newcomer, after taking their vows, is given a home, a job, and a clean bill of health to help create the life that they have always longed for.'

'We were told that there was no need for money in this land, so . . .' thought Jake, 'Why is there any need to work?'

Trickster smiled at the innocence of the boy that stood the same height as himself, and explained that in order for their society to work properly, each individual had to put in as much as they took out.

'Seems fair!' said Peter, and Trickster smiled at him.

They walked for a short while talking about the differences between the people who were born in Pixity and people who took their vows and stayed, and what Helen was hoping to find out was why they were only allowed to visit their past for an hour only. But as she was about to ask, Trickster pointed to a lovely little cottage on the other side of a field.

'Here we are!' he said, 'The residence of Marcus Bullman. Dairy farmer, artist, and a member of the committee for Pixity.

'A committee?' asked Helen. 'So you have no pixie king or queen?'

'No! Never have, never will. We like to think that a committee represents the thoughts and ideas of the individual better than one. Don't you think?'

'I do!' said Peter.

'Young man!' said Trickster, 'We are going to get along just fine, you watch!' he said, and they walked down a long path to meet the boy who they had read about and played with Helens granddad at the summer school.

Trickster knocked on the front door with what must have been a secret knock that told Marcus who was at his front door, as before the door was open, they heard Marcus shout . . . 'Come in Trickster, the door is open!'

They followed Trickster through the front door and into a room that reminded Helen of the house her granddad lived in when her grandmother was still alive. There was a TV, but it looked like one of the first black and white televisions that was ever on the market. The radio that was in one of the alcoves looked like one she had seen in a museum once, and she noticed that all the decoration and the furniture was all styled from the nineteen fifties, and she realized that this Marcus would not have known any different. He had what every young boy would have ever wanted in his bedroom at the time, and she wondered what it would be like for herself if she ever took the vows.

'I see you have companions Trickster!' said a voice that came from behind and Helen spun round to get the first glimpse of the man that was her granddad's best friend.

Helen was confused as the person that stood before her had to be in his early twenties. *'You never grow old, and you never die!'* she was sure her granddad told her, yet this boy had obviously 'aged a little in the fifty eight years he had been here' she thought, but didn't want to ask anything until she had learned more about this strange land they all found themselves in.

'Yes my friend,' said Trickster, 'and you'll never believe who this lovely lady says she is!'

'Oh?' asked Marcus, 'And who might that be?'

Helen stepped forward to introduce herself and she nervously reached out to shake his hand.

'Hello Marcus, I am Helen, I don't know if you remember, but my granddad said he and you were best friends long ago. You both stayed at the summer school back in . . .'

Marcus looked at Helen, and was smiling before she had a chance to say who her granddad actually was, and he interrupted her in mid sentence.

'Fifty two?' he asked.

'Yes, do you remember your best friend . . .'

Marcus interrupted her again.

'Monte!' he said with a look of having fond memories. 'Good old Monte. Has it really been that long? We have no real meaning of time here!'

Trickster looked at his best buddy and decided that it would be best for him to leave and return at a later time, as he knew that the longer visitors stayed, the harder it was for them to leave.

'I'll leave you to it Marcus.' he said and closed the front door behind him.

'Marcus walked over to the window and watched as Trickster strolled to the end of the meadow, and as soon as he was out of sight . . . .

'You must leave! Listen to me, this is not a good place!' said Marcus, and Helen looked at him with total bewilderment, as all the stories she had heard *must* have been true.

'I don't understand Marcus, why? What about all the stories granddad told me about this place? Are you trying to tell me that he was lying all of this time?'

'No, Monte never knew the truth! No-one finds out the truth until it's too late!' he said, and he ushered them all into the garden at the rear of the cottage where he knew they could not be heard.

'Helen is it?' asked Marcus as he looked around his surroundings.

'Yes, I'm Monte's grandchild.

Marcus was silent, he was looking at the young woman that stood before him and he couldn't believe she was who she said she was.

'What year is it on the other side Helen?' he asked.

It's 2012 Marcus. You are now about seventy years old and looking about twenty two. I thought that nobody aged in this land Marcus, as I don't think you were twenty two when you were at summer school. I assumed you were the same age as granddad.'

'It's hard to explain Helen. You see, the ancients decided that humans were at their peak at the age of twenty one, and they didn't allow ageing to carry on after that age!'

'The ancients?' asked Peter, 'who are they?'

'In your world you have a God. In this world we have the ancients. They decided at the beginning what was meant to be and what wasn't!'

Helen didn't know what to say even if there were three questions in her head she was dying to ask. The first two could not be asked as Peter and Jake were still in their presence, so she asked the boys if they would like to go and watch TV, but that didn't go down too well with Jake.

'What? TV?' he moaned, 'I didn't come all the way here to watch TV!'

'Please Jake, this is very important.' she asked.

'Well is it ok if we explore nearby? I promise we won't go far.' asked Peter, as he knew it would calm Jake enough for them to talk in private.

'Yes ok, but don't go anywhere where I can't see you. You know we're in a strange land, and I don't want you to talk to anyone without talking to me first! Do you both understand?' she asked, but at the same time feeling bad for not keeping them close to her side like she should have been, but the need to ask Marcus was too great, and she wondered what were the best words to use.

'Marcus?' she asked after the boys had walked away.

'Yes Helen?'

'Who is it you represent in this committee that you're a member of?'

'I represent the newcomers Helen! They don't have as much say as the pixiborns, but I represent them well, and it was a unanimous vote! Or so I hear.' he said proudly.

Ever since she could remember, Helen wanted to ask the question she was about to ask, and she couldn't believe she was about to ask the one person that would know the answer.

'Marcus?' she asked.

'Yes Helen, what is it?'

'What about my parents? Are they here? They must be! And if they are, you represent them, so you must know!'

Marcus thought for a short time, and Helen was trying to hurry him for an answer.

'Their names are Winifred and Edward Montgomery!' she added.

Marcus could see how important the answer was to Helen, and he had to chose his words wisely.

'Helen, listen to me carefully!' he said, which didn't make Helen feel any better. 'When new comers visit more than once, they get to know a lot of the pixies, and sometimes the pixies don't want them to leave!'

'What do you mean Marcus?' asked Helen. 'Does that mean you *know* my parents, or *knew* my parents? I must know whatever the answer!'

Marcus drew a deep breath as he knew he was about to disappoint her, and he placed his hand on the side of her arm.

'I met your parents Helen! They *were* here, on more than one occasion, but after they announced that they would not be staying, a few of the pixiborns tricked them into taking their vows!'

'How do you mean tricked?'

'It's quite easy considering you only have to say a few certain words in a certain order, and I'm afraid the elders in the committee sometimes turn a blind eye to those who have added to the population!'

Helen knew that her parents wouldn't have left her alone all those years back, but an awful thought entered her mind.

'But if they became what *you* call newcomers, and they're not here, then . . . they must have turned to stone!' she said as best she could with an ache in her throat.

'I'm sorry Helen, but yes!' said Marcus behind a sad face.

Helen, through her sadness of becoming so close, but yet so far from seeing her parents again, thought about where her parents statues may be. She thought of the pixies they had found in the house, and there *was* a female pixie among the four they had found. But what were they doing in the house?' she thought.

'Marcus?' she asked. 'We found four statues in the house, and . . .'

'House? What house?' he interrupted.

'The old summer school you attended with my granddad! It's the boys home now and I work for their father.'

'Oh, and these statues were definitely in the house were they?' he asked, and Helen wondered what he was thinking.

'Why Marcus? What difference would it have made?'

'They'll be small statues then?'

'Yes, why?' she asked curiously.

'The moonlight Helen!' he said, and the look on Helens face asked him to explain. 'If their time is up and they're indoors, the moonlight can't restore them to their original size. But if they are outside, they at least change back to the way they were!'

'But still a statue?' she asked.

'Yes.'

'So what's the point in that?' she said, and she thought of Jake as she tutted.

Helen asked Marcus to walk with her as she needed to go and look for the boys. She couldn't believe she had allowed them go exploring in a strange place like Pixity, and the more she learned about the place, the quicker she wanted to get them out of there.

They walked towards a stream at the bottom of the next field as she could hear the boys laughing and splashing about, and she remembered the third question she wanted to ask.

'Tell me Marcus, why would all the statues be inside the house? Because it looked like they were all looking for something.

'They were all probably looking for the recipe!' said Marcus with a smile.

'Recipe? What kind of recipe?' she asked.

'Well it's an antidote really. You see, when Trickster came to visit me in my room one night, he brought with him this recipe for changing back the previous pixie I accidentally kept from returning back to Pixity!'

'So it is possible to change the statues back to their original form then?' she asked with excitement.

'Yes, but it has to be decided among the committee members whether or not they deserve a second chance or not first, and if they are, it then has to be brought forward to the elders.

'I see!' she said thinking hard. 'So how does it work?'

'First of all, you have to get the statue through the gate, with the recipe of course, and you need to know the melody that they used to enter. Then under our moonlight, we say a certain verse. It's as easy as that!'

Helen needed to get the boys together and hurry back to the gate, as she knew there would still be time to get the statues together and bring them through the gate. But she forgot one major problem in her plan.

'Do you know where the recipe is Marcus? It's very important.'

'Yes, I put it underneath one of the floorboards in my bedroom. I had the room . . .'

'In the attic, I know. That's where you hid your diary! But I know there wasn't anything else under that floorboard Marcus, could you have hidden it elsewhere?' she asked, 'Like in the games room?'

'The games room?' he asked, 'I didn't know a games room when I stayed there. Believe me, we weren't allowed anything like that when I was at that place!'

'That's where we found a piece of paper with a riddle, and some musical notes on it!'

'My my,' he said, 'I completely forgot I had written that. Have you got it with you?' he asked. 'I would love to see it again.'

'I don't know, I think Jake might have it with him.

'Was it in a small book about pixies?'

'Yes, yes it was!'

'Then the recipe should be in that book Helen! I always tried to keep my diary and the pixie book together as they were the only ones I ever used!'

Helen knew exactly where the book he was talking about was, as she had kept it aside to read later, and then she hurried over to the stream where she heard the boys playing. She heard them singing a song she had never heard them sing before and got a fright when she heard Marcus shout . . .

'NO!' he shouted before they had a chance to finish their line.

Helen noticed that as soon as Marcus shouted 'NO' there were two pixies running away and giggling to themselves like she heard in the maze.

'Peter, Jake, you must never sing that song do you hear? There are things about this place that you may still be too young to understand!'

'But why? I quite like it! said Jake, and he went over to Helen and Marcus humming the tune he was told not to sing.

'Stop!' said Marcus, which upset Jake a little. 'Even humming the tune can have severe consequences! Now do your best to forget it. Your lives depend on it, believe me!'

Peter and Jake looked at Helen, and she knew there were questions they needed answering, so when Marcus was looking the other way she placed her finger over her lips and winked. The boys knew that that meant she would tell them later on and they followed Helen and Marcus back up the path to Marcus' cottage.

'Before you return Helen, would you and the boys like to visit our town? It's only a short detour and I'm sure you'll meet some lovely characters along the way!'

Helen knew she couldn't use the excuse of not having enough time, as in her own world only ten minutes had passed, so reluctantly she agreed and the boys cheered.

The sun was still high in their sky, but it wasn't at all hot considering there wasn't a cloud in sight and Helen allowed the boys to explore as long as they were within her sights. She wanted to know more about what Marcus had said to her earlier about this place not being a good place, and what did he mean by *'no-one finds out until it's too late!'* so when she thought the boys were far enough away to not be able to hear them, she was about to ask Marcus.

Marcus looked around a full three hundred and sixty degrees and looked as if he was about to tell Helen something important when he saw someone walking towards them who he knew was the of gossip of Pixity.

'Good morning Mrs Atkinson.' said Marcus.

'And good morning to you Mr Bullman!' she said while looking at the three strangers before her.

'Oh,' he said, as he could see she was hinting to be introduced to the strangers. 'Peter, Jake, and Helen, their nanny!'

'Nanny?' she said, 'My you must have busy parents?' she said, but put it as a question.

'Er, yes.' said Marcus, 'My friends are just visiting and they are anxious to see our land.' he said as he didn't want to stay and talk too long to the equivalent of the Pixity morning paper.

'Oh, just visiting?' she asked, 'well I hope you enjoy your visit, and no doubt we'll see you again in the future.' she said and went her own way, wondering who she was going to tell first of their meeting.

'Don't take any notice of her.' said Marcus, 'Although, word will be around the town that there are visitors before we even get there!'

Helen let out a nervous laugh and wondered what this Mrs Atkinson meant by *'no doubt we'll be seeing you again in the future.'* She didn't know if it was because of what Marcus had said, or if she was just being plain paranoid, and decided to repeat the questions she had earlier not received an answer from.

After another quick glance around, Marcus invited Helen to sit on a nearby park bench, and 'like a gentleman' Helen thought, held her hand until she was sat comfortably. He joined her and took a deep breath.

'It is only the pixiborns who lead a good life in this land, not the newcomers Helen. Although the newcomers do not have a *bad* life here, sometimes they realize the life they once had wasn't so bad after all! This place has a habit of helping you realize that!'

'What do you mean Marcus?' How don't they have as good a life as the pixiborns?'

Marcus stood and once again looked around, but this time it was only to get his bearings. He helped Helen out of her seat and pointed south.

'Do you see the lake Helen?' he asked.

'Yes.' she smiled as the view reminded her of her holidays that she spent with her granddad at the lake district.

'Do you remember the stream we have just came from?'

'Yes, but why Marcus? What has that to do with anything?' Helen asked.

'Salt water Helen!' he said.

'Salt water? You mean all the water in this land is salt water?'

'Yes, all the fresh water has to be brought up from the deep mines in the forbidden zone.' he said, 'A long time ago there was a newcomer who was hear to stop our way of life, nobody knows exactly why, but he found a way, by pure chance I'm led to believe, and he blocked the source of our fresh water. Now we have to mine it, as one would coal, or gold, you know?'

When Helen heard Marcus use the words 'forbidden zone' it didn't take her long to work out who it was that was bringing the fresh water to the surface.

'So . . . The newcomers are basically slaves then!'

'Well . . . In a way, but not really as they can leave if they want!'

'Yes,' said Helen, 'if they want to be turned into stone, that is!' she said, and Marcus could see the anger inside her.

Helen didn't want to hear any more, for now anyway, and all she could think about was to get back to the gate.

'Peter, Jake, come on, we're going back now!' she said, and she heard the 'tut' from Jake who was stamping his feet on the way back to her direction.

'Do we have to go now Helen?' asked Jake.

'Yes, we do, but we will return soon, I promise.' she said in the hope that this would stop Jakes pet lip showing.

'But we've got lots of time Helen!' said Peter while twisting his neck to look at his fathers watch at the top of his arm.

'In our world there's only eleven minutes passed since we've been gone!'

Helen wished that Peter wasn't as bright as he was, and couldn't think of an excuse to why she wanted to leave so soon. Then Jake asked Marcus a question that both Helen and Peter wouldn't have minded knowing the answer to.

'Marcus?' he asked.

'Yes Jake?'

'I don't know if you know but, the letters of the notes Peter had to whistle to open the gate spell out something rather odd!' said Jake, who was about to tell Marcus something he thought he never knew.

'I know Jake, and there's a reason for that!'

'Oh yeah? and what's that?' he asked as he was a little disappointed that he knew.

'There isn't just one melody that opens the gate Jake, but there are a few. Each melody tells whoever goes to open the gate where that person probably came from! In your case, the summer school!'

'So every time someone entered using that tune, you knew the person was . . . .'

'A bad egg!' Marcus interrupted, and Jakes face told them how much he didn't appreciate that last comment.

'What I was going to say was . . .' he said sarcastically, 'A person who found that piece of paper in *'our new home!'*

'You're right Jake, sorry, which reminds me, do you happen to have my diary with you?' asked Marcus.

Jake knew that he had the diary in his back pocket, but didn't want to hand it over as he hadn't read it all yet.

'Er, no. I think Peters got it!' he lied.

'I haven't got it Jake, you know I haven't! Anyway, it's not on the check list so it's probably still in the house.' said Peter who realized why Jake didn't want to hand it over.

'We'll bring it the next time, won't we boys?' said Helen trying to hurry them up.

'Yes, of course we will Marcus,' said Jake, 'Any more messages you want us to do while we're out?'

Jake felt a dig in the back of his left leg which seemed to come from Helens heel, and Marcus didn't answer the sarcastic question he had just been asked.

'Come on,' said Marcus, 'I'll walk you to the gate, it's just up this path.'

Helen was relieved that they were all on their way back to the house for a number of reasons. Firstly, there was a chance that two of the statues they had found might actually be her parents, secondly, she wanted to find a way to release all the newcomers who wanted to leave without becoming a statue, and the third reason was that she needed more proof of a theory she had before she would tell the boys what it was.

As they walked up the path that led to the little green gate, Peter had a few questions of his own that he wanted answering, and he jumped on the opportunity.

'Marcus?' he asked.

'Yes Peter, what can I do for you?'

'Where could the other tunes be found that can open the gate?'

'Good question, and it's one I have never known the answer to! Trickster knows, as he is usually the one who opens the gate. I've only ever heard the one you know!' said Marcus, but Peter didn't believe him. There was 'something missing' he thought, and he couldn't put his finger on it.

'Ah, here we are!' said Marcus, 'I trust you'll all return soon?'

'I hope so Marcus.' said Jake, 'there's just so many places that need exploring, and I might bring my camera next time!'

'I'm afraid that is not allowed Jake! But you can draw as many pictures as you like!'

'Marcus turned to head towards his cottage, and he nearly forgot one important thing they needed to know to be able to return to the house.

'Oh, and by the way,' he shouted from a distance, 'to exit through the gate, you have to whistle the tune backwards!' and he was soon out of sight.

'Whistle the tune backwards?' they all said together in disbelief.

'How are we going to do that?' asked Helen, 'I can't even remember the tune forwards!'

'Leave that to me! said Jake, and he wrote the notes backwards on the back of the paper that Helen had found in the games room.

Jake hummed the new tune a few times in his head until he knew he got it right, but before humming it out loud to Peter, he stopped.

'What's the matter Jake?' asked Helen, 'Why aren't you showing Peter the tune?'

'I don't know.' he said. I've got a bad feeling!'

'What's wrong Jake?' asked Peter.

Jake hummed the tune once more in his head just to make sure, and now he was convinced.

'It's exactly the same tune those pixies were teaching us down at the stream!'

'So!' asked Peter.

'Jakes right!' said Helen, 'Don't even hum it out loud!'

'Why? What aren't you telling us Helen?' asked Peter, who was becoming tired of all the secrecy.

Helen noticed a seat next to the gate and she asked the boys to sit with her.

'I'm afraid I haven't been straight with you both!' she sighed. 'The thing is, I applied for the position as your nanny, not just because I needed the money, but . . . You see, *my* parents also went missing, and it had something to do with the house, or so my granddad told me. I needed to get into the house and see if there were any clues to prove that my granddads stories were true, and not just children's stories like I believed. Even after I grew up, granddad still said that they were true and that I should go there as soon as I had the chance.'

'So why didn't you tell us straight away Helen? Instead of lying to us like everybody else?' asked Jake.

'I have come to search for my parents, and I didn't want to build up your hopes up on also finding your mother. I wouldn't know if I could live with myself if I led you to believe there was a chance that she was here!'

The boys sat quietly, and Helen didn't know if it was because they were upset or annoyed at her. Then Jake stood up.

'Do you believe our mother is here? somewhere?' he asked.

'I don't know,' she admitted, 'but I'll tell you everything I found out when we get back to the house, I promise. Let's just concentrate opening this gate without whistling that tune ok?'

'What's so bad about whistling that tune backwards anyway Helen?' asked Peter.

'Do you remember Marcus asking you not to sing that song?'

'Yes,' said Peter, 'he told us never to sing that song, or even hum it. Why?'

'The lyrics to that song you nearly finished singing, were really the vows a person takes to be a life long member of Pixity! And without knowing it, an hour after leaving the maze, you'd have both become two little stone statues!'

'Phew . . . That was close!. said Jake, but . . .'

'But what? asked Peter.

'If Marcus, well . . . Saved our lives by stopping us, why did he tell us to whistle the tune backwards in order to leave, he must have known it was the same tune!' asked Jake, but there was already a plan brewing in his head about getting out of that dilemma.

'Maybe he's one of the ones that are tricking people into staying!' Helen suggested, and the boys agreed.

'But *I* have a way of getting around that problem!' Jake said proudly, and he whispered into Peters ears.

'Jake?' said Peter, 'You *are* a genius, you just don't know it! Helen? If you whistle the first four notes, and I'll whistle the last three, that way the gate should open without any of us whistling the full tune!'

'What a bright pair you are!' said Helen, and nearly told them that their mother would have been proud.

A couple of goes each later they stood facing the gate with their fingers crossed, and Helen began to whistle her first four notes. They were closely followed by Peter whistling the last three, and they waited.

'It's working!' shouted Jake, and they watched the little green gate open as wide as its hinges would allow.

Helen made sure the boys were safely through before she cautiously walked through the gate, as she didn't know when she would once again become her adult size. She crawled through, stood, straightened her back, and realized instantly that everything was back to normal as she looked down onto the tops of Peter and Jakes heads.

'Look Jake, daddy's watch still tells the right time and it's only twelve minutes past twelve!'

'Amazing, no wonder the pixies live forever!' said Jake, and he was the first to notice that the dead end they had earlier been trapped in was now open. 'It's as if they wouldn't let us go until we had visited their land!'

'Yes, you're right,' said Helen, 'but let's be getting back, there's a lot more planning to do than there was on our first visit!'

'Why Helen? And when are we going to visit again?' asked an over excited Jake.

'I'll tell you both before your father comes home, but for now, I have to think!'

It didn't take them long to exit the maze as it did to find their way in, as Peters map reading skills had come along tenfold, and as Helen came out of the maze, she watched the boys race away towards the house. Even though they were running their fastest, she could hear them talking about the land they had just witnessed, and they were making a new list for the second adventure they knew they were going to have.

Helen started walking up the slope to join them when she stopped, and she looked at the full size statues that stood before her.

'I wonder!' she said to herself as she walked over to the statue that was obviously female.

The dress she was wearing, the long hair, the shoes, and the stone wedding ring told her that before this person was a statue, she was someone's wife! Someone who either hadn't realized the length of time she had been gone, or had taken some vows she had not known she had taken, and Helen didn't know if she had found the boys mother or her own. 'She certainly looks like the woman in the photo I've seen!' she thought, and she noticed something in the statues right hand, then Helen saw what looked like a note pad with a riddle of some sort on it. 'It's got to be the recipe!' she thought, and she tried to read part of the writing that was still legible.

CHAPTER NINE

The recipe

Helen finally reached the large front door of the house where Peter and Jake were waiting eagerly, and they were still adding to their list of things they'd need for their next adventure. Helen smiled to herself as she knew that what she was about to tell them would have them jumping with excitement, and although some of the writing on the stone notepad wasn't legible, she could work out enough to give them a head start. She turned the key and as soon as she pushed the door open, Peter and Jake scrambled down the hallway towards the kitchen.

All the things that Helen had learned about Pixity and their visit was going around in her head, and she didn't know where to begin when she would sit the boys down for their chat. 'They know there's a chance of their mother being there,' she thought, 'so is there really any point in keeping anything else to myself?' she wondered. She didn't want to lie to the boys any more, but at the same time she didn't want the boys to get over excited about maybe finding their mother, and she decided just to answer the boys questions as best she could for now.

Helen sat with the boys who were all of a sudden quiet, and she guessed that they were waiting for her to tell all from the land they had returned from.

'Helen?' asked Peter, 'Earlier in Pixity, I remember that you winked at us and put your finger over your mouth, why did you do that? Have you got something to tell us?'

Helen tried to remember that specific moment in time, but there were so many things she had found out that she didn't know where to start.

'I can't remember what happened at that point, but I'll do my best to tell you both what I found out!' she said and she watched the boys get themselves comfortable in their seats. Helen went through from the beginning as well as she could and the boys sat quietly with their mouths agape and eyes wide open. They didn't interrupt once and Helen was glad there were no more secrets between them.

'Wow!' said Peter.

'I don't know if I want to go back now!' said Jake, and he thought for a bit longer to try and convince himself that it would be alright if they were careful. 'And I don't trust that Marcus person!'

'I know.' said Helen, 'I don't know what to make of him either. Especially as he tricked us into whistling the tune that he warned us about!'

'Maybe you have to sing the lyrics for their plan to work though, so I don't understand why it can be bad even if you hum the tune.' said Peter still thinking hard.

'Best not chance it, said Helen, 'until we learn more about the place.'

'So we're definitely going back there then Helen?' asked Peter.

'We have to Peter! We are so close to finding the ones we love, I think we should take every opportunity to visit!' said Helen, and she saw that Peter was pleased. Jake on the other hand was still thinking hard.

'Marcus told you that the newcomers didn't have to stay, didn't he Helen?' asked Jake.

'Yes, that's right Jake, why?'

'If they were allowed to leave, even if it was for just an hour, Why didn't your parents go to your granddads house to tell him what was happening?'

'Good question Jake!' said Peter.

'I don't know, maybe it was too far to travel there and back in just one hour! They'd have been very small remember.'

'Hmmm,' Jake sort of agreed, 'but mummy must have tried to get back to the house though! Why didn't she warn anyone?'

'I think it's because of the time difference between our two worlds Jake!' said Peter. But Jake didn't understand his older brother and waited for him to explain more. 'We don't know when exactly mummy went in the maze, but she obviously spent a lot more time there than we did, and Maybe when she got a chance to come out, the summer school had been closed down by then!'

'You could be right Peter!' said Helen, and she thought that now would be the best time to give them the best news. 'But I haven't told you the best bit yet!' she said, and the boys were once again wide eyed and mouths open.

'What?' Jake said quietly.

'Are you ready for this?' she teased them.

'Yes! Come on Helen, tell us!' said Peter.

'There is an antidote!' she plainly said.

'An antidote?' asked Jake.

'An antidote Jake is another name for a . . .'

'A cure I know Peter!' shouted Jake, and he let out the biggest 'tut' they had ever heard. 'An antidote for what though Helen?'

Peter smiled uncontrollably as he thought he had guessed what Helen was going to say.

'To bring the Pixie newcomers back to their original form!'

Although the boys knew this was the best news they'd heard, they sat there quietly for a moment thinking of the possibilities that lay ahead.

'What was it that Marcus said about the moonlight and being indoors Helen?' asked Peter.

'Erm, let me think . . . If the pixies time is up, and he or she is indoors, er . . . When they turn to stone, I think that they remain small! I think!' Why?'

'So if they were outdoors, the moonlight would at least make them their original size, is that it?' asked Peter.

'Yes, I think that's right.' and Helen thought she knew where he was going.

'So what about the two large statues in the garden?' asked Jake.

'My thoughts exactly Jake!' said Peter.

Helen was very impressed with their thinking, and she decided to tell them about the notepad in one of the statues hands that had also turned to stone.

'Peter was out of his chair with Jake not very far behind, and Helen needed to know what was on their minds.

'The recipe Helen. We have to find the recipe!' said Peter.

'But I told you, It's in the hand of the statue in the garden, and only half is readable! Helen reminded him.

'If it was me Helen, I'd have made a copy! I think we should look through the book about the pixies again!' said Peter, and as soon as he finished speaking, the race was on for the entrance to the games room.

Helen allowed them to run ahead as she got out of her chair to follow them. She didn't think they would find anything as she was convinced at what she saw in the statues hand was probably the original, but she thought she'd like a proper look at the book, now that she had seen the land it was about.

'I won!' said Jake as he performed his tribal ritual dance, but didn't realize that Peter had already entered the games room and was looking for the pixie book. 'Wait for me Peter,' he shouted.

Peter noticed that all the books were placed on the shelves in order of their size, and he remembered the book being a small one, so he started at the right hand side where the small ones were.

Helen soon entered the games room after going straight to the bedside cabinet next to her bed to find the book they were looking for and walked towards the boys

'Is *this* what you're looking for?' she asked, and the two boys ran to her fighting over who was going to look through it first.

'Let me have a look first!' said Jake.

'No! You're always first, let me have a look Helen.' said Peter, and gave Jake a sarcastic smile as Helen handed the book over to him.

'You'll not find anything! I didn't see anything the first time *I* looked at it!' said Helen, but she soon had to eat her own words as when Peter started looking from the back to the front, out fell a piece of paper that was smaller than a pixies handkerchief. Jake picked it up and wished he had his magnifying glass with him, and didn't notice that Peter was doing his own tribal dance that he was making up as he went along.

Helen laughed, as she had never seen Peter dance before, and it reminded her of a group of dancers on a pop show she had seen on the TV when she was a child, and Jake noticed what he was doing.

'Hey you, only I do that! Stop copying me now!' he shouted.

'Jake?' said Helen, 'I think we may need your magnifying glass again! Go and get it and *you* can read it out!'

Jake had to ran along the hallway to the kitchen where he had left his bag after they returned from the maze. He grabbed it and didn't bother opening it to find the magnifying glass, but ran straight back to the games room in case he missed anything.

'Here it is Peter, pass the paper over!' he said between gasps.

Peter handed over the piece of paper and Jake placed it on the floor. They all knelt down in front of it and waited for Jake to start reading it out loud.

'It's much smaller writing than the last one!' he said, but after getting the magnifying glass the right distance from the paper, he started to read what was on it.

RECIPE

*For those that feel the need to feed
their mind of the knowledge to cure.
The lost and the found,
be it human or hound,
you must first trek little Thornton moor.*

*There you must find, a fern of one kind
to pick when it's young and ripe.
no other will do
as the wrong potion will brew
a most hideous and terrible sight.*

'Woah!' said Peter, 'does that mean if we get the wrong fern it'll work, but change the way that person used to be?' I don't like the sound of that!' he said with a worried expression.

'We're just going to have to be very careful Peter!' said Helen, but was a bit worried about what she had just heard herself.

'Do you want to hear the rest of this or not?' asked Jake, who was eager to carry on. 'Ok, it goes on . . .' he said.

*Once picked it will wither, so try not to dither
for time is a thing you have not.
Then bring it on over
with a fist full of clover
to place in a cooking pot.*

> *Then Come to the land with ingredients in hand*
> *and wait for the moon to appear.*
> *with the concoction that's pulped,*
> *heed not to be gulped,*
> *but spread with an evenly smear!*

'This is amazing!' said Peter, 'If we follow this to the word, we could have every pixie we've ever found back where they belong. Is there any more Jake?'

'There's two more verses on the other side!' he said, and started to read before there were any more interruptions.

> *The song will be sang, then a clutter and bang,*
> *will show that the spell will awaken.*
> *The statue will move*
> *then stand up and prove,*
> *that the potion has certainly taken.*

> *When stood straight and tall*
> *and then asked above all,*
> *what it is that they can remember.*
> *If a look of confusion*
> *shows real disillusion,*
> *then freedom it is, no longer a member!*

'Well that sounds pretty straight forward!' said Peter half joking.

'So!' said Jake excitedly, 'What are we waiting for then?' and the boys ran as quick as they could, but neither of them could even make it to the front door as Helen was calling them back.

Peter? Jake? Come back! Helen shouted, 'Aren't you forgetting something?'

Jake looked at Peter, and then down to his hand that held the paper. He suddenly realized what the recipe had explained in the second verse of the recipe.

'We can't do this until the morning Peter!' said Jake with a frown.

'I know!' said an also disappointed Peter.

'Listen boys.' said Helen, 'There are a lot of things we have to prepare before we can start making the recipe! Like who are we going to get to sing that song the recipe told us about for a start!'

Jake was thinking hard, and he came to the conclusion that they'd have to make another visit to the maze before they could start to help the statues.

'I think you're right Jake!' said Peter, 'But how do we find out the words and the melody of the song that has to be sung?'

'Not only that!' said Jake, and the others wondered what *they* had missed that Jake hadn't.

'What Jake?' asked Peter, 'What else?'

'What fern are we looking for Peter? It doesn't say what the name is, or even what it looks like!'

Peter realized that Jake was right, and he looked over at Helen who obviously realized the same. But then Helen had an idea that led to another tiff between Peter and Jake about who would look through the pixie book first.

Helen decided the only way to stop the bickering was to look through the book herself. And as she did, she soon noticed that it wasn't words she should have been looking at, as on every other page there were pictures of pixies dancing and chanting, and it didn't take long for Helen to see what they were all dancing around.

In most of the pictures, the pixies were dancing among flowers, or, 'what looked like flowers,' Helen thought, and she went to another part of the shelf where she knew there was a book on 'local flowers and ferns!' The fern was very alike one she had seen before, and that was in the garden of her granddads house. Although it was missing the very small blue flowers, she was sure that if they went to the moors, she could spot the fern easily enough when they were there.

'Ok Boys,' said Helen, 'meeting in Peters room in one minute. On the double!' she said, trying her best to sound like a sergeant major, and the boys ran as fast as they could up the staircase. The idea of another adventure that afternoon had them standing to attention at the side of Peters bed awaiting instructions.

'Permission to speak freely serge?' Jake asked with a straight face that was slowly turning into a frown.

'Granted!' said Helen.

'Why can't we have the meeting in my room?' he asked.

'Because . . . er,' Helen thought quickly, 'I need a desk to write on, and you haven't got one!'

'Oh!' said Jake and thought about asking dad why he hadn't and Peter had.

'Ok men, we need a list. I want you to write down everything we're going to need for our next mission into Pixity! And remember that we have to carry everything, so no silly things or things that are too heavy. Can you do that, men?'

'Yes serge!' Peter and Jake shouted at the top of their little voices, and they sat around Peters desk where Helen was now sitting with a pen and some of Peters drawing paper.

Jake tugged at Peters sleeve and when he turned, he whispered to Peter . . .

'Next mission Peter! This is going to be the best ever adventure, I just know it.' said Jake with a huge grin, and Peter agreed by shaking Jake by the shoulder and grinning from ear to ear. But once again, the boys were about to be disappointed as Helen had overheard them.

'I hate to be the bearer of bad news men, but I think we'll have to wait until your father leaves for work in the morning. We have a lot to get ready, and I expect we will be in Pixity for a very long time, no matter on what the time difference may be. We need plenty of rest before we go there again, so relax, and do your best to get everything together for the mission. Now, what have you got on your list so far?'

Jake was especially disappointed they were not going on another adventure that day, but did as he was asked in a slightly less excited manner.

'Ok then.' he said and couldn't help give a small tut, 'First on the list is food and drink, then we've got . . . . A torch, watch, compass, paper, string, pencils, my screwdriver,'

'Screwdriver?' asked Peter.

'Yes screwdriver! It came in handy before remember!' said Jake, and he carried on.

'A copy of the recipe, a copy of the riddle, and er . . .'

'What are we forgetting boys?' asked Helen, and the boys scratched their heads trying to think of what it was they had forgotten.

'What else are we going to need?' asked Peter.

'Oh, just the most important thing we haven't discussed yet!' she said, and got a fresh piece of paper ready as if she was about to make a new list. 'We need to make a list of questions and things we need to find out in order to help the statues return to their usual form!'

'Oh!' said Peter, 'Of course we do. Like what are the words to the song we have to sing?'

'Yes,' said Helen, 'and what the tune is!'

'Why don't we just find some pixie that will tell us!' suggested Jake, 'There's bound to be someone we can trust!'

Although what Jake had suggested sounded too easy, Helen and Peter thought about it and couldn't think of a reason for why they shouldn't just do that, then Jake thought of something else.

'We should have to stay there for a much longer time this time if we're going to have to get to know more pixies though!'

'He's right Helen, it takes a lot longer than a few hours to gain someone's trust!' said Peter, and Helen had to agree.

'Peter?' asked Helen, 'Have you got a calculator handy at all? I need to do some mathematics!' and the boys knew what it was that Helen was trying to work out.

The sound of her tapping fingers filled the silence in the room, and the boys eagerly waited to find out how long they could stay in Pixity while father was at work. After what seemed like an eternity to the boys, Helen put the calculator on the desk and sighed a tired breath.

'Well?' asked Jake.

'How long Helen?' asked Peter.

'This morning we were there for what seemed like five hours, and when we returned only ten minutes of our time had passed! So, if my calculations are correct, If we go to Pixity at nine in the morning and return for Five in the afternoon, we are able to stay there for a total of . . . . Six and a half days! Roughly that is!'

'Six and a half days?' screamed Jake, and an extra week off school pleased him greatly.

'Imagine the amount of adventures we could have in all that time Jake!' said Peter.

'Missions Peter!' said Helen, 'We are now on a mission remember. This is to restore all the statues to their former selves don't forget!'

'Yes Peter! And don't forget we are doing this for our Parents!' said Jake, and the others didn't know quite what to say. It wasn't as if they had forgotten about the possibility of finding their parents, but they were all too scared to talk about it in case there would be great disappointment after all of their efforts, so from then on it was treat like a real mission, and they did their best to write down all the important questions that they needed to make sure the recipe would work.

CHAPTER TEN

A favour to ask

That afternoon, all that was on Helens mind was to work out a way to find the words and melody to the song that had to be sung under the Pixity moonlight. 'We could always ask Marcus!' she thought, but then she remembered how he tried to get them to whistle the tune that he had earlier said not to. 'There must be another way.' she thought, and before she knew it, a plan was coming together that couldn't possibly fail.

When the boys father returned from work, Helen made an excuse to leave for half an hour as she had someone to visit, then got a few things together and left with a spring in her step.

'The boys are going to love this!' Helen thought as she walked up the path to her granddads front door, and she searched for the keys to let herself in.

'Granddad!' she shouted, 'Granddad, it's me. Where are you?' she asked, but there was no reply.

The kitchen was the first place that Helen checked, then the sitting room, and she looked out of the window into the garden. She couldn't see her granddad anywhere, and part of her panicked as she ran up the stairs.

'Granddad!' she whispered in case he was having an afternoon nap, but he wasn't in bed either, and there was only one more place where he could have been.

Helen knocked on the bathroom door, but once again there was no reply, and she stayed silent for a moment to hear if he was in the bath. Again there was no sound, and she was just about to enter the bathroom when she heard someone put a key in the front door.

'Is that you granddad?' she shouted down the stairs, but knowing at the same time it couldn't have been anyone else.

'Helen!' he shouted, 'Is that you? Where are you?' and Helen came down the stairs showing the relief of knowing he was ok.

'Yes it's me! Where have you been? You had me worried!'

'I nipped out for some bread and milk as I was getting a bit low, and when you didn't show this morning I thought you might have been too busy for me to bother you. Did you forget dear?' he asked, but he didn't want to seem a burden and giggled a little.

'Oh, I'm so sorry granddad, I forgot. A lot has happened today and it completely escaped my mind. Come on, sit down and I'll make you a nice cup of tea. I've got something I need to tell you!'

Helen went through to the sitting room where here granddad had got himself comfortable in front of the TV, and handed him his drink with a few biscuits. She wondered how she should bring up the subject that had been on her mind all day and decided that the reason why she had forgotten about running his errands that morning was the best way.

'Granddad!' she said, 'I'm sorry about forgetting to pop around earlier but, ... well basically, ... I've spent five hours in Pixity with the boys this morning and we need your help!'

Granddads drink nearly went down the wrong way and he stared at her with wide eyes. Helen didn't know if he was shocked or annoyed for doing something dangerous like her parents did, and was about to start from the beginning when she heard her granddad say something she wasn't expecting.

'Helen Helen,' he said smiling, 'you know those were just stories I told you when you were young, they're not real! Why would you say something like that?'

'No granddad honest, I've seen it. And when we got back, only ten minutes had past. We even spoke to your old friend Marcus Bullman! We found his diary, and a riddle that helped us to enter the gate! Look granddad.' and she got the diary out of her handbag to prove that the stories he told were in fact true.

Monte stared at the diary in disbelief, and he quickly glanced through the old book that had once belonged to his best friend. His eyes darted from left to right, and Helen noticed the side of her granddads cheek rising as he began to believe what Helen had told him was true.

'So the old boy was telling the truth all along!' he finally said, and he asked to see the riddle that Helen was holding in her other hand.

Monte took the paper and unfolded it carefully. He placed it on his lap and took his reading glasses from their case and put them on.

'This is unbelievable!' he said. 'So the statues are really little pixies then?' he asked as he studied the small writing.

'Yes granddad, we found four all together, three male and one female!' she said, and watched for his reaction.

'Female?' he asked.

'Yes, but in the garden are two full size statues granddad. Do you realize what that might mean?'

Monte took off his reading glasses and looked Helen in the eye.

'Edward? Winifred?' he asked, and Helen could see there was a shine in the eyes of the old man that sat before her.

'I'm not sure granddad.' she simply said. 'This is why we need your help!'

CHAPTER ELEVEN

Monte on board

Helen handed over to the boys father his briefcase, Thermos flask and lunch box as he headed towards the front door to leave for his meeting, and as usual, he was thanking her for the excellent job she was doing so far with Peter and Jake.

'Oh they're no bother at all Brian, we're getting along just fine!' she said with a smile, and secretly wishing him to hurry.

'You all seem to be getting along very well! he said, 'And if luck goes my way today, who knows how long we will have you as part of our little family!'

'Our little family.' Helen thought, and she wondered how it would be if she were to find her *own* parents. 'How would they adjust to life as it is now? And would they ever become a normal working family after what they had been through?' she thought, and decided to cross those hurdles when, or if, they ever came along.

'Not as long as I would like!' said Helen, and she hoped that it was the last of the conversation they were going to have, as it was nearly time to expect a certain visitor.

'Goodbye Helen!' said Brian as he climbed into the drivers seat, and Helen just smiled and waved as she watched the car disappear through the trees of the long driveway.

'I'll give him a few minutes in case he's forgotten anything!' she thought to herself, and when she was convinced he wasn't going to return, she locked the door from the inside and ran up the stairs to where the boys were still sleeping. Or so she thought!

'Is it not time to leave yet?' asked Jake as he bounced on the edge of Peters bed.

'Has daddy left yet?' asked Peter, who was also becoming very fidgety.

'Yes it is Jake, and yes he has Peter! . . . Now then boys, I have some good news and some bad news! So which is it you would like to hear first?' asked Helen.

'Tut! I hate it when you tease Helen. Just give us the bad news first, as the good news might cheer us up after!' said Jake, and Peter was pleased that Jake was now starting to think like *he* did. Only recently, Peter thought, had Jake started to use his mind as well as he ever had, and as every day went by, he no longer thought of himself as being the brighter of the two.

'Ok.' said Helen, 'There is still too much to learn before we pay our next visit to Pixity,' and as soon as Helen spoke, their shoulders slumped with disappointment. 'But we still have an adventure on our hands!'

Peter and Jake once again sat upright as if to attention, as they now knew with experience that every time Helen spoke of an adventure, It was going to be a good one, and they sat quietly waiting to hear what the good news was.

'We have someone coming along with us today, let's call him . . . someone who knows a bit about gardening, and . . .'

Helen wasn't surprised that there was going to be interruptions at that point, but she allowed them to moan a little as she knew that once they knew who it was, they would soon forget that they weren't going into the maze that day.

'Gardening?' asked Jake.

'But we know our way through the maze Helen!' said Peter, and when Helen smiled and shook her head, the boys knew they had misunderstood what she had meant.

'We are going to search for the fern boys!' she said, 'Remember what the recipe said?' and Helen tried to remember what they read just the day before. She tried hard to think. 'It was something like . . .'

> *We must find the right kind*
> *to pick when it's young!*
> 'Or something like that!' she said.
> *No other will work,*
> *or a most hideous and awful sight!*

'That couldn't have been it!' said Jake, 'That doesn't even rhyme!' and he folded his arms in protest.

Just then, a sound from downstairs took Jakes mind off his protest.

Dong!!

'Oh good!' said Helen, 'Run downstairs boys and open the door. That'll be the gardener!'

They did as they were asked, but moaned about having to have an extra person on 'the team' for the day.

'Helen!' shouted Peter. 'You've locked the door from the inside. Where is the key?'

Helen had forgot that the door was locked, and started to make her way down the stairs.

'Look Peter.' said Jake excitedly as he looked through the letter box.

'Let me see.' said Peter as he crouched a little. 'It's Monte! Monte's the gardener!'

Helen placed the key in the lock and smiled as she saw the happy faces on the two excited boys at her side.

'Hi granddad.' said Helen.

'Monte!' shouted the boys.

'I'm so glad it's you Monte, and not some boring old gardener!' said Jake, and Monte was pleased the boys were happy for him to tag along that day.

'Hello everyone,' said Monte, 'so whose up for a trip up to the moor eh?'

'Me me!' shouted Peter. 'Look Monte, I've got my Wellingtons on just in case it's a bit boggy up there!'

'That's good Jake.' said Monte.

'I'm Peter!' he corrected him.

'Oh I'm sorry, my memory isn't so good these days!' he said, and looked at Jake. 'So *you* must be Peter then.'

'I'm Jake!'

Monte laughed a little out of embarrassment, and he shook the boys hands.

As they all headed down to the end of their driveway, Jake whispered in Peters ear when Monte wasn't looking and said . . . .

'I hope he doesn't get us lost on the moor Peter, his memory doesn't seem so good!'

'It's ok Jake, I've got my compass with me!'

'Good! I feel a lot better now!' said Jake, and he ran ahead to catch up with Monte who was leading the way.

They had only been walking for about ten minutes when Monte told them that the moor started on the other side of some trees they could see that were just ahead, and as they climbed a small wooden fence, Jakes keen eye noticed something in the tall blades of grass.

'Look look,' Jake yelled, 'I've found another one!'

Monte, Helen and Peter ran to Jakes side, who was kneeling down in front of the little statue that was stood up, but leaning forward with his hands on his knees.

'He looks as if he was trying to catch his breath!' said Peter, and the others agreed.

'Have you moved him at all?' asked Helen.

'No, not yet, why?' he asked.

'I want to see which way he is facing!' said Helen, and she noticed that the little statue must have been heading back to the maze when he had run out of time.

'Do you think he was looking for the same fern as we are Monte?' asked Peter.

'Hmm, it's quite possible Peter!' he said, and he suggested that they leave the statue where it was until they returned a little later.

Monte stood away from the others and scanned the area while slowly turning on the spot. He knew the fern they needed existed, he had seen it before, and he told the others to look for a kind of bluish purple colour.

Peter and Jake stood on a large boulder to get as good a view as the adults had, and Peter wished he had brought his small binoculars. Jake was trying his best to be the first to spot the fern, but gave an almighty 'TUT' as he heard Helen shout.

'Granddad!' she shouted, 'I think I've found some!'

'Ok, good.' he said. 'But don't pick it out the ground yet, It may be the only fern of the right kind around!' and when Monte knelt down next to Helen, the first thing he did was to smell the bluish purple flower within the fern.

'Is this the same as what's in the book granddad?' asked Helen, and Monte ran his fingers through the fern to study the leaves.

'I believe it is Helen! There are lots of ferns with leaves like these, but only one with this blue flower!'

'What's it smell like Monte?' asked Jake.

'Awful Peter!' he said, and Jake didn't bother correcting him.

'Does that mean it's no good? Has it gone bad or something?' asked Peter, and wondered if they were going to have to search all day.

'No, not at all!' said Monte, 'in fact it's good news! The worse the smell, the younger the fern. But like the recipe says, It must be picked, then rushed to the maze as it will wither quickly!'

'Oh, I see.' said Peter, 'But now that we've found some, why don't we just pick some and go straight to the maze! We must have at least six days left before daddy gets home Helen!'

Helen wished that Peter wasn't as bright as he was, and she couldn't think of an excuse quick enough before her granddad said something that wouldn't change the boys minds.

'Maybe *I* could tag along! said Monte, 'I want to see Marcus again, and I bet you that I can persuade him to teach us the song we need!' and the boys were just about jumping on the spot. Helen could not refuse now that the boys were so excited, but insisted on one thing.

'Ok, but I insist on one thing!' she said, 'That we go back to the house for a quick bite to eat and a short rest. We don't know when we will get our next meal, or where we will be sleeping come to think of it!'

'Yes yes,' said Peter, 'but won't the fern wither by then?'

'Probably!' said Monte, 'But we're not far away! So if we do what Helen says, then we can pop back and grab a bunch of fern later'.

They all finally agreed, and they made their way back to the small fence where Jake had spotted the statue. Helen placed the statue inside her coat, making sure no damage would come to it, and they were soon back at the old oak door at the front of the house.

Once safely inside, Helen Gave the statue to Jake and told him to put it carefully in the box with the others, but Jake was confused to why he wasn't asked to bring the box downstairs, as he thought they were going to start bringing the pixies back to life.

'No Jake,' said Helen after a bit of thought, 'we have to convince Marcus to help us first! What if we picked the fern and Marcus refuses to help for some reason?' she asked him, and the boys realized that they would have to make at least two trips to Pixity before their father came home.

'I never thought of that!' said Monte, and he asked the boys to lead him to the kitchen as he was going to make them the most filling breakfast they'd ever had.

As they all sat around the table, they discussed do's and don't's, which of the seven statues they knew about were they going to help first, and how to convince Marcus he'd be doing the right thing. They wondered if Marcus himself would like to return to the world he came from, and what would happen if he did. 'Would he remain looking the age he was in Pixity?' they thought, or 'Would he all of a sudden return to the age he would have been if he never went there in the first place?' They decided that there were too many questions to be answered before they began their mission to free all newcomers from where they are entrapped, and they all tried to rest as best they could before leaving for Pixity.

CHAPTER TWELVE

The first mission

The old clock in the hallway chimed to reveal to all that it was 10 o'clock, and no one actually *had* got any rest. Even Helen and Monte were getting excited about the mission, and after going through their list one more time, they all marched up the hallway to the front door.

'This is it boys,' said Helen, 'It's now or never! Now let me make sure the front door is properly locked and then we can begin our mission.'

Peter and Jake led the way to the gardens at the rear, but had to slow down a few times so Monte could keep up. When Monte stood and saw the maze, he paused for a while. He couldn't believe he was about to see his old friend Marcus soon, and that he was only an hour away.

'Are you alright granddad?' asked Helen, but Monte didn't answer. He just started walking towards the maze again, and the others were close behind him.

Just in front of the entrance to the maze, they all stopped at the two large statues. Nobody said anything at first, as it was possible they were Helens parents, who were also Monte's son and daughter in-law, or could have even been the boys mother. But then Jake broke the silence.

'Don't worry.' Jake said softly to the statues, 'It'll not be long now!' he said, and the others smiled at Jake as they walked away, but none of them saw the tear that had fallen from one of the eyes of the female statue.

Peter got the map from his bag and lined it up to face the same direction as the maze. They walked slowly into the maze and kept tightly together, as they remembered that the pixies liked to play tricks on visitors by moving the hedges around.

The sun was becoming hotter, and Helen was glad she had brought her small umbrella, as she remembered the lack of shade as they neared the clearing in the center. The further into the maze, the more everyone was keeping an eye on Monte. They had walked for about fifteen minutes now and the temperature was increasing rapidly, and the boys knew what Monte's breathing was like, as it was the first thing they had noticed about him the first time they had met.

'Are you ok Monte?' asked Peter, 'Any time you need a rest just say so, ok?'

But Monte carried on until they reached the clearing in the center of the maze. It was as if he was on a mission of his own, and Helen was worried that this 'mission' was maybe too much for him to handle.

Peter and Jake sat at one of the stone benches in the clearing and waved their hands in front of their faces. The heat was affecting the young as well as the old, and even the boys rested for a longer period than normal, but a quick bite to eat and a glass of pop later, they were soon back on track in search of the little green gate.

'If I remember correctly, The gate should be around the next corner!' said Jake, and he ran to the next turning. But as he looked around the corner, the little green gate was not where they had seen it last.

'That's strange!' said Jake, 'I could have sworn it was in that corner the last time we came!' and neither Peter or Helen could say that they thought he was wrong.

'What's different about it this time?' asked Peter.

'Nothing, I think!' said Helen. 'But I was expecting something that hasn't happened yet, and that is that we haven't heard any giggling, or seen any pixies yet!'

'That's right Helen!' said Jake, 'Maybe it's because we have already been here!'

'Yes!' she said, 'It's as if we don't need any more encouragement to carry on any further!'

Then, just like the last time, they looked back at the direction where they had came, and noticed that the last turning was now blocked. This didn't bother them too much, as they were able to leave the maze as quickly as they entered the last time, and it wasn't long before they all heard a single snigger coming from a corner in the hedge row behind them. Their heads turned quickly to the direction of where the sound came from, and their search for the gate was over.

'There it is!' shouted Jake, 'It wasn't there before, but there it is now!' he said, and they all went over to Jake who was already reminding himself of the tune that had to be whistled.

'What are you doing Jake?' asked Peter.

'I'm trying to remember the tune. I've got the notes in front of me!' he said.

'What's the point in that Jake? You can't whistle, remember?' said Peter, and took the paper out of Jakes hands, then looked at the notes.

Peters memory was always good, and he just had to look at the pattern of notes to remember the melody that was needed. He whistled the tune once, and the little green gate slowly opened with a loud creek.

Monte stood to the side as the others edged towards the gate, and he tried to see over and around the entrance to Pixity, but all he could see was more hedges. Then he remembered what Marcus had told him about the other dimension.

'After all these years,' thought Monte, 'I thought that he was making it up as he went along, and here we are!' He knew that he had told Marcus that he believed every word he had said, even if it was to help stop him from going insane, but 'never in a million years,' he thought, would he have ever thought that *this* was possible!

Peter and Jake were through to the other side, and Helen stayed with her granddad until *he* was sure about going through.

'Your turn granddad!' she said, smiling to try and show that there was nothing to worry about.

'Ok Helen,' he said nervously, 'Let's go and see Marcus shall we?'

'Mind your head there granddad.' Helen said softly, and couldn't wait for him to meet his old pal from nearly six decades ago.

When Monte was through to the other side, he looked at Peter and Jake, and was a little confused.

'Why have I shrunk, and you two haven't?' he asked.

'Sorry Monte,' said Jake, 'we forgot to tell you that everyone is the same height in Pixity. No-one taller or shorter than the other!'

'Oh,' he said, 'I don't know if I can get used to this. This is weird!' said Monte as he shivered, but the thought of seeing Marcus again took his mind off the weird feeling he had, and he followed the others down the winding path that led to a luscious green meadow.

When the path made it's first turn, from behind an old tree stump walked a figure, and it was the figure of someone they had met before.

'Greetings!' said the funnily dressed man who stood before them.

'Isn't that the one called Trickster?' Jake whispered to Peter.

'Yes! I recognise the odd socks he wears!' he said.

'You never said anything about that before!' said Jake, as he stared at the green sock and then the red one.

'I know, said Peter, 'I didn't say anything at the time because I was dying to laugh!'

'I see why!' said Jake, and they were interrupted by the one who was called Trickster, and he said . . .

'It's rude to whisper gentlemen!'

'I wasn't going to whisper 'gentlemen!' said Jake in a sarcastic tone, and once again he felt a heel dig into the back of his leg. He knew where it had came from and he apologised to Helen before he even made sure that it had came from her.

'I see you have decided to return!' said Trickster, 'It's been a lot longer than we expected!' he said, 'What's it been, a couple of weeks?' he asked, then he stared at the man who was with them that he thought he recognised. 'Hello sir' he said, 'Haven't we met before?'

Monte knew they had never met, but came to the conclusion that Trickster must have recognised him from the old summer school when he was visiting Marcus.

'No, I don't think I've had the pleasure!' said Monte, as he felt he didn't have time for a deep conversation.

Trickster looked again at Monte, he knew he *had* seen him before, and he knew *why* he was here!

'You've come to see your old friend Marcus, haven't you?' he asked, and Monte didn't know what to say next, except . . .

'Yes. How is he?'

Trickster smiled at the old man that stood before him and held his hand out in a fashion that said . . .

'Come friend, I have no doubt that he will be as glad to see you as you are of him!'

They all started walking towards Marcus' house, but Helen had something nagging her in the back of her mind. 'What did he mean by it's been a lot longer than we expected!' she thought, 'who's we?' and she quickly did some sums in her head to try and work out how long they had been away from Pixity as it is measured in *their* time.

'Roughly,' Helen thought, 'one of our hours is equivalent to one of their days, so we've been gone for about twenty five hours, erm . . . that'll be nearly three and a half weeks!' but she still wondered what Trickster meant by 'longer than *we* expected.'

'Not long now Monte!' said Peter, and offered him his bottle of water. 'Do you need to rest before we get there?' he asked, but Monte was determined that he wasn't going to stop until he reached the front door of Marcus' house.'

Trickster opened the gate that led up to the front door of Marcus' house, and Helen took hold of her granddads hand as they slowly approached. She thought that before the door opened, she'd better explain something else they had forgot to mention.

'You still might not recognise Marcus granddad!' she said, 'He *has* aged since the last time you saw him, but he stopped ageing like everybody else, at the age of twenty one!'

'Twenty one?' asked her granddad, 'Why twenty one?'

'I don't know exactly, I'll explain better later!' she said, and Trickster knocked his knock on the front door.

For the first time in over fifty years, Monte heard the voice of his best pal from the summer school, and he didn't know whether to laugh or cry. He recognised the voice instantly, and didn't know if he was dreaming, or why he had been so stupid as to not believe his best friend all those years ago.

The door opened, and Monte stared at the young man who had answered it. He knew inside, that it was him, and when he saw the look on Marcus' face, he knew hat he himself was recognised also.

'Monte old boy! he shouted, 'Could it possibly be you? You've never changed. How are you old boy?' he asked, and he put his arms around the friend that he had missed so much.

Monte's mind was racing. 'What does he mean 'you've never changed!' he thought, and he wondered for a moment if he himself had the looks of a twenty one year old since he entered their land.

He looked to Helen who was on his side, and Helen had a feeling of what the question might be.

'No granddad!' she whispered. 'You're still the same!' she said, and she noticed a slight look of disappointment on the tired old man who raised her.

Monte looked at Marcus, and even after all the years that went by, he didn't know what to say to him.

'Marcus!' he finally said, 'Forgive me, but you *do* look a lot older than I remember!'

Marcus laughed and he threw his arms around his old pal once again and invited them all in for a drink.

Monte walked into Marcus' home first and he looked around to see how Marcus had been living for all of the time he'd been 'missing'. His home reminded Monte of his friends parents home when he went to stay there after the first summer at the school. It was the same TV, the same old decoration, the same carpet, and he noticed there wasn't any records in the rack that were written after the last stay they had at the school. But he thought he knew why, and he didn't mention his thoughts on his lack of modern taste.

'Black tea with no sugar wasn't it Monte old boy?' asked Marcus, proud that he still remembered.

'Er, yes!' he said, and he didn't have the heart to tell him that he was more of a coffee drinker these days.

They all sat down on the fifties style two piece suite, and Trickster put the radio on quietly to ease the silent tension. Monte stayed in the kitchen with Marcus while he made tea, and the others stayed where they were to let the two friends get to know one another again. Peter and Jake were becoming bored with the old style of music that was repeatedly being played on the radio, and asked Helen if they could once again explore nearby.

'Er, I think not boys!' she said, 'Remember what nearly happened the last time?'

Trickster listened to what Helen had said to the boys, and wondered about what she had meant. He wondered if she was talking about his *own* two friends that nearly converted the boys to a lifetime membership of Pixity, and if she was, he would have to choose some other visitor to convert to get the one hundred he needed to live with what would now be his great great great nieces and nephews in the 'old world!'

Marcus and Monte entered the room with trays that were full of cups of tea and biscuits, and that were made in the very area they were visiting, then Trickster looked at Monte. He looked how his health was, and how his breathlessness was much older than his state of mind, and he knew he had a chance of converting an old man that would be grateful of a new bill of health.

No one could get a word in edgeways, as the two friends exchanged stories about things that had happened nearly sixty years ago, and the two boys couldn't help but snigger at the wild tricks they used to play on people. It reminded them of themselves and the last school they were at, where they had swapped identities on numerous occasions to confuse anyone and everyone. The boys completely forgot they were stuck in the 1950's and were enjoying their visit more than ever.

'Any more stories?' asked an excited Jake, and Peter also showed his enthusiasm by repeating the question Jake had just asked.

'Have you? Any more?' Peter asked, but their expectations were interrupted by Helen, who was trying to think of the best way to get rid of Trickster.

There were lots of important reasons why they had all visited that day, and she knew nothing could be done when a certain individual was in their company. In order to continue with 'the mission', they had to get Marcus on his own. They had to get Marcus on his own because granddad was going to try and find out about the song needed in the ritual!

When the conversation became more quiet, Trickster concocted a plan, and it was a plan that was going to get him out of there for good. There was 'no room for mistakes' he thought, and this time he thought he had the right person for the job!

Trickster made an excuse for leaving, and as he walked passed Monte, he tapped him on the shoulder and motion him to follow. Monte wondered what he had wanted, and he wondered if he had anything to say about Marcus, so *he* too made an excuse to see Trickster to the front door.

'I'll see you out Trickster,' he said, 'I need a bit of fresh air! I don't know if I'm in my early teens, or seventy!'

Helen giggled and the boys smiled. They were so glad that Monte had been reunited with Marcus, but Peter was curious to why Trickster had slyly asked him to meet him outside.

Peter stayed behind the front door as Monte and Trickster walked to the garden gate, and he did his best to listen in on the conversation that was obviously meant to be between Monte and Trickster only.

'Monte My dear friend!' said Trickster. 'You know you don't always have to suffer from your health!' he said, and he eagerly awaited the response from Monte, who was still a bit out of breath.

'What do you mean?' asked Monte.

'Come, live with us!' he half whispered, 'You'll be given a clean bill of health! No more puffing and panting! and we'll make sure you have everything you need to enjoy a carefree and happy life! he said, and he didn't know if Monte had taken him seriously or not, as Monte slightly shook his head and declined.

'Trickster!' said Monte with all seriousness. 'I have come here to collect my son and daughter in-law! and I'm not leaving until I do that very thing!' he said with a stern look that said he wasn't going to budge until he had found a way to get what he wanted.

'But Monte!' said Trickster, everything you need is right here! Why would you want anything more?'

'Because Trickster, I believe you are just that!'

'What?' asked Trickster.

'I believe you *are* a trickster!'

There was a silence, he knew that Monte was right and wouldn't settle until he got the truth!

'Monte!' said Trickster, and breathed out a heavy sigh 'Join us, and the boys get their mother back!'

'What? when? Where?' were the only things that came into Monte's head, and he knew the conversation was going to last a lot longer! 'Are you trying to make a deal with me trickster? Because if it's that easy, where is my son and his wife? Tell me, now!' he said as the volume of his voice increased.

Please Monte, not so loud. You don't want your Helen to hear now do you?' he asked, and after a short deep thought he asked, 'How long are you all staying?' he asked.

'As long as it takes, why?'

'Meet me in the morning at nine o'clock by the gate, and we'll talk in private. If I am to help you Monte, you must help me!' said Trickster with a slight smile as he concocted a plan that would help them all.

Peter quickly flushed the lavatory that was situated next to the front door, and entered the sitting room where all the others were still giggling at Marcus as he told more stories of their wicked childhoods, and Helen noticed that Peter had been gone for quite some time.

'Are you feeling alright Peter?' she asked, and although her question embarrassed him a little, he just smiled and nodded.

Jake on the other hand was keen to fill Peter in on the stories he had just heard from Marcus, but Peter didn't take much notice as what he had just heard outside was more important, and he wondered if he should tell Helen now, or follow Monte and Trickster to the gate in the morning to hear what it was that Trickster had to say.

'The boys get their mother back!' replayed in his mind over and over, and to Peter, he knew that he was going to be reunited with his mother that he had always only imagine from pictures. He didn't want to say anything to Jake yet, as building up Jakes hopes would not be the best thing to do in case anything had gone wrong. Then the next thing Peter remembered was . . . 'I help you, you help me!' and then that statement kept echoing through his mind. 'What was it that Trickster wanted in return?' he asked himself. Was it a sacrifice? he didn't know, and decided that before he told anyone what he had heard, he was going to follow Monte and Trickster to the gate in the morning to find out more.

'Are we staying here tonight Helen?' asked Peter.

'Oh please Helen, I want to hear more of Marcus' stories. Please Helen!' Jake begged.

Helen was glad of what the boys had asked in a way, as she didn't really want to ask Marcus herself, and was happy when it was Marcus who answered the boys questions.

'What a brilliant idea!' he said. 'I've never had anyone stay over since I've been here! Would you all like to stay over? I've plenty of bedding, and it never gets cold in Pixity.'

Monte was also pleased that they were all asked to stay over as he had just agreed to meet Trickster in the morning at the gate, and was relieved when Helen agreed that they would all stay.

'Are you sure you don't mind Marcus?' she asked, 'I mean, where would we all sleep? You only have one bedroom!'

'Two bedrooms Helen!' he corrected her, 'I have one upstairs, and one downstairs! The bedroom downstairs hasn't been used as a bedroom before but I'm sure we can make it look like one once I've taken all my junk outside. You Helen, can have my room upstairs, and us boys will make ourselves comfortable downstairs. how does that sound?'

'That sounds great Marcus thank you.' she said, and she suggested that they should all go for a short walk before they had lunch.

'Yeeey!' shouted Peter and Jake together.

'An adventure! come on Peter, said Jake, 'let's go explore!'

CHAPTER THIRTEEN

A trip into town

Marcus and Monte led the way down the path and the others followed as the two old school buddies joked, laughed, and reminisced about old times they had as young men. Marcus talked about Pixity and what he had been doing since he arrived, and Monte talked about all the things that have happened in the world since Marcus had left. Marcus laughed when Monte told him of new inventions and gadgets like mobile phones and microwave ovens as if he didn't believe him, but when Monte told him about man landing on the moon, Marcus stopped where he was and asked him to repeat what he had just said.

'What did you say Monte? That's impossible! How could man have possibly achieved that?'

Ever since Marcus was able to look up at the sky, the moon fascinated him. He wanted to know what it would be like up there, what it was made of, and most of all, what would the machine that would take man up there look like? Marcus knew he had missed a lot of the old world he had left, and often thought about visiting there himself again one day. But knowing he would only have an hour, and the thought of turning into a statue like many of his old friends had put him off greatly, and had decided that it would be best never to take the chance.

'I said that 'Man has gone to the moon!' Monte repeated, and Marcus realized just how long he must have been in Pixity. The idea of asking the elders for permanent freedom was becoming a real thought again, but he remembered what their answers were the other times he had asked.

They had walked for another fifteen minutes and over the brow of the hill, they could see rooftops with chimneys belching out smoke. Helen thought she was looking at a photograph of old days gone, and imagined what she was looking at to be in black and white.

'It's beautiful!' she said in awe, and the others agreed. Monte just slightly nodded and stared for a while. 'A clean bill of health?' he thought to himself.

'Come everyone,' said Marcus, 'I'll take you to the high street!'

They all followed with a quickened step as they imagined a busy wide street, with lots of shops and funny little people to meet. But when they got there, all they could see were little houses with flowers in the window boxes and brightly coloured window shutters. There was no sign of a bustling little market town like they had all imagined.

'Where are all the shops Marcus?' asked Jake with a little disappointment.

'When you get to know everyone, then you'll know where to look Jake!' said Marcus. 'If you'd like a loaf of bread, you'll know where to go, and if you need milk, you'll know where to go! That's the way it is in Pixity.

Just as Peter was going to ask Marcus a few questions of his own, a lady walked by who he knew he had seen before.

'Well hello there!' said Mrs Atkinson, 'Visiting again eh?'

Helen remembered that this Mrs Atkinson was know as the local gossip, so decided to keep their conversation to a minimum if she could.

'Hello again!' she said, 'Lovely day isn't it!'

Mrs Atkinson looked at her strangely and wondered what she had meant. But Helen had soon realized that what she had just said, wasn't completely understood because it was always bright and sunny in Pixity.

Marcus intervened by changing the subject rapidly and asked her if there was anything that had happened since the last time he was in town.

'Well!' she said, and she began to reel off everything that she had heard or witnessed over the last week or so. 'Mrs Frannigans dog had four pups, beautiful little creatures might I add, and Mr Parker has asked if he can have extra flour for his new blueberry cakes he is making! But best of all,' she whispered, and asked Marcus to come closer, 'the latest, is that . . .'

She looked around to see if anyone else was listening, and when she was happy with the lack of company, she said . . . 'Apparently . . . Trickster has applied for an audience with the elders!' and as soon as she said it, she was away. Away to gossip with anyone and everyone she could see before she would retire to her home.

'An audience with the elders?' Marcus thought to himself, 'But why?' and he thought that he'd keep that question for the next time he'd see his 'buddy'.

'Why would he want to ask the elders something rather than himself?' he thought, and he knew there was something not right. 'Did it have anything to do with his visitors?' he thought, and as soon as he thought that, he remembered what Trickster had said to him a long time ago. 'If I could only enlist a certain amount, I'd be free and return to my family!'

'Marcus!' Monte called.

'Yes Monte?'

'I hope that Tricksters meeting with the elders doesn't have anything to do with our visit!' he said, and could tell that Marcus was thinking hard for an excuse for the topic of conversation with Mrs Atkinson.

'Oh, take no notice please Monte,' said Marcus, 'Mrs Atkinson is one of the longest residents of Pixity, in fact, in human years she is about Four hundred years old! She craves gossip like a small dog craves it's ball!'

'I realize that Marcus,' said Helen, 'But for what reason would Trickster want to see the elders for? It must be something important!'

'I know!' he simply said, 'And I promise you all, as soon as I find out, You'll know!'

'Four hundred years old!' though Monte, but then thought that Marcus' mathematics had to be wrong. 'The maze certainly hadn't been around for that long, nor the house come to think of it!' he thought, and he decided that he would sit and chat more with Marcus that night . . . alone.

As they all walked along the high street, they noticed first of all that everybody knew Marcus, and he knew them. They were also doing their best not to stare at the visitors to their land, so Peter and Jake tried their best not to giggle at the residents clothing as Helen was keeping a close eye on the pair of them. They smiled, pointed, and failed to keep their shoulders from making it obvious of what they were thinking, and every now and then they both received a kick in the side of a leg from the side of Helens foot that was telling them to stop. Peter had a question for Marcus and he tapped him on the arm, but before he got the chance to ask, Helen wanted to know what the question was before she allowed him to ask it.

'Oh!' said Helen, 'Good question Peter, go ahead, ask.'

'Marcus!' asked Peter.

'Yes Jake?'

And Peter thought, 'Not again!' but he carried on with his question.

'I was told that there were newcomers, like yourself, and there were Pixiborns! So, there must be children in Pixity, right?' he asked, and already Marcus was trying to think of an answer for what he knew what was coming next.

'Yes Jake there are!' he said.

'It's Peter!' he had to tell him, and nearly found himself giving a huge 'tut' like Jake would have done.

'Sorry Peter,' he said, 'I think the next time we meet, you and Peter, sorry Jake, will have to wear different colours!' and he laughed a little.

'So?' asked Peter still waiting for an answer, 'Where are they then?' and didn't realize how sarcastic he had put that last question to Marcus.

The others noticed the tone in which Peter had asked Marcus, but even Helen didn't say anything to Peter as she looked around the town searching for at least one other child, but there weren't any, and they all waited for an answer.

'Why Peter,' he said, 'They're all at school!'

Peter, Jake, Monte and Helen tried to hide their embarrassment as the most obvious answer in the world escaped them, and Marcus smiled to himself realizing that they didn't know that there were no schools as such, in Pixity.

Even Monte thought no more about the misunderstanding, and asked Marcus if there was a cafeteria near by, as he was getting a little parched with the permanent Pixity weather.

'Cafeteria?' asked Marcus, but soon knew what he had meant as Monte was using one of the 'old' words.

'Yes Marcus, you know? A sit down with a cup of tea and a scone?' he asked, and Marcus had to explain that there was 'no such thing in this land!'

'What?' No tea rooms?' he asked disappointedly.

'Yes Monte old boy, there are lots! but you just have to decide on which one you want to visit!'

'What do you mean Marcus?' asked Jake, who was also feeling a bit peckish.

'There is a tea room in every house in Pixity Jake!'

And Jake was glad that he had got his name right.

'I see!' said Helen, 'You mean that you just choose who you want to visit?'

'Yes Helen!' said Marcus, 'The elders decided that there were some times that you didn't want to bump into certain pixies, and this way gave you the option of who you would like to have tea with!' he told them, but didn't expect what question he was asked next.

'So,' said Jake thinking hard, 'You just knock on the door and demand a cup of tea? Is that how it works?' and Marcus hadn't thought of it like that, and he got a bigger shock when Jake asked his next question. 'But what if *you* were the Person that *they* didn't want to have tea with? Can they tell you to go away?'

Helen, Monte and Peter smiled at Jake whose mind was improving by the hour since they started visiting Pixity, but Marcus was becoming more tired of the two boys and their questions that he couldn't answer, and was secretly wishing he hadn't stopped them from singing a certain tune that day.

Helen and Monte noticed that the more the boys asked their awkward questions, the harder it was becoming for Marcus to answer them. They could see that he was starting to stumble further into submission as the bright pair learned more about their surroundings, and both Helen and her granddad knew that he could not be trusted.

Tea and scones were delayed until they had all reached Marcus' home, and when they arrived, Marcus put his deck chair, and anything else he could find to sit on, out in the rear garden. They all sat drinking their tea and nibbling on what Helen thought were the best scones she had ever tasted, and the Boys were pestering Marcus and Monte to tell more of their childhood stories.

'I think we have told you all of them now, unless you, Marcus, can think of ones I seem to have forgotten!'

Marcus thought hard, he couldn't think of a story, but he thought of a question he had wanted to know the answer to for a very long time.

'So Monte,' said Marcus, 'what ever happened to that old blighter Brannigan eh? Please don't tell me he's still alive! What would that make him now, ninety something?' he asked, but Monte Waved his finger at Marcus wanting to ask him not to mention him, as he was in the middle of swallowing his last gulp from his cup.

'I afraid I can't talk about him Marcus!' he said as he wiped his lips with his hand.

Helen looked over to her granddad and wondered why this 'Brannigan' had upset her granddad enough for him to say that. Then she remembered the words in Marcus' diary. *'Monte got ten because he told him it didn't hurt!'* and her instinct made her instantly go over to him as she tried to hide the water welling in her eyes as she thought about the beatings they received.

'It's alright granddad, you don't have to talk about him! I know what he did to you all, I read about what he did to you in Marcus' diary!' and as soon as Marcus' diary was mentioned, Peter and Jake went to get it out of Jakes bag as they forgot that there were still pages that they had not read yet.

Helen wasn't quick enough to stop them, as she remembered that Marcus wanted to see it again. The feeling of mistrust with Marcus was increasing, and she wanted to read it herself from front to back before it was given back to it's rightful owner.

'We've got a surprise for you Marcus!' said Jake.

'And if you guess what it is, you can read it to us!' said Peter, and Jake gave a humongous 'tut', as Peter had given away their surprise. But before Marcus could even hasten a guess, Monte interrupted, and told them that it wasn't the beatings he received that made him dislike the man, and they stayed silent until he told them the real reason why Brannigan had reappeared in his thoughts after all the years gone by.

'I had seen Brannigan on a number of occasions since those summers ago,' he finally said, and Helen didn't know if she wanted to hear.

Monte looked inside his cup, and with a disappointed look, asked one of the boys to fetch him a glass of water.

'I'll get it Monte!' said Jake, 'But don't start till I get back ok?' he asked, and ran as fast he could to the kitchen. He found a glass that was in one of the cupboards and looked around for the sink ... There was a sink, but there were no taps! He looked everywhere in the kitchen, but there were no taps in sight! 'Strange,' thought Jake, 'a kitchen with no taps! How are you supposed to wash dishes?' he thought, and just then, Marcus came in and took a large bottle from one of the cupboards to fill the glass with water.

'There!' he said, and Jake took the glass of water to Monte who was mopping his brow with his handkerchief.

'You were saying granddad, er . . . I mean Monte.' said Peter, and hid his face.

Monte smiled a smile he couldn't control, and patted Peter on the shoulder.

'I wish I was Peter,' he said, 'and you too Jake!' and ruffled his hair like Helen had done once or twice before.

'Stop it.' said Jake, but in a childish way that told him he didn't mind, really.

Monte sighed a big sigh, and the others thought that he was going to tell them all something that he wanted to get off his chest for a long time, but they couldn't have been more wrong. Because Monte, in the last day or so, had found out something terrible.

'Brannigan, I heard, was the main suspect in the disappearance of the children that went missing from the summer school!' he said, 'It was because he received so many complaints from the children and their parents because of the drastic measures he took upon himself as adequate punishment!' said Monte, and immediately stared at Marcus to see his reaction.

Marcus inhaled quickly and deeply, as he knew instantly what it was that Monte was getting at.

'So they think it was all down to him?' asked Helen, and Monte nodded.

'He's innocent Helen!' said Monte, and bowed his head. 'Twenty years taken from him for something he always denied, and when he was released, no one ever saw him again!'

Marcus remembered all the lashes to his hind, and the bullying, and the name calling, and wondered how on earth Monte could have any sorry feelings for this brute that tried to make their lives a misery.

'But Monte, you remember how he treat us don't you?' asked Marcus, 'He had to pay!'

Monte couldn't believe what he had just heard, and the others could tell that he was getting annoyed. He rose from his chair and paced around the others, especially Marcus, and let out what was brewing inside since he heard what had happened to him.

'He's no murderer Marcus!' said Monte. 'I said that I'd seen him on a number of occasions?' he reminded them, 'Well, those occasions were on the television! You now know why! And although I didn't know for sure at the time about the stories, you . . . Marcus especially, had told me, with what I've learned recently, I don't care how bad this man had treat us, that should not have happened!' he said, and he had one more thing to say to Marcus.

'I don't know if it's souls you have to collect, but if you want to get out of here Marcus, we're your only hope! So . . . from now on, no lies, truth only, and I'm sure we can all leave healthy, guilt free, and be able to get on with the lives that we should have!'

Everyone was quiet, Helen had never heard her granddad make such a speech as powerful as that before, and she pretended to be as serious and forceful as the granddad she was so proud of.

Peter and Jake sat, not knowing whose side to be on until they remembered about the tune that had to be whistled to exit the gate, and it was Jake who decided to demand an answer to that question.

'Marcus!' he said with as deep a voice he could. 'Why did you stop us from singing that song, or even humming that song, when it was exactly the same tune as the tune that was needed to exit the gate?'

'Is it?' he shrieked, and the others thought that he really *didn't* know, and wondered if all the bad thoughts they had about him were justified.

'You mean you really didn't know?' asked Jake.

'No, certainly not! I'm surprised you even thought that I would have known.' and Marcus felt hurt as they all stared and wondered. 'It was Trickster that told me that years ago!' and he pondered a little before what he said next. 'I've known for a long time that Trickster has been waiting for the right time to 'enlist' more outsiders though, but I didn't think He'd target a relative of old Monte here! You've got to believe me.'

Monte, even after all these years, still believed that he knew this man well, and he couldn't believe that Marcus would do such a thing. He searched his feelings, and decided that it was Trickster that was the one to be weary of and not Marcus.

'Trickster *did* try and tempt me earlier!' Monte thought out loud, 'He said I would get my health back.'

'There!' said Marcus, 'You see? He only needs a few more and they will let him leave!' he said, and his begging eyes looked into all of the others eyes one by one to see if he was believed.

All except Peter, were beginning to believe that Marcus was telling the truth, as there were still a few questions he had for Marcus. He put his hand up as if he was in a lesson at school and looked at Helen to see if she was going to silence him again, But Helen wanted to know all the answers Marcus might have and she allowed him to carry on.

'Marcus!' he asked, 'You said that all the children were at school! But, I never even saw any children that were too young to even go to school yet! Where are they all Marcus?'

Monte, and Helen especially, stared at Marcus after realizing they should have thought of that very question.

Marcus looked at them all, bowed his head and said . . .

'Ok, the truth it is.' he said, and before he could answer, Helen remembered something he said on their first visit.

'The mines!'

The others wondered what it was she was going on about, and the two boys asked the same question at the same time.

'Mines? What mines?' they asked.

Monte stared at Marcus as if to remind him that it was all the truth from now on.

'The children . . . .' he went on, 'The children work the mines!' he said, and in a strange way he felt relieved that there was nothing left to hide. 'When a child becomes five years old, and apart from being the same size as an adult don't forget, they help down the mines with the other adults, and after their duty is over, it's school for a few hours then home. There aren't many children in Pixity under five at the moment, and that is why you probably didn't notice any. Most of the people who came here from the outside were older when they arrived, this is why when a school was built next to the portal, every pixie in the land was keen to enlist unsuspecting boys and girls who entered the maze. Anything to increase the population!' he said, and there was a silence while everyone tried to get their heads around all the confusion.

'So,' said Monte, 'If you arrive young, you stop ageing at twenty one! and if you arrive say . . . . my age, you stay the same! Is that how it goes?'

'That's pretty much it Monte! said Marcus, and he thought he knew what he was going to ask next.

'So Trickster lied when he said I'd get my health back then?' asked Monte, and was annoyed at the fact he thought about trading with him.

'On the contrary Monte!' said Marcus, and he regained Monte's attention. 'One will look the same as one did when one arrived, but will regain ones health of when one was at his or hers best! Do you understand old boy?'

'Who's one?' asked Peter.

'I understand!' said Jake, 'But what is it they're mining?' he asked, and Peter gave a 'tut' and said . . .

'I was going to ask that!'

And as soon as he said it, he wondered what was happening to himself and Jake.

'I just tutted! and complained that you said what I was going to say! It's always been the other way around Jake! Always has been! What's going on?'

Marcus sat in between them and explained that it was nothing to worry about.

'Am I turning into Jake?' asked Peter.

'No Peter.' he said, and asked Jake not to take offence at what he was about to say. 'You are both evening out! You Peter, are toughening up a little, and Jake is becoming a bit smarter. That's how it is in Pixity!' and Peter remembered something Trickster said on their first visit. *'No-one smaller or taller than the other!'* 'Did that mean for every difference that people had from their own world?' he thought. 'No-one smaller or taller, no-one brighter than another, no girl prettier than another!' He began thinking that this Pixity isn't as tempting a place as he first thought. 'A world needs differences!' he thought. 'Does that mean there would be no sports days or competitions? No-one faster or slower? No-one better than another?' and he decided that the quicker they got the pixies back to their former selves the better.

Peter went over to Monte and stood in front of his chair where he was sitting. He was worried about him meeting Trickster in the morning, and he hoped he was doing the right thing by telling everyone what he had heard.

'Monte!' said Peter. 'I don't think you should go alone to meet Trickster in the morning, I don't trust him! And I don't think anyone else does either.'

'Granddad!' said Helen a little alarmed. 'Weren't you going to tell us? And why? Are you going to join this place?'

'No Helen,' he tried to reassure her, 'I was only going to see if I could make a deal!'

Helen was going to ask him 'What kind of a deal,' as she had nearly forgotten the reason why they had all gone there in the first place, But it was Jake who thought he'd guess first.

'It's because we need to know the words and music of the song that has to be sung for the recipe, isn't it Monte?'

'Yes Jake, I thought we could trade a few of the statues we have!' and he looked into Helens eyes to see if she knew what he had in mind.

'How many do you have?' Marcus asked.

'Five small ones!' said Peter.

'And two large ones!' said Jake. 'Why?'

'Hmm,' said Marcus, and thought for a while that was a little too long for Peters liking.

'What do you have in mind?' asked Peter, And Marcus had an idea that was sure to please them all.

'Do you think you could bring them to the gate so I could see them?' he asked, and the others wondered what good that would do. They still needed the song, and without the song, they didn't know which of the pixies could be the ones they loved.

'Because everyone,' he said, 'I know every pixie there is! Both the pixiborns and the newcomers, I'm bound to recognise them when I see them!'

'How can you recognise what's turned into a little stone statue Marcus?' asked Jake.

'Please, let me explain.' he said, 'Don't think of them as little statues, as they look exactly as they did when they were transformed! Every curve, cheekbone, ear size, foot size, are never changed. It is an exact image of what they once were.

'Well I think that's a great idea!' said Monte, 'We'll go and get them straight after a nap!'

'A nap?' asked Peter, 'Is *this* not more important?'

'If we take a nap here Peter, we only use up a few minutes of *our* time. If we got tired and had a nap in our world, who knows how long we will have wasted.'

'Good point Monte!' said Jake, and the thought of a nap made him yawn.

'Then it's settled then?' asked Marcus.

'Yes Marcus!' said Helen, and after doing some quick sums, told Marcus that they should be back by the time his clock says six o'clock.

'Oh and Marcus?' asked Monte, 'You *do* know this song we need, don't you?'

Marcus smiled back and tapped his finger on his temple twice, but Monte had to ask . . .

'And we *can* trust you Marcus, can't we?' he asked.

'I invented the recipe old boy!' he said, and Monte smiled.

CHAPTER FORTEEN

Back for the statues

Peter was very proud of himself for remembering the tune that he and Helen had to whistle, and as they all exited the maze, they stood and stared at the two large statues that were just outside of the entrance.

'Whoever she is,' said Monte, 'she's beautiful!'

'Whoever *he* is,' said Helen, 'he's butch!'

'Whoever *they* are,' said Peter,'we'll all find out soon enough!' and he had wished that he brought a photograph of their mother to be able to compare with the statue.

'Wait for us Jake!' shouted Helen as she saw him race towards the front door of the house. 'Granddad can't run as fast as you can!' and Jake was standing at the large oak door waiting for the others to catch up,

'Can I go and get the box Helen?' he asked.

'Yes,' said Helen, 'but my granddad will go with you. The box should be quite heavy by now, and we don't want to forget what the box is carrying, do we?'

'Ok, come on Monte!' Jake said excitedly, 'Follow me, it's in my bedroom.' and he ran up the stairs forgetting that it wasn't Peter he was racing.

Jake felt a little guilty doing his tribal victory dance as he saw the state that Monte was in as he finally reached the top of the stairs.

'Are you making fun of me?' asked Monte as he saw the dance, and Jake immediately stopped.

'Sorry Monte, just a habit . . . that's all!'

'So where's this box with the pixies inside Jake?' he asked while mopping his brow with his handkerchief.

Jake knelt down beside his bed and reached far underneath. He slowly dragged the box out and unlocked the small padlock that was keeping the statues safe. He opened the lid very carefully, and he noticed that Monte's eyes widened.

'Do you recognise any Monte?' Jake asked.

Monte didn't answer, as his attention was brought to one of the little statues. He held it as gently as he could, and he looked at the clothes it was wearing. 'These don't seem to be pixie clothing!' he thought, and he placed it carefully back in the box with the others.

'Do you recognise any Monte?' Jake repeated.

'No Jake, it's still too hard to tell.' but Monte's thoughts were different as he then saw the female statue lying next the the one he had just held.

He picked the box up, and walked slowly to where the others were waiting. Jake, this time, didn't race like he normally would, but instead stayed by Monte's side and he helped him down the stairs.

Helen and Peter were in the kitchen, they were putting together more sandwiches and bottles of pop to get ready to meet Marcus at the gate, and they stopped what they were doing as Monte and Jake entered the kitchen. Monte placed the box on the kitchen table and opened it, carefully took out each statue, and lined them up in a row next to the box.

They all stared at them and each wondered which, or if any were their loved ones. Jake stared at the only female statue, and he pretended in his mind that she was his mother. He stroked her hair and smiled at the little statue for a while, until Helen asked for them to be placed back in the box.

Peter looked at Monte, and he had an idea.

'I know!' he said, 'Wait here and I'll be back in a moment.'

The others wondered where he was going, but didn't have to wait long, as Peter entered the kitchen with his skateboard in his hands.

'Peter,' said Helen, 'you can't take that with you!'

'It's not for me Helen.' he said, and he put the skateboard on the kitchen floor.

'Put the box on top of the skateboard Monte, and we can push it to the entrance at least!'

Monte smiled, as he wasn't sure if he could have carried the box all the way to the gate.

'Your a bright boy Peter!' he said, and Jake wondered if they were becoming normal again since they left Pixity. So Jake had an idea of his own. He got the ball of string from his bag and tied one end to the front of the skateboard, and he cut the string at about two lengths of his own body and wrapped a bit around his hand.

'There!' he said, 'Now I can pull, and someone else can push!' and he was pleased, as Monte gave *him* a pat on his head as well as his older and smarter brother.

With the heavy front door closed and locked behind them, Helen made her hand into a fist and held it out in front of her with her arm straight.

'To the gate!' she shouted, and the others giggled and copied.

Jake pulled and Peter pushed as Monte shouted heave hoe to them. They both thought that this had been one of the best days since they arrived at Little Thornton, and secretly hoped it was going to be the best day they had in their lives ever, as the possibility of meeting their mother came closer than ever before.

Helen checked her watch, and after some quick calculations, revealed to the others how much time in Pixity they had left.

'five days gentlemen!' she said.

'Loads of time!' said Peter.

'To the gate!' shouted Monte with his fist held tight like before.

'I think we should leave the skateboard here, It will be hard to move over the grass!' said Jake, and decided to try a little of the way first.

With the sun being hot for the last few days, and the rain staying elsewhere, the ground was hard, and the skateboard rode along easily enough for them to carry on. The length of time it took to find the gate was becoming shorter each time they visited, and before they knew it they were standing on the outside of the other land. Monte was lifting the box off the skateboard and waiting for Peter to whistle the tune.

'Hurry Peter,' said Monte, 'This is getting heavy!'

'What's the matter Peter?' asked Helen.

'I've forgot the tune! I can't remember what the notes are! I think it's because we're nearing Pixity, and I'm turning into a kind of Jake again!'

'Hey you, what do you mean by that?' shouted Jake, but couldn't be bothered to waste any more time on arguing so he told Peter what the notes were.

'A bad egg Peter!' he said, then saw the confused look on Monte's face.

'A..B..A..D..E..G..G! said Helen, and Monte put two and two together and giggled as he realized at the reason for why *they* were the notes.

'So they can tell who the caller is from eh?' he asked and shook his head. 'Which reminds me, there is more than one entrance and one tune! We must find at least one other tune and entrance in case of an emergency!' he suggested, and Peter took a mental note in his head.

He then went through the notes in his head a few times before giving it his best shot.

'See! I haven't lost it yet Jake!' he said as the little green gate slowly opened with a loud creek.

In crawled Monte first on his knees as his arms were starting to ache with the weight of the box, then Peter, and then Jake. Helen entered, and she screamed with horror, as lying on the ground in front of her was her granddad, under a pile of statues that were now the same size as themselves. Jake couldn't be bothered to explain that they themselves were now the size of the statues and not the other way round, and he ran with the others to help Monte back on to his feet.

'Granddad, are you alright?' said Helen in a panic.

'Actually Helen,' he said, 'I feel fine, I was just caught unaware that's all!'

Helen sighed with relief, but checked her granddad over anyway, and once she was happy, she suggested that one of them should go and fetch Marcus.

'I'll go.' said Peter.

'Me too!' said Jake, and they ran down the path towards the meadow as a race was now on.

Helen sat with her granddad near the gate waiting for the boys to return with Marcus and she was still making sure that he hadn't been hurt.

'Are you sure you're ok granddad?' she asked. 'That looked as if it hurt!'

'I'm fine Helen, stop fussing, you sound just like your grandma did!'

'Sorry, I can't help worrying about you.'

'To tell you the truth Helen, I feel great! I think it's this place. I start to feel forty years younger every time I come here!' he smiled, which worried Helen.

'Oh please don't say you're thinking about living here granddad! You know something is not right about this place!' she said, and she didn't know if she wanted to hear the answer.

But before Monte could answer, they saw the silhouette of someone they didn't trust.

'Well hello again!' said Trickster, I thought you were at Marcus' house . . . and, what do we have here?' he asked as he saw the statues in a heap.

There was no way that Helen and Monte could hide the statues in time, and they didn't quite have time to think of a reason why they were at the gate with them.

Meanwhile, the boys were running as fast as they could to Marcus' home, and it was Peter that noticed something out of the ordinary first. While they were still racing, for the first time in his life he was still keeping up with Jake, and for a moment he thought that he would never again see the tribal victory dance that he secretly liked.

'No-one faster or slower eh Jake? Getting tired?' he asked sarcastically.

Jake didn't answer, he knew what was happening because of his new found intellect, and they both slowed down together.

'I could get used to this Jake!' Peter said happily.

'Well I don't like it!' Jake huffed, and he folded his arms in protest.

They opened the gate at the bottom of Marcus' garden and they saw Marcus coming out of his front door.

'Marcus!' shouted Jake, and Marcus looked over.

'Peter, Jake!' he said, and they wondered if he had the names the right way around. 'Are they here? I mean the statues?'

'Yes Marcus,' said Peter, 'They are at the gate with Helen and Monte.

'Oh good!' he said pleased, 'Let's get there as soon as we can before Trickster sees!'

'Do we have to rush!' Jake moaned as his legs were aching from the race.

'Why don't we want Trickster to see the statues Marcus? Are we doing something wrong?'

'No no Peter, It's just that I don't trust him! Since *you* all showed up he's been acting a bit strange that's all.'

'What? Only since we turned up?' asked Jake who thought that Trickster had always been a bit strange.

'Yes strange! You remember that he only needs to enlist a few more and then the elders of the committee will allow him to leave for good!'

'Do you think he's going to try and trick Helen and Monte?' asked Jake.

'I wouldn't put it past him Jake! Come on boys, we've no time to loose!'

Jake couldn't believe he had to run all the way back up the path to the gate, but this time he didn't mind if Peter led most of the way.

When they arrived back at the gate, to their horror, Trickster was looking over the statues that they brought back to Pixity, and Marcus tried to think of something quick.

'Trickster! What are you doing here old buddy?' he asked and tried to act as if he were pleased to see him.

'I answer the gate Marcus, you know that!' he said, and Marcus began to stutter as he had no reply to the answer.

'It's alright Marcus old boy, I told him everything! There's no need to hide anything any more. This is the best way!' said Monte, and he turned to Trickster. 'We might as well pretend that it's nine in the morning Trickster,' he said, and Trickster coughed and stumbled his words.

'Er . . . no. er, I don't know what you're talking about! Don't listen to him Marcus, I wasn't going to do anything of the sort! Believe me . . . old buddy?'

'Yes you were!' said Jake. 'Peter was listening in when you tried to tempt him to live here!'

'Lies!' Trickster protested, but he saw the look in Marcus' eyes and he knew he had to come clean.

'You arranged to meet, Trickster, to make some sort of a deal! We know all about it!' said Marcus, and Trickster fell to his knees and sighed.

'Am I ever going to get out of this place?' he cried, and Helen's mother instinct made her want to go over and console him, but then she thought of him trying to take her beloved granddad away from her and she no longer felt the need to mother him.

'I thought you loved it here! You said it was a perfect place to live!' said Monte.

'It is it is!' he said, 'But only for the right kind of person though, and I'm afraid that I'm not that kind of person. I am now a hundred and fifty two years old, can you believe that? And I still long for the world that I left behind. Fresh running water, sports, a bit of bad weather, the list goes on!' he said, and the others couldn't help feel a little sorrow for the man who was on his knees in front of them.

'It's fresh water they're mining! Isn't it Helen? That's why Marcus doesn't have any taps in his kitchen isn't it?'

'Yes Jake.' said Helen, 'The Lake, the stream, It's all salt water!'

Monte still wanted to do a deal with Trickster, but not all for the same reasons as before. He thought, while Trickster was pouring his heart out to Helen, that there must be a way in which everyone could get what they want. 'Trickster needs only a few to enlist!' he thought, 'We want my son, daughter in-law and the boys mother back, and we've got a few pixies left over that he can have!' And as soon as he thought about the boys mother, he remembered what Trickster had said to him. but Peter got there first.

'Trickster!' said Peter.

'Yes Peter?' he said, and wiped away a tear.

'You said to Monte . . . *'Join us, and the boys get their mother back?'* he asked loudly. *'Correct?'* he whispered.

Trickster dipped his head and quietly answered . . .

'Yes.'

Jake was annoyed that Peter didn't tell him what he had said, but wasn't annoyed for long, as he knew he couldn't have handled his own temper at the time., and Peter went on . . .

'And what did you mean by *'If I am to help you Monte, you are to help me!'* How can we help you Trickster? And how can you help us?'

'Took the words right from my own mouth Peter!' said Monte, and they all waited for an answer from the man that, if he wanted to, could put everything right.

Trickster stood and paced around for a while thinking about doing what he wasn't allowed to do by strict instructions from the elders, and he came to a decision he never thought he'd have the courage to do.

'I'm going to need a lot of help if we are to do this right!' he said, and he had all of their attention.

'Anything Trickster!' said Marcus.

'Just tell us what we have to do!' said Monte, and they listened carefully to what plan it was that Trickster had.

'First of all, I need you Marcus, to accompany me to the forbidden zone!'

'The forbidden zone?' asked Jake, 'What's that?'

'The mining fields Jake!' whispered Helen.

'But why would they call it that, Trickster?' asked Marcus, 'I'm sure they would all like to know the answer to that part!' he said making sure that he didn't leave out any important bits.

'Because everyone, not all miners just work there. Let's just say that it's sort of . . . er, our prison!'

'Prison?' asked Jake. 'Here, in Pixity?'

'Yes Jake. The ones who can't leave are so' because they have repeatedly tried to con their way out, which is what may happen to us incidentally if we get caught!'

'I can't believe it!' said Peter.

'Believe it!' said Marcus. 'This is why I told you to leave Helen, remember? As soon as you arrived I told you that you should go, and that it wasn't safe here!'

'Ok ok,' said Monte, 'We've all gathered that this is not the kind of place it seems, so lets just cut to the chase eh Trickster, what is it you need us to do?'

'Nothing yet, until Marcus and I return with the song we need for the ritual!' said Trickster.

Marcus smiled, and so did Monte, as they thought that they had their first little problem solved. But Trickster had news for Marcus about something he hadn't told him.

'I know Marcus that you yourself wrote the recipe and the song for the ritual, but after a lot of pixies escaped one year, the elders decided to change the tune and the lyrics every year! So I'm afraid your song is a little out of date now Marcus!'

'But the recipe Trickster, is the recipe still the same?' he asked.

'Yes I believe it is. They decided to keep the recipe as no-one had ever seen the right kind of fern needed for a lot of years, so they didn't see the point!' he said, and it was Monte, Helen and the boys that jumped for joy.

'Do you know of any?' asked Marcus.

'Heaps of it!' said Monte. 'You and Trickster concentrate on the song, and when you return, leave the rest to us!'

After they all carefully covered the statues with the many leaves that lay around, Marcus and Trickster set off on their long journey to the forbidden zone, accompanied with some pop and some sandwiches from the 'real world'. As Trickster explained to Marcus the plan he never had the courage to do on his own, and Helen, Monte and the two boys went back to Marcus' home to wait for their hopefully successful return.

CHAPTER FIFTEEN

To the forbidden zone

Trickster led the way down the winding path and through the overgrown bushes that led to what was known as the 'forbidden zone', and Marcus wondered how he knew the track so well. 'How many other times had he been this way?' thought Marcus, as Trickster took every turn as if the map was imprinted on the inside of his eyelids.

Marcus no longer recognised where he was, as he had never ventured into what they had called 'the forbidden zone' before, because if caught without first consulting the elders, the forbidden zone may just as well become home.

Marcus was becoming increasingly more nervous with every step towards their destination, and he wondered why Trickster didn't look as if he had a care in the world. 'Why isn't he as nervous as I am?' Marcus asked himself, and he went through Tricksters plan out loud.

'According to you,' said Marcus, 'there is only one guard at the entrance of the mine,'

'Yes!' said Trickster.

'I take it we're going to have to overpower him then?'

'No no, Marcus old buddy, we are going to ask him to retrieve the new ritual song for us!'

'How? Are you just going to plainly ask him for it?'

'Yes!' he said, and smiled.

'I don't get this at all!' said Marcus. 'Anyway, why is the information we need kept there?'

'It is the only secure place in Pixity Marcus! With no money there are no need for banks, with no theft there is no need for safes. Where else would the elders keep their secrets hidden away, hmm?' asked Trickster.

Marcus realized that he was right, but was still wondering why the only guard would happily go and get the words and music and give it to us, and he had to ask.

'Trust me Marcus!' said Trickster, 'You'll see!' and Marcus didn't know if he should ever trust Trickster.

A short distance later, Marcus and Trickster came to a small meadow that rose up the side of a hill, and Trickster smiled.

'Ah, perfect!' said Trickster, and he picked a few of the weird looking flowers that Marcus had never seen before, and placed them very carefully in his pocket without sampling their aroma.

'What are you going to use those for?' asked Marcus, but never got an answer as they had reached the other side of the meadow.

Trickster held his arm out in front of Marcus to stop him from going any further and asked him to keep out of sight.

'What is it?' he asked.

'The entrance to the mine is just over those rocks, do you see?'

'Yes, but don't you want me to come with you?'

'No, from here you can see every route to the entrance and keep hidden! I need you to stay here and keep look out. I mustn't be seen anywhere near, so I need plenty of warning if you see anyone else ok?' whispered Trickster.

'I see,' Marcus whispered back, 'but how will I let you know if anyone *is* coming?'

'Throw a stone or something, that will do!' he said, and tiptoed to the rocks.

Looking back at Marcus, Trickster was given the all clear, and he casually strolled up to the guard at the entrance. Marcus couldn't believe he was approaching the guard, and wondered what he was going to say.

The guard stood immediately in front of the opening to the mine, and when he saw Trickster, he stepped forward a couple of paces and shouted . . .

'Halt! State thy purpose!' he said in the deepest voice anyone had ever heard.

'Hi there!' said Trickster, 'Were you not informed of my visit this afternoon?'

The guard looked puzzled and checked a sheet of paper he had folded in his pocket. His eyes looked up and down each side of the paper, and Trickster put his hand in his pocket to crush the flowers he had picked earlier. He rubbed, and he crushed the flowers until they were like powder, then waited until the timing was just right.

'No!' said the guard, 'There is no mention of a visit today! I'm afraid I must inform the authorities about this!' and he stood firm in front of the mine.

'What?' said Trickster with his voice rising sharply, 'I can't believe they've done it again! Well, now that I am here, my name is Trickster.' and he held his hand out to shake his hand. The guard, who wasn't the brightest fellow in the land, came forward to shake Tricksters hand, and when he was close enough, Trickster pulled his hand with the crushed flowers out of his pocket towards his mouth and blew as hard as he could. The dust and pollen sprayed into the guards face, and it made him sneeze.

Marcus couldn't believe at what he had just seen, and he began to look around nervously in case *he* would be caught. He then saw Trickster whisper into the guards ear. 'What in Pixity is he doing?' he thought, and he saw Trickster blow another handful of dust into the guards face. Again he saw him whisper to him, and after a few seconds the guard rose. 'Oh no!' thought Marcus, but he watched the guard turn, and march into the mine as if he was obeying an order.

Trickster looked around and did his best to get the residue of the concoction free from his hands, and it wasn't long before the guard returned with what looked like a scroll of some sort. He handed the scroll to Trickster, reclaimed his place to the entrance of the mine, and Trickster ran as fast as he could to where Marcus was keeping look out.

'You did it!' said Marcus, 'I'd have never believed it if I hadn't seen it with my own eyes! How did you do that?'

'Forgetmewil!' he said.

'What's that?' asked Marcus.

'The flower I picked!'

'There's no such thing! I've heard of a forget-me-not!' said Marcus.

'Same thing dear boy! Only with an added ingredient of my own! Whoever inhales the pollen from this plant along with the crushed leaves, will have a few hours missing from their life without ever knowing about it! Oh, and they do as they're told too, which comes in very handy!'

'Well, I don't care how you found that out,' said Marcus, 'but let's get back, the others will be waiting.' and off they went through the meadow to retrace their former steps.

CHAPTER SIXTEEN

This years ritual song

'Here they are!' shouted Jake as he looked out of Marcus' window, and the others ran to the front door to welcome back the two buddies from their dangerous mission. Helen was first at the garden gate, and she was studying their faces to see if she could work out if they were successful or not.

'Nobody struts their stuff like that if they've failed a mission! Am I right?' asked Monte, and Trickster held the scroll high in the air.

The cheers must have been heard for miles around, which made Trickster quickly place the scroll back in his pocket before anyone had seen.

'Quick, indoors!' said Marcus, and as soon as they were inside, the scroll was opened, and a separate piece of music paper fell on to the floor. Both were laid on the table for everyone to read, and Jake took the music sheet for himself to learn later. Monte put his reading glasses on and began to say out loud what was written in front of him.

The ritual song number 34.

Our moon you shine, so clear and fine,
by the clouds so soft and white.

May you hear this chant
so our wish you may grant,
on this special clear moonlit night.

Ingredients top grade have been evenly weighed,
and mashed to the desired texture.
They're now in the pot,
and not too hot,
and waiting the required temperature.

Moon do your stuff, not too much, just enough
to reverse the effect of ones plight.
And as we smear
this paste with no fear,
we beg you what's changed you put right.

Give thanks to the great, for the affected will wake
from a sleep that was as cold as stone.
And return to a life of trouble and strife,
in a world they insist they call home.

'These riddles and songs get stranger every time I hear a new one!' said Jake, and he started reading it again quietly to himself.

The others arranged, talked and planned about the order of events to take place in their near future, and Marcus left them for a short time to bring Jake something that he hoped could help him work out the tune that they had to sing the ritual to.

CHAPTER SEVENTEEN

The chosen one

'Here Jake,' said Marcus, 'I don't know if this helps but . . . here you are anyway!' and Marcus handed him some type of wind instrument. It 'looked like a recorder' Jake thought, but it had extra holes and a few levers for the purpose Jake didn't yet know. He picked it up and blew softly into the mouth piece.

'*Toooot!*' It sounded as he blew, and the others turned to see where the tone had came from.

'What's that?' asked Peter, 'I've never heard a sound as nice as that before!' he said, and the others agreed instantly.

'It's what *we* call a reverbawindercordian!' said Marcus as he looked over at Trickster to see his reaction. '*I*, in all these years, have never been able to extract one blooming note from that thing!' Marcus lied, 'I was going to throw it out years ago, but now I've heard it, I might just keep it!' he said with a smile. 'Jake?' he asked, 'See if you can make some kind of tune from it will you?'

They were all quiet, waiting to see if the maestro among them could work out the fingering on such a weird instrument, and after a few mistakes, and ear wrenching screeches, Jake played one of the tunes he had learnt at piano lessons when he was younger.

191

The sound filled the room with a tone they had never heard before, and when Jake had finished, Monte, Helen, Peter and Marcus, stood to give the soloist a huge round of applause. Trickster on the other hand *had* applauded, but not with the enthusiasm that the others had given, and only Marcus knew why.

Trickster had given Marcus the instrument as a gift, as he himself received it as a gift the year before from someone else who couldn't manage to toot a note out of it! Yet Jake, had found it to be one of the easiest instruments he had ever played, and he couldn't stop himself from trying out another tune.

'You have a gift my dear boy!' said Marcus as he looked at Trickster again to see his reaction.

'This is great!' said Jake, 'what is it again? A reverba . . . . what?'

'A reverbawindercordian!' Marcus was pleased to remind him, and as Jake practised more, Trickster whispered into Marcus' ear.

'Do you realize what this means Marcus?' and he didn't say anything else until Jake had put the instrument down to give his lips a rest.

Trickster winked at Marcus, then announced that he was going into the garden for some fresh air, and waited for Marcus to follow.

'He's got to be the one Marcus!' Trickster whispered. 'In all the years of being stuck in this ancient forsaken place, I've known that instrument to be handed to at least twenty or thirty people, and that's only the third time I've heard a sound come out of the stupid thing! And this boy can already play whole tunes?' You know what this may mean Marcus don't you?'

Marcus looked at Trickster, and Trickster looked at Marcus, and neither of them knew what to say at first. Then Trickster shook his head in disbelief and mumbled to himself.

'He's got to be the chosen one!'

'What? The chosen one? What do you mean Trickster? That's impossible!' said Marcus, who was as confused as he was when he first set eyes on a pixie. 'But Jake isn't even from Pixity, he's neither a Pixiborn *or* a newcomer!'

'It doesn't make a difference Marcus, it's the instrument that chooses the player. That's what I heard anyway!' said Trickster.

'But this doesn't make any sense, why should it choose him? And what do we do now?'

'I don't know.' said Trickster, 'But we now have massive leverage over the elders Marcus. You know how long they have waited for a player to be found don't you? And I think we can get them to do anything that we want in exchange for the 'player' to give them what they want, don't you?'

'I think your right Trickster. We may not even need to do this ritual secretly, and have their blessing instead!'

'We'll talk again later, but don't mention anything just yet, I have to think!'

Just then, Jake came into the garden rubbing both of his cheeks with one hand, as he had been practising more on the instrument.

'You know it's rude to whisper!' he said to Trickster in a sarcastic manner.

'Jake,' said Marcus, 'how are you young man? You know, *you've* got a talent my boy, do you know that?'

'Why thank you Marcus!' said Jake. 'Er . . . is this mine to keep? Or are you just lending it to me?'

Marcus looked at Trickster, and wondered if he was thinking the same as he was, and Trickster smiled and nodded.

'I'll tell you what Jake!' said Marcus. 'If you do a certain little task for us, you can keep it for ever and ever! How does that sound?'

'Yeeey!' shouted Jake, and he ran through to the room where the others were to tell them his good news.

'No, wait Jake!' said Marcus, but he was too late.

Trickster placed his head in his hands, as he knew he was going to have to explain to the others what the task actually was.

'Hey everyone!' said Jake excitedly, 'Marcus said I can keep this, as long as I do a task for him!'

'A task? And what kind of task would that be?' asked Monte, who was weary of everything as he stood in the land that took his son and daughter in-law away.

Marcus and Trickster entered the room, and Marcus asked everyone to gather round. By the look on Marcus' face, they all knew it was serious, so they sat quietly wondering what this task was.

'Is this task dangerous?' asked Monte, 'Because if it is, I won't be wanting Jake to do it!'

'No, It's not dangerous Monte,' said Trickster, 'but it will involve talking to the elders!'

'That reminds me,' Marcus butted in, 'don't you already have a meeting with the elders soon?'

'Yes Marcus,' admitted Trickster, and he wondered how he knew. 'But this, as you know, is much more important!'

'What is?' asked Helen.

Trickster sighed and took a couple of deep breaths as he was doing his best to Keep to the truth. He didn't want to lie any more, he had done that for years and he knew this could be a way out for them all.

'We need Jake to play the reverbawindercordian in the forbidden zone!' said Trickster, and before he could explain more, there were more than one or two objections that were let known.

'I asked you if the task was dangerous Trickster! Now you want Jake to go to the forbidden zone? I think not!' said Monte.

'And neither do I!' said Peter, and all the time Jake listened, he wanted to do the task, even if it was just to prove himself of being more mature than the rest had thought he was.

'But I want to do it!' he announced.

'But Jake,' said Peter, 'you don't even know what it is yet! What if they want you do play whilst jumping off a mountain eh? would you do that?'

'Oh, I never looked at it like that!' said Jake, and he waited to find out more about the task.

'But why there?' asked Monte. 'What will happen if the reverba . . . . thingy is played there? and why does it have to be Jake?'

'Because Monte,' Trickster went on, 'Only Jake can get a note out of the stupid thing! It's a long story but, the instrument chooses the player! Not just anyone can play it, it's up to Jake to save us all!' he said, and was glad that there was no more to hide.

Nobody said anything. The last few words that Trickster said were repeating in their heads, 'Save us all, save us all, save us . . . 'From what?' Marcus tried his best to continue where Trickster had left off, as the thought of being back with his family after six generations was becoming too much for Trickster to comprehend, and as the tears fell, he rose to leave the room, but before he left, Marcus knew he had to explain the need for the chosen one.

'Ok,' said Marcus while trying to compose himself. 'you all know what I told you about the water here? The fact that all the water in the lake and the streams is all . . .'

'Salt water?' said Peter.

'Yes, salt water Peter.'

'So?' asked Jake.

'And you know about what the people in the mines are there for?'

'Extract fresh water!' said Helen.

'Yes!' said Marcus, 'Well the only way I can explain it is that, the instruments sound, if played at the entrance to the mine shaft, can release all the fresh water we need, and give Pixity the most important luxury since the dawn of our time!'

'What? How?' asked Monte.

'What if he plays a wrong note?' asked Peter, and Marcus smiled.

'I don't think it matters peter. But to answer your question Monte, the reverbawindercordian contains certain tones that will set off a vibration in the mines! A vibration that will shatter the walls that have held the fresh water there since they were wished there by a certain individual a long time ago!'

'So Pixity can finally have running water?' asked Helen, and she smiled because unlike some of the others, she realized that if they could give Pixity this, then they could bargain for the lives of every statue and newcomer that ever entered their land.

'But I'd rather someone else went there Marcus, I don't like the sound of Jake going to that place!' said Monte, and again Jake protested.

'No,' he said, 'I *want* to do it! It's not every day you're chosen by an instrument, and I insist anyway! I'm not handing this instrument to anyone until I'm finished with it! So there!' he said and folded his arms in protest.

'Very mature!' said Monte.

'Very brave!' said Helen.

'Very stubborn!' said Peter.

'I don't care! Show me the way Marcus, I'm ready!' said Jake, and he picked up the instrument and held it tight in his arms before anyone could take it from him.

After Monte tried to talk him out of it, he had to finally give in. There was no point, he thought, of trying to change this young man's mind, but promised himself that where ever Jake went, he would follow. Peter and Jake were becoming more like the family he had missed so much, and although he wanted to protect them as if they were his own, he knew that Jake held the key to his reunion with his son and daughter in-law.

Trickster entered the room after drying his eyes and Helen went to him. It wasn't in her nature to ignore someone's tears and her heart went out to him.

'Marcus, Trickster, we'll all soon be back, I just know it!' she said, and when Trickster heard that Jake wanted to do the task, he had to leave, as there were more happy tears to fall at the good news.

'So when do we do it?' asked Jake who was keen to get started.

'Soon Jake, soon.' said Marcus, 'But first we have to tell the elders about you and the instrument!'

'Why?' asked Jake, 'Couldn't we just do it now and surprise them all?'

'You'd surprise them all right!' said Monte, 'You'll drown all the miners Jake!'

'Oh yes! I never thought about that!' he said, and felt a little silly.

'This is why we have to wait until Trickster goes to see the elders!' said Marcus.

'So when will that be?' asked Peter.

'I don't know!' said Marcus, and Trickster came back into the room.

'Now!' he said. 'This can't wait, it is far too important!'

'Can I come too?' asked Peter, 'I want to see one of the elders!'

'So do I!' said Helen.

'We'll all go with Trickster!' said Monte, 'I want to make sure we all get our loved ones back!' he said, but secretly it was because he didn't trust Trickster one tiny morsel.

CHAPTER EIGHTEEN

To the elders

Marcus stood at his front door and waited for the others to follow him outside, as they were about to make the long trip to where the elders lived. Although the sun was now lower in the sky, it was still warm and he hoped they could make it there and back before darkness had set in.

Jake held the instrument tightly to his chest and was wondering what tune he should play to the elders to show how clever he was at playing it, and Peter tutted at him, as he was a bit jealous of the fact that it was Jake that was the chosen one and not himself.

'Can I have a go Jake?' asked Peter, and before Jake had a chance to answer, Trickster interrupted as soon as he could.

'No Peter! *That* would not be a good idea!' he said, and Peter was a bit taken aback by his sharpness.

'But why?' he moaned.

'If you try, and fail, then *you* have to pass on the instrument to someone different, and it might be another fifty years before another player is found! So now we know that Jake can play, it's best he keeps it until our mission is complete!'

'Oh, I see!' said Peter, and he was glad that Trickster wasn't actually being mean to him like he first thought.

Helen could see that Peter was displeased, and she tried to think of a task that he could have for himself.

'Peter!' said Helen, 'If all goes well with the elders, there's a good chance we will have to return to our own world. I need you to remember how we got back through the gate, and more importantly, the way to the moors where the fern for the recipe is, can you do that for me?'

'Yes Helen, I sure can!' said Peter, and he smiled as he now felt as important to the mission as Jake was.

As they reached the top of a hill, Trickster stopped and told the others to rest a while, as they were about half way to their destination. Monte found a place to sit and took in the view, and he realized how he wasn't as out of breath as he normally was. He enjoyed feeling like he was twenty one again and he half dreaded how he would feel once they returned to their own world.

'Are you alright dear boy?' asked Marcus, 'Do you think you can make it there alright?'

'Yes, I'm fine!' he said, and took a sip of water from the bottle Marcus had given him.

Trickster pointed towards the horizon, and the others went to him to see.

'You see the valley?' he asked, 'See the field with the red flowers?'

'Yes!' they all said together.

'Look slightly to the right, and within those trees, lives the highest member of the elders!'

'What's he call Trickster?' asked Monte.

'Er, now let me think,' he said after removing his cap and scratching his head, 'er . . . Titchietot, that's it, Titchietot!' he smiled, 'Nothing wrong with my memory! Come on, it's all down hill from now on!'

In the middle of a small brook sat a house, a very small house with a thatched roof and brightly coloured curtains that were drawn. Although it was the only house for miles around, they all wondered why there was a number one on the front door.

'Number one?' asked Jake. 'So where's two and three?'

'Two and three are elsewhere Jake. The number one isn't part of the address like in *your* world, This number one means that it is number one that lives hear. You know? Top man? Top dog? Chief of chiefs?'

'Oh, I get it.' he said, and he walked towards the front door.

'Wait Jake,' said Marcus, 'no guest or newcomer is allowed to knock on the door of the number one, Trickster will have to knock!' he said, and Jake came back to join the others.

Trickster breathed deeply, and slowly neared the yellow painted door and took hold of the knocker.

'He we go!' he said to the others, and they all nervously waited to see if the door would answered.

They all heard footsteps getting louder, and were glad that their journey wasn't a waste of time. The door opened, and there stood the smallest man they had ever seen.

'I thought everyone was the same height in Pixity!' said Jake, and was quickly hushed by Helen.

'Ah, Trickster!' he said smiling, 'I'm so glad that you're two days early!'

Trickster was happy that Titchietot was at home, and was even happier that he was in a good mood. This small man was a man that was very hard to please, and if they were to succeed, It greatly depended on him not being grumpy at all.

'Oh? Why is that sir?' Trickster asked nervously.

'Because my friend, you've been a naughty boy haven't you?' and the smile disappeared from his face.

Tricksters rosy cheeks faded quickly as he followed Titchietot through the front door and into his house. The others stayed where they were as they were not asked to follow, and they wondered what was going to happen to Trickster.

What seemed like a very long time had gone by and Monte was about to knock, when the door swung open, and the little man stood there and apologised for his rudeness.

'Come in come in,' he said, 'come in and sit down, would you all like a drink?' he asked politely, and Monte was the only one who answered.

'Yes thank you Mr Tot! Just a cold drink of water for me please!' he said.

'Please,' said the little man, 'the name is Titchietot. It's all one name, no first or second name!'

'Oh, I apologise.' said Monte, 'I assumed your first name was Titchy!' and for the first time it was Monte who received Helens heel in the side of his leg.

Titchietot tried not to take offence of the remark given because of his small stature, and ignored the same feeling that he used to have before he became someone of great importance.

Only Monte sat with a drink as Titchietot stood in front of them all with his back to the coal fire that was burning softly. His hands were behind his back and he was smiling at everyone, looking left to right and back again.

'So,' he said, 'you must be Jake, the maestro in this little band of travellers. Am I right?' he asked, and he stared at Jake.

Jake stood to attention, and he held the reverbawindercordian out in front of himself as if he was about to play it.

'Yes sir,' he said, 'I am Jake! Would you like me to play it for you?' he asked.

'No Jake, not yet! I still have to sort out the little matter of a certain naughty little man in the room!' he said, and he looked straight at Trickster.

'He's calling *him* little!' whispered Peter, and Helen had to try and hide her smile.

'Sir!' said Trickster as he got to his knees, 'In my defence, may I say how deeply sorry I am for disobeying the rules, er sorry, 'your rules', but . . .'

Trickster was thinking hard. He knew he was about to lie, and hoped that the others would confirm his story and not let on.

'But,' he went on, 'when we found out that young Jake here had the gift, my ideas went into overdrive! You see sir, young Peter and Jakes mother was lost here when they were very young, and Monte here lost his son and his daughter in-law also. They have come

203

here to see if there is any way of taking them back home. Oh, and Helen is Monte's granddaughter by the way, so you see sir how my thinking at the time wasn't about rules, but, well my heart went out to them sir, and forgive me for saying, but even after being here now for over a hundred and fifty years, there is still a big part of me that is human!' and he bowed his head for forgiveness.

Although they all knew that not all of what Trickster said was the whole truth, Helen took in every word, and and she wiped away a small tear from her cheek. Titchietot *had* listened carefully to the man kneeling before him and he paced left to right, right to left, with his hand rubbing the soft facial hair that grew from his pointed chin.

'You know it was fifty seven years ago when the last player was found, and we've had good fertile soil ever since!' he said, and Marcus smiled as that was *his* doing, but Titchietot was still pacing. 'Twenty six years before that is when we lost the fresh water because of that vermin intruder we took in from the school!' he said, and both Monte and Marcus wondered if it was anyone they had known.

They knew that when they had both stayed there, the house had been a school of that sort for a very long time, and then realized it was obvious that they could have never known this 'intruder!'

'Excuse me Mr Titchietot!' said Peter, 'So this reverbawinder . . . thingy, is not made for just one purpose then!'

'No Jake . . .'

'It's Peter!' he decided to say for the last time.

'Sorry Peter, no! Every so often, a player may be found to right a wrong, or add to this lands well being so to speak. When there is a need that is great, or a wrong needs putting right, the instrument, given to us by the ancients, is placed in the hands of one they think is worthy of wisdom!'

'So they placed it in the wrong hands that time?' asked Jake.

'No, whoever handed it to him last placed it in the wrong hands! That newcomer came with great ideas and suggestions, but to this very day, no-one knows why he turned and tried to destroy us!' Titchietot explained.

'So it's not the instrument that chooses the player then?' asked Peter.

'Not really no.' he said, and Peter exaggerated a smile that was directed at Jake. 'It's the ancients!' Titchietot carried on, which made Jake exaggerate a larger smile towards Peter.

'You're so immature!' said Peter, and he realized that the 'Jake' inside of him was popping out more than ever.

'Never mind all that boys!' said Monte, 'So are you going to trade then Titchietot?' he asked, and everyone was pleased that someone had the nerve to ask what it was they had all went there for in the first place.

Titchietot stopped pacing. and he looked at Jake once more with a straight expression.

'That all depends on what this young man desires!' he said, and he never took his eyes off the boy who was holding the giver of wishes.

Jake stared back at the little man in front of him and didn't know how to put into words what it was he wanted.

'You get your fresh water,' said Jake, and Titchietot somehow knew that he wasn't going to stop there.

'And you get your mother?' asked Titchietot.

'Yes, and . . . . Helen gets her parents back!' Jake finally said.

'Two for one?' Titchietot protested.

'Take it or leave it!' said a stubborn Jake, and the others were proud of him.

'This is all very well,' said Titchietot, 'but first you have to find them! Are they here? or are they on the other side in a state of rest?'

'The thing is sir,' said Trickster, 'they have seven statues in total, and we are confident that some of the five we have here are at least some of who we are searching!'

'I see!' said Titchietot, 'And where are they now?'

'They are well hidden by the little green gate sir.' said Trickster.

'Hmm, and the other two?' he asked.

'The other two sir,' said Peter, are beyond the maze in the garden of the old summer school!'

'I take it that those two are full size then?'

'Yes sir!' Trickster confirmed.

The pacing began again as the highest of the elders tried to decide on what was the best course of action, and Jake began to pace with him. Everything was taking too long for Jakes liking, and he was itching to blow the instrument to show Titchietot how good he was, and he silently blew a single note to remind himself of what it felt like to play.

Jake blew so softly that he was sure no-one would hear, but as soon as air entered the weird contraption, there was a loud knock on the door, and the owner of the house knew who it was. He looked at Jake, and although he was cross because he blew when he asked him not to, didn't say anything and headed towards the door.

'Jobberbob, Bumbad! How nice it is to see you both! You've heard then I see!' asked Titchietot.

'Yes, the sweet sound filled my pointed ears the instant it sounded!' said Jobberbob as if the sound was nectar itself.

'It's so good to hear the sound of wishing tones again Titchietot! How long has it been?' he asked, but then remembered. 'Fifty seven years! *You'll* remember, won't you Marcus?'

Marcus smiled and nodded, and he glanced over to where Jake was so Bumbads eyes would follow.

'Ah! There he is.' he said, 'So *you* are the chosen one are you? Let's hope you use your tune with the tones that do good eh?'

Jake smiled and nodded to Bumbad, then Titchietot whispered into his ear.

'*You* called them here when you blew! Now *I'll* have to convince *them* also!' he said, and Jake couldn't work out if he was being nasty or not.

'No-one is going to reject having fresh water!' Jake thought, and he asked Trickster if there would be any problems.

'Trickster!' he whispered when the three elders were quietly talking, and he came over slowly while watching them.

'What is it Jake?' he asked.

'Would the other two elders have a problem with fresh running water? Because Titchietot told me that he'd have to convince *them* also!'

'No Jake, not at all! I think what he meant was that he was going to let me off and say nothing to the others about what I did. Now he has to tell them, and they may not be as forgiving. That is why it was Titchietot who I visited first Jake.'

'Oh, sorry, I hope I haven't got you into big trouble Trickster!' said a very sorry Jake.

'It's alright don't worry Jake, we have the tool that will solve this lands greatest problem! As long as you use the instrument for that reason, we'll *all* be out of here soon. I promise!'

'Great!' said Jake, 'It's even far too hot when it's starting to get dark here!'

Trickster didn't realize how long they had been there, and he noticed that Marcus was looking at his watch and out of the window. But when Titchietot spoke, they all knew that they would be returning to Marcus' house soon.

'Ok, listen all!' said Titchietot, 'We must consider! So if you all return to where you came, we shall give you our decision in the morning!'

Monte, Helen, Marcus, Trickster and the boys, all looked at each other, and it was Monte who thought out loud.

'What is there to think about? Don't you want fresh running water or not?' he said and cringed as soon as he said it, and the number one began to loose his patience.

'Yes we do, whoever you are!' shouted Titchietot, 'We have to decide on whether or not to turn a blind eye to the use of Forgetmewil by a certain member of your party! And incidentally Trickster,' he went on, 'how much did you use? The poor man is still under the spell, and under the watchful eye of Doctorment!'

'I wouldn't like to meet this Doc Torment Helen!' whispered Peter, and Helen touched her two lips with her finger.

'Doctorment came here when he was a doctor Peter,' said Marcus, 'but wasn't needed as a doctor! You understand?' whispered Marcus.

'I think so Marcus!' said Peter.

'I'm sorry sir, er . . . the second blow was when I sneezed!' Trickster lied.

'I'm sorry to have angered you sir,' said Monte who didn't think he should apologise, 'but we just want our loved ones back, and then we'll be out of your sight forever.

Jake knew he had what they wanted, and only *he* could give it to them. So he picked up the courage and faced the three elders.

'Yes, we want our mother! And yes, Helen wants her parents! But there is one more thing we want in return for my task!' he said.

They all looked at Jake and wondered what he had meant. Never before had there ever been someone who would try to bargain with the elders in such a manner.

'Trickster is now a loved one, and he's coming with us! Like it, or leave it!' he said and faced the others. 'Come on it's nearly dark. let's get back!' he said, and as they walked out of the house of the number one, he had one last thing to say. 'And *we'll* see *you* at Marcus' house first thing in the morning!'

209

Everyone waited until they were a safe distance from the brook, and when they reached the meadow with the red flowers, there was an almighty cheer from Monte, Peter and Helen. The biggest cheer of all came from Trickster. Finally after over twelve decades, he now felt he was going to see the world he had missed so much, and the tears started falling once again.

CHAPTER NINETEEN

The trial

The boys hadn't slept much with all the pacing that Helen and Monte were doing during the night, and as they sat at the window waiting for their first glimpse of the Pixity sunrise, they heard Trickster enter the sitting room where they were supposed to be asleep. He looked as troubled as Helen and Monte were, and as soon as he entered, he paced back and forth, left to right, and mumbled to himself about how long he had been stuck in this ancient forsaken place. Peter and Jake never realized before how much this Trickster was desperate to get back to where he came from, and the boys wondered if there was anything left of Tricksters old world for him to go back to.

'No wonder he was doing his best to enlist more!' said Jake, and Peter nodded.

'I don't like the fact he was trying to get us though!' said Peter, as he still he didn't trust him as much as the others.

'Trickster!' said Jake, 'If you *do* get back . . . . Where are you going to go?'

'I don't know Jake, it's been that long! But I know where to look. Little Thornton mustn't have changed that much over the years!'

'Your right Trickster,' It still looks really old, and it has no cinema or anything!'

'Cinema?' asked Trickster.

'Moving pictures Trickster!' said Monte.

'Oh! So what's the difference? Do you mean like Marcus' magic box?' and they realized he had meant Marcus' TV set.

'Never mind, you'll see,' said Peter, 'soon enough you'll see!' and hoped he'd remember in the future that in Tricksters old world, things were a lot different now.

Trickster didn't mean to keep Peter and Jake from sleeping, nor did he mean to wake up Marcus as he paced with his heavy feet, and it wasn't long before Helen joined them all at the window, looking and waiting for the elders to arrive with a decision that could change all of their lives forever.

'Move over Peter!' groaned Jake, and as Peter did so, he blocked Monte's view.

'Not there! I can't see.' said Monte, and before the others could have their say, a certain pointed hat was seen coming over the horizon.

'That's Jobberbob!' shouted Peter, 'I recognise the stupid hat!'

'But where are the others?' asked Jake.

'There's someone else with him, look!' said Helen, and she squinted her eyes to see if she could recognise who it was.

'That's that Bumbad!' said Monte, 'Look at the roundness!'

'But number one isn't with them! I hope it isn't bad news!' said Marcus, but forgetting about Titchietot's size, he soon realized that Titchietot would have been the last to emerge over the horizon, and there he was.

They all ran to the front door, and then on to the gate at the bottom of Marcus' garden to greet them. Marcus opened the gate and stood to the side and held his arm out to invite them all in.

'Titchietot, Jobberbob, Bumbad, welcome to my humble abode! Please come in and rest.' he said cheerfully.

'Thank you Marcus,' said Titchietot, 'but we'll wait for the others before we talk!'

'The others?' Marcus thought, and he noticed the look on Tricksters face. It was a look of panic, unrest, and confusion all at the same time. 'This might not be good news!' he thought, and he offered them all a cold drink to try and take his own mind off the slight panic he was also feeling.

Jake, knowing that *he* was the one who had what they wanted had more confidence than the rest, and he had a question that everyone else wanted to know the answer to.

'Er, sir Titchietot!' he said.

'Yes maestro, what do you want to know?' he asked.

'Why are there others coming?' he asked, 'And *why* should there be others? Have you not yet decided if you want fresh running water in your streams, rivers and lakes?'

Trickster was shocked at the way Jake had spoken to the number one of the land, yet he was curious also to how Titchietot would reply to the way of questioning.

But the number one just smiled, and he knew he didn't have to answer as the other two elders were only a few seconds away.

Helen was still searching the horizon, and it wasn't long before the others heard her say the words . . .

'Who's this coming this way?' she asked, and they all spun to see two more weird looking characters walking up the path towards them.

'Grumptious, Hipocritter!' shouted Jobberbob, 'This way!' he said.

'I don't like the sound of those two!' said Peter, and Helen agreed, wondering if their names had anything to do with their personalities.

'Well Marcus,' said Titchietot,' we're all here now so let's get down to business shall we?' and Marcus wore a hidden smile, as the word business to him, also had a connection with the word 'deal'.

The small sitting room in Marcus' small house was cram packed, as Marcus, Monte, Helen and the two boys sat and waited to hear what the elders had to say.

There were four on the sofa that was built for two, Marcus stood near the window, and Trickster sat at the side on the three legged stool, so if it *was* bad news, he wouldn't be sitting with the humans or the elders, and he felt better in between them all for that moment in time.

Titchietot stood in front of them all with Jobberbob on his right, and Bumbad on his left. Grumptious and Hipocritter stood next to the entrance to the kitchen, and everyone then knew who, of the five elders, were four and five.

'Order!' said Titchietot, 'This meeting is now in session!' he shouted, but no-one was actually making any noise. 'The request being for the return of loved ones, in exchange for the running of fresh water to our streams and lakes, has been put to us by no more than four humans, who are hear *only* as visitors. Not Pixies, not even newcomers!' he said, and the others didn't like the way things were going already. 'But, my fellow elders,' he went on, 'one of the visitors has a bargaining tool that I'm afraid we cannot ignore! and that is that he has the gift of the reverbawindercordian!' he said.

Grumptious and Hipocritter were wide eyed and open mouthed, as Titchietot wasn't allowed to inform them of everything until the hearing, and they listened eagerly to what Titchietot had to say.

Jake felt proud, and he held the instrument tight in case he was all of a sudden asked to prove his worth.

'As you know fellow elders,' Titchietot went on, 'it is not allowed for us to question his intentions, but to realize the potential it may have upon us! What say yee Jobberbob?' he asked, and the visitors waited with anticipation and hope.

'I say aye!' said Jobberbob.

'What say yee Bumbad?'

'I say, what have we got to lose?'

'And what say yee Grumptious?'

'I suppose so!' he huffed.

'And finally my friend, what say yee Hipocritter?'

'Well . . .' he said, 'I would just let him try anyway!'

'That's not what you said the last time Hipocritter!' Titchietot reminded him.

'Yes, but that's just me though, isn't it?' and Trickster remembered what he said the last time he asked the elders to set him free.

Titchietot paced for a short while and approached the sofa where the visitors were sitting. He breathed out loudly and closed his eyes.

'Monte, Helen, Peter and Jake?' he said quietly, 'I have some good news, some more good news, and I'm afraid I have some bad news! Which would you like to hear first?' he asked, and there was still silence in the room. Then Jake spoke.

'Good, then bad, then good again!' he said, and they all wondered why. 'Good first because we all need cheering up!' he said, 'And good last because it will cheer us up after the bad news!'

Titchietot smiled at the tall young man that stood before him, and he delivered the news as requested.

'First of all, Trickster!' he said, and Trickster was so glad that he had nothing to do with the bad news. 'My friend!' he said softly, 'You have served your time here, you may leave if you wish!' he said, and Trickster was stunned at how easy it was. Was it because he helped find the maestro for the instrument? He didn't know, but Titchietot was going to tell him anyway. 'Nobody Trickster, has to stay longer than one hundred and twenty years after they've enlisted if they don't want to my friend, but we're not allowed to tell you that until you ask! I was about to tell you this in a days time or so, if that is why you requested an audience?' he asked.

'Yes actually,' he said and swallowed hard to try and remove the lump that was swelling in his throat.

'So,' said Monte, 'care to tell us this bad news?'

Titchietot looked to the floor as he knew that the news he was about to give would upset.

'The bad news my friends is . . .' he paused, 'that we can't find a way to help the resting beyond the maze! We realize that they may be, or may not be your loved ones, but a way has not yet been found to prescribe the recipe beyond our maze. We do not yet know if your moonlight has the same effect as our own, it has never been tried before!'

Their hearts sagged low enough to make them feel as if the end of their dreams were cut short, but they tried their best to keep good spirits up by hoping some of their loved ones were actually within the small group of statues they had hidden at the entrance of the gate.

'And the third piece of news?' asked Helen.

Monte sat that close to the edge of his seat that he nearly slipped off, and Helen had to hold on to him as she knew that the news would be as important to him as it was to herself. Then Titchietot smiled at them all and began to speak.

'And thirdly,' he said, 'We need volunteers to go and fetch the recipe, as we begin the ritual at midnight!'

'Does that mean I now get to play for you?' asked Jake, and he was about to pick his instrument up and give it a tune.

'No, no Jake!' said Jobberbob, 'We must first work out the timing between our two worlds so that we will all meet at the gate at the same time! As you know, the fern wilts very quickly and will wither if left too long, so timing is of the greatest importance Jake!'

'I understand!' said Peter, and he handed his calculator to Helen for her to work out exactly how long they had to retrieve the fern and the clover.

Helen tapped away for a few seconds, and they were all relieved that there was more than enough time to achieve their goal.

Throughout the cheers and celebration of most in the room, Peter sat on his own and smiled at Helen, as he knew that now it was his turn to prove his importance of the mission, until Monte announced one slight problem.

'So does Jake perform his task before or after we try the ritual on the statues?' he asked, and Helen was instantly back on the calculator to see how much time they had left in the land that they were visiting.

'If he has to release the water beforehand, it must be achieved in the next three hours!' she said, and watched to see if the elders would know if that length of time was long enough.

Titchietot, Bumbad, Jobberbob, Hipocritter and Grumptious conversed quietly for a moment or two before addressing the others, and when they did, the elders and Jake were on their way to the forbidden zone where Trickster and Marcus had taken that same route not so long ago.

They had only been gone for a couple of minutes when they heard Trickster calling to them from a small distance away.

'Sir, sir!' he shouted, 'I think you may need this!'

The elders wondered what the hold up was, as they stated before how time was of the greatest importance.

'What is it Trickster?' said a slightly annoyed Titchietot, and Trickster handed over the scroll that contained the latest ritual lyrics along with the music.

'Trickster!' said Titchietot, 'that is for the ceremony at the gate!' and He blushed which put the colour back into his cheeks.

'I apologise once more sir!' he said as he took back the scroll from the number one.

Titchietot patted his friends shoulder.

'You know Trickster,' he said quietly, 'these visitors have taught us a few lessons on how our land should be governed, and if you ever decide to stay, welcome aboard!' he said, and Trickster realized that he was being offered a place on not just the committee, but had been asked to become one of the elders themselves.

There were two things in the last hundred and twenty years that Trickster ever thought about, and although each one was of a different world, what he had just heard was one of the most tempting things he had ever been offered. He wanted to find his relatives, he wanted to be of importance like the elders, but he just couldn't choose between the both ever, and he pretended not to hear the offer that was just given to him and returned to the others waiting for him.

CHAPTER TWENTY

Jakes finest hour

As one mission started in the real world, another started in the land of Pixity, and as Jake got nearer to the forbidden zone, the excitement of playing the instrument in front of the elders was quickening his pace. The thought of being the first chosen one for nearly six decades made him feel like he had never felt before, and he felt proud because it was *he,* and not Peter, that would give what the Pixies had wanted for so long.

As they came to a meadow that rose up the side of a hill, Jake noticed that it was beautifully adorned with a weird sort of flower, and he quickly realized that it must of been the flower that Trickster had told them about, and he lagged behind a few meters. When they weren't looking, he placed a large handful in his pocket without crushing them, and quickly caught up so they didn't notice anything.

Jobberbob reached the brow of the hill first, and he pointed to the entrance of the mine. Jake wondered where the guard was, as there were supposed to be prisoners and such like working in the mines.

'Where is the guard?' he asked.

'The guard, Jake, is still under observation at Doctorments house, thanks to Tricksters escapades earlier this afternoon!' said Titchietot.

'Oh!' said Jake. 'So who's guarding it now then?' he asked.

'No-one!' Grumptious replied. 'We've only got one guard, as there is no need for another!' he said, and Jake was more confused than ever, and Jobberbob noticed.

'Jake dear boy, do you think we are going to let you blow the reverbawindercordian down the shafts and allow you to drown all our staff?' asked Jobberbob.

'I didn't think you would sir!' said Jake.

'Well, because we have found *you* Jake, we've let them all off! Gone home! Back to whatever they did in Pixity Before we lost the water!'

And although he was so pleased that he also had something to do with the release of the miners, the pressure to perform well was increasing, but still he couldn't wait to blow the instrument into the many miles of tunnels that lay underground.

As they walked around a mound of rocks that were just in front of the mine entrance, Jake exercised by cracking his knuckles, and by intertwining his fingers and bending them backwards. He wanted to make the instrument sound as nobody in Pixity had ever heard before, and finally decided upon a tune to play. It was a lullaby that he learned at piano lessons when he was younger, as it was his favourite tune ever. He had heard from his father that mother used to sing it to them when they were only a few months old as it soothed them to sleep every night.

Titchietot looked at Jake, and the other elders copied. Then altogether they nodded to him.

'This is it!' thought Jake, and he took a few calm breaths as the tune he had decided upon was a soft and slow piece, and needed what *he* called respect.

Jake stood at the entrance of the mine and put the instrument to his mouth. then blew softly. The notes came naturally to him as he had never forgot the tune that reminded him of having a mother once so much, and as he played, the beautiful sound floated down the many shafts that lay before him, and as if in response, an equally beautiful tone echoed back to him as he played.

Jake was only half way through his recital when he started to notice the echo that was returning to him started to overlap itself, and he began to think that he didn't like what he was hearing. The elders nodded and smiled to encourage him to carry on, but the longer he did, the messier the tones entangled as semitones started to overlap each other, and ring with an awful resonance that was urging Jake to stop playing.

Jake didn't stop playing until he was asked to, and when the elders knew that enough vibrations had been injected into the mines, they all pointed towards the rear of where Jake was standing.

'What?' he asked.

'Run Jake, Back to the hill!' they said, and Jake didn't know what they were expecting, but did as he was told and ran with his head facing towards the mine entrance behind him.

He couldn't see anything, but he did notice a rumbling sound getting louder and louder, and just as Titchietot, Jobberbob, Grumptious, Bumbad and

Hipocritter joined him, there was an almighty gush of torrent from the entrance of the mine. It wiped away the mound of rocks that stood at the entrance once before, and quickly found it's way to the lowest point that was nearest to the mine.

Grumptious, who was nearest the torrent couldn't help himself, and he knelt down beside the new river and cupped his hands to sample the taste.

'Just as I expected!' he said, and the others were curious as they wondered what he was doing.

'Does that mean it's no better?' asked Jake, thinking that his task was not achieved.

'On the contrary Jake!' said Grumptious, 'It's as good as our bottled!' he said, and the others shook their heads.

'It's exactly the same as our bottled you silly man!' said Titchietot, as he then realized that their plan had in fact actually worked.

CHAPTER TWENTY ONE

The second mission

As one mission started in the land of Pixity, another started in the real world, and as Peter and Helen got nearer to the gate, they tried to remember how they exited the last time.

'I wish Jake was here!' said Peter, and he worried Helen a little.

'Why Peter, can't you remember how to get through the gate?' she panicked.

'Yes Helen, But Jake knew the tune forwards *and* backwards! he sighed.

'Oh yes!' realized Helen, 'We have to whistle the tune backwards, I forgot.' she said.

'And,' Peter added, 'we have to split the tune into two, so neither of us whistle the whole tune!'

'Ok Peter,' she said as an idea came to mind. 'You write 'A BAD EGG' down backwards, and we'll give it our best shot from there!'

Peter did as he was asked, but with no instrument to Practice the tune on, Peter didn't have any clue on what tones they should be whistling. So Peter decided to run back to Marcus' house and ask if he had any sort of instrument at all in his house.

'Helen, I'll be back in five minutes, I need something that sounds a few notes!' he said, and he ran as fast as he could.

While Peter was away, Helen uncovered some of the statues and searched to see if her feelings could identify any of them. She looked mainly at the female statue and tried to imagine her being her mother. She remembered Marcus telling them that 'they are an identical image of what they once were', but that didn't help much, as the clothes she was wearing were not one of their own worlds fashions. She uncovered some of the others, and she stared at the face of one that she thought had her granddads looks. 'Square chin' she thought, 'Pointed nose' she noticed, and she wondered if she was staring into her fathers eyes. 'Can he hear me?' she thought, but her mind was taken away from her thoughts as Peter ran back up the path clutching a harmonica that Trickster had given him.

'Here!' he gasped as he had never ran so fast for so long in his life.' Let's see if this works shall we?' and first he tried to play the tune forwards a few times before he learned it backwards.

After lots of practising, and being out of breath, Peter finally decided he was good enough to be able to explain properly to Helen on what to do.

They stood in front of the gate and looked at each other with their fingers crossed behind their backs. Helen whistled the first four notes, then Peter timed it perfectly so there was no gap placed in the tune as he whistled *his* three notes.

They waited, but not for long, as the familiar creaking noise of the gate opening made them laugh with relief.

'You did it!' said Helen.

'No, *we* did it Helen!' shouted Peter, and they made their way out of the maze as quick as their legs would carry them.

One more turn later they were standing in front of the two large statues in the garden, and they wondered to themselves how they were going to get them through the maze and to where they could be saved.

'Come Peter.' said Helen, 'there's no time to lose.'

Around the side of the house and down the driveway they quickly walked, and on to the main street of little Thornton. Peter took over, leading the way through the rights and lefts that would lead them to little Thornton moor. They came to the fence that stretched in front of some trees and Peter recognised it as the place where they found the last pixie.

'It's just through these trees Helen!' he said, and a few minutes later, they were standing on the moor that grew the fern that they were looking for.

Helen knew instantly where she had spotted the fern with the little blue flowers, and she headed in that direction. She stopped, turned around slowly, and there it was.

'I see it!' she said excitedly, and as Helen and Peter went to the spot where the fern lay, their hearts felt as heavy as one of the statues had became as it crossed the boundary between their world and Pixity.

'Is it dead?' asked Peter.

'I don't know Peter, it doesn't look very healthy though!' said Helen, 'Quick, look for some more!'

And as soon as Helen gave the order, their search became a frantic search as time was not one of their leisures.

Peter stood on the boulder he had once perched himself upon to get as good as view as the others, and after a short while his tactics had worked.

'Helen!' he shouted, 'Three o'clock!'

'What? Three o'clock?' she panicked again, 'We're going to be so late!'

'No Helen!' Peter explained, 'Over there!' he said, and he pointed to his right.

'Oh, I see!' said Helen, and they ran to the spot where there was a hint of blue.

The fern was young, the flowers were bright blue, and there was no doubt in either of their minds that they had found exactly what they were looking for, as a horrid smell reminded Peter of the last time they came across the fern, and before Peter could pick some, Helen interrupted.

'Wait!' she said, and Peter asked why.

'What else do we need?' she asked, and Peter quickly went through the recipe in his head until he came to the point where it had said . . .

'A hand full of clover!' he remembered, and he knew exactly where to pick some.

'Are you sure Peter?' asked Helen, 'Because we shouldn't pick these until we have the clover, as the fern will wither quickly!'

'I know Helen, trust me, There is lots of clover in our garden! Especially around the bases of the two statues, come on!' he urged, and Helen took some small scissors from her bag and gently snipped away until there was no more fern in that area.

'Ok Peter, let's hurry back. There's one more thing we need from the house!'

'What's that?' he asked, as he knew he had everything on *his* list.

'A cooking pot!' said Helen, 'I'm not taking a chance on any of the boys remembering one!'

'Good point!' said Peter, and slightly faster than a fast walk, they made their way back to the kitchen in the old house.

Helen rummaged around inside the cupboards and found what she thought was a cooking pot of an adequate size, and they quickly left to find the clover that Peter had said was at the base of the statues.

'Here Helen, look!' said Peter smiling, and they both got down on their hands and knees to gather as much clover as they could carry.

Into a separate bag went the clover, and into the maze they went. Peter raced ahead and stopped at every turning to give Helen a chance on catching up, but Peter stopped at a corner and looked around himself with a look of puzzlement.

'What's the matter Peter?' asked Helen, 'Have you forgotten the way?'

'No!' said Peter, 'The way we would normally go has been blocked!'

'What? Blocked?' asked Helen, and she began to panic slightly. 'But we've got to get back to Pixity before the fern withers! What are we going to do?'

Peter thought hard, but his thoughts were interrupted by some giggling that was coming from behind one of the hedges.

'Did you hear that Peter?' asked Helen, 'Listen, there it is again!'

'Peter and Helen followed the giggling to the next turning, and when they got close enough, Peter pounced and caught two pixies, one in each hand.

'I know you two!' said Peter, 'You two tried to get me and my brother to sing a certain song that would enlist us to be members of Pixity, am I right?' he asked.

The pixie in his right hand finally admitted to teaching them the song, but then started to giggle again as the pixie in Peters left hand stuck his tongue out at him.

'What a nasty pair!' said Helen, 'What do you think we should do with these two Peter? Shall we keep them here until their hour is up?'

The pixies soon changed their mood and begged for forgiveness from the large boy that held them.

'It's up to you boys!' said Peter with a sly grin. 'Take us to the gate, or hold that position until someone finds you and keeps you on their mantelpiece forever! So what is it?' he asked, and it wasn't the hardest question the pixies had to answer.

'Go straight forward!' said the first pixie.

'Then the second left!' said the other.

Soon they were all at the gate, and Peter was glad that he held an easier way of opening the gate.

'*You*' can do the honours!' said Peter to the pixies, 'And I'll let you go as soon as we're inside, I promise!'

'Very well!' sighed one of the pixies, and he whistled the tune that Peter had secretly forgotten.

The creaking of the gate seemed to be louder than ever, but the gate was now fully open and as they went through one by one, nobody was taller than anyone else, and as soon as the pixies fell out of Peters hands, they giggled and sped down the path and out of sight.

'I hope we don't bump into those two again!' said Peter, 'I don't like it when they're the same size as me!'

'I know what you mean Peter,' agreed Helen, 'but let's look for the others, they should be on their way back by now if everything has gone to plan.'

CHAPTER TWENTY TWO

The decision

No sooner than Helen had finished speaking, up the path came Jake, Jobberbob, Grumptious, Bumbad, Hipocritter and Titchietot. They walked with pride in their step as they marched towards the gate, and as they got nearer, Peter could see that Monte, Trickster and Marcus were only a short distance behind them.

'Well?' shouted Helen, 'Did it work?'

But Helen soon knew the answer to the question as Titchietot and Jobberbob lifted Jake high up onto their shoulders, and did what looked like one of Jakes tribal ritual dances.

'Jake *must* have done it Helen!' screamed Peter, 'You know what this means don't you?' he asked.

'I know, I can't believe it, I just hope that the statues that we have contain our loved ones!' but as soon as she said it, Helen realized that there was only one female among the smaller statues, and she didn't know what to say next.

'Yes, I realize that too Helen,' said Peter. 'but we still have the two larger ones outside the maze, don't we!'

'I know Peter, but we still don't know how to get them to the gate, they must weigh half a tonne each at least!'

'If it comes to that Helen, I'm sure we'll think of something!' said Peter, and he ran towards his younger brother to congratulate him on his success.

'Jake,' Peter shouted, 'well done, I knew you could do it!' he said, and Jake leapt from the top of the elders shoulders and rushed to his older brothers side.

Jake had never before felt like he did right now and he and Peter went straight over to the mound of statues that were in a dark corner next to the exit of the maze.

'When do we start?' he asked Titchietot who was close behind him.

'We have an hour at least to get the recipe ready,' he said, 'And then all we need is a clear sky and a full moon!'

Monte looked up to the sky, but all he could see were clouds, and he wondered if tonight was the night or not.

'But what if the moonlight can't get through?' asked Monte, and he also wondered if they would all have to wait for both a clear sky, and a full moon also.

'The ancients will decide dear boy!' said Jobberbob, And Monte noticed that Jobberbob didn't seem all that bothered if it was clear that night or not.

Titchietot gathered the fern and the clover off Helen, and commented on how well they had done on gathering so much. He took half of the fern and half of the clover, and then shook his head as he had forgotten one of the most important things.

'Bumbad!' he called, 'Fetch us something to mix the recipe in will you?' he asked, and Bumbad tutted a large 'Jake type tut', and turned around to start the journey back to his larder that was near half the way that it was to the forbidden zone.

'No, wait Bumbad!' shouted Peter, '*We* have one!' he said, and the elder stopped where he was.

Helen presented the large cooking pot to Bumbad, and he sighed with relief as he thought he had already done his fare share of walking that day.

'Women eh?' he smiled, 'You can't live with them, and you can't live with them!' he said, and Peter was itching to put him right on his last quote, but decided not to confuse one of the elders at this point in time as it was easier to be forgotten,

Monte in the meantime, was placing the statues in a line next to the entrance of the porthole that they all got to know as 'the gate' as Helen, Peter and Jake were going over the latest ritual song that Trickster had stolen from the mines.

'It seems pretty straight forward to me!' said Jake, 'Doesn't *seem* to be any hidden tricks or anything like that!' he said, then he tried to grab Helens attention as he wanted to discuss something with her in private, as he still wasn't as good as mathematics as she was.

Helen didn't notice Jake trying to grab her attention and carried on with what she was doing.

Although Jake's newly found intelligence was driving him crazy, as with every new dilemma they came across, he felt as if he had a hundred and one questions and answers to. But he did his best to confine his curiosity as not to embarrass his older brother Peter, who in his past, had always been the brighter one of them both.

'You know it's rude to whisper!' said Trickster for the third time since he had met the boys, but then instantly went about what he was doing before hand.

Trickster hoped that Jake had just taken his comment as a bit of fun and nothing more than serious, after all, Jake *was* 'the man of the hour!' he thought.

Titchietot stood on the highest spot of the area and he cleared his throat to grab everyone's attention.

'Er hum!' he coughed, 'May I have all of your attention please?' he said, and he waited until all who were around were facing his direction. 'We gather here to repay a deed that was so gallant, and executed in the most mature and honest way, to say an eternal thank you from the people of Pixity. Jake! Please step forward.' he said, and Jake proudly stood in front of Titchietot as if he was about to receive a knighthood. 'Jake!' said the number one, 'We thank you from the bottom of our hearts! You did as you promised and restored our fresh water to the people of this land when you could have used your gift for whatever purpose you desired.'

'You're welcome!' said Jake, but instantly wondered if he could have used the instrument to bring back their loved ones, but he still grinned from ear to ear from all the attention he was receiving.

'I number one, and numbers two to five, have decided to grant your wish to bring back the former selves of these five statues.'

'Er, no wait!' Jake interrupted, 'We have seven statues Mr Titchietot, seven!'

Titchietot lowered his head as he knew he was going to disappoint the one who they owed so much to.

'I'm so sorry Jake, we can't do anything to help the statues that are outside of this world. You see, we are sure it's only *our* moonlight along with the recipe that bears the magic combination that is needed to perform the ritual of reselfinisation!'

Jake, Peter, Helen and Monte felt as if their hearts had been torn out by a spoon again, as they all knew it was probable that the two larger statues were either the boys mother and someone else, or Helens Parents. But Jake with his new found intelligence was already concocting a plan that would wipe out that dilemma in the future.

'But what if we got the two larger statues here ourselves at a later date?' he asked.

Titchietot glanced at the other elders to see their reaction to this question, and when Bumbad and Hipocritter nodded, Bumbad said . . .

'It's because of this boy, er man,' he said, and Jake smiled harder, 'myself and Hipocritter can now go fishing in the stream again after fifty seven years!'

Then he saw that both Jobberbob and Grumptious were also nodding, and Titchietot asked for their reasons for allowing a second night of ritual.

'Sir!' said Jobberbob, 'We can all remember how we lost our fresh water all those years ago, yes?' he asked, and all the other elders remembered how hard it was to cope at first.

'Yes Jobberbob, and?' asked Titchietot.

'I think this boy, er man sorry Jake, should have what he desires! We only lost our water, which we found elsewhere! These visitors, have lost a lot more than that. Mothers, father, son and daughter in-law are what these who have helped us have lost, and I see no excuse for not granting them their every wish . . . Sir!' he said, and he turned to Grumptious for agreement.

'Here here!' is all that Grumptious said, but it was enough for Titchietot to make up his mind, and he put his arms in the air as he was about to give the decision of the council.

'Very well!' he began, 'It is now decided that we, the elders of the committee of Pixity, shall hereby grant the two nights of ritual to restore the former selves of the seven statues! Five under this moon, and the other two under the next moon, provided that the two large statues can be brought here by no later than the next moon!' he said as he looked at the visitors.

'No problem!' said Jake, and Peter especially, wondered what plan it was that Jake was thinking up to get the larger statues through the gate.

Titchietot nodded to all the elders, and as soon as they acknowledged, each one knew what they had to do. It was as if they had 'done this ritual every night,' thought Monte, and he watched as Jobberbob and Bumbad made a small fire with twigs and dried out bramble that was scattered around the area. Grumptious and Hipocritter collected the fern and clover that Helen and Peter had freshly picked from the outside world and began to mash and crush and grind the ingredients into a pulp that almost made Monte and Trickster gag because of the aroma the recipe was unleashing on all in the vicinity. And while Helen, Monte, Peter and Jake gathered around the cooking pot that was starting to gently cook the ingredients in their own juices, Titchietot took the folded pieces of paper from his pocket that held the words and the tune of the latest recipe. He stared at the words for a short time and he had a puzzled look about his face.

'Who wrote this last recipe?' he asked, and he looked at the other elders who were either shrugging their shoulders or shaking their heads. But one of them started whistling a tune that he was making up as he went along and looking in the other direction. 'Bumbad! Are these your words?' he asked, 'Very good! Up until the last verse that is!' and Bumbad was slightly embarrassed.

'Sir!' he said. 'I'm sorry about the last verse, I was running out of time!'

'Er hum!' Titchietot coughed and shook his head. 'Well I suppose they'll do for this once, but I insist on new lyrics for tomorrow night!'

'Sir!' said Bumbad.

'Er, I think not yourself this time Bumbad, um . . . Jobberbob?' he asked, 'Your task for tomorrow eh?'

'My pleasure sir!' he replied, and he gave Bumbad a look that told him he should have tried harder.

CHAPTER TWENTY THREE

Magic moonlight

Titchietot cleared his throat once more and began to read the lyrics that were on the folded piece of paper. None of the elders knew why they always had the tune written down on manuscript, as they had used the same tune since as long as they cared to remember.

Everyone who didn't have a job to do was silent and waited for Titchietot to begin, then Monte looked up to the sky and noticed that the moon was nowhere in sight. 'There's not even a break in the clouds!' he thought, and he was about to stop the proceedings when Titchietot began his chant.

'The ritual song number thirty four!' he announced.

Our moon you shine,
so clear and fine
by the clouds so soft and white.

Monte looked again at the sky above him, but there still was no sign of the Pixity moon that held the magic that was needed, but he decided to wait until Titchietot had finished the whole song as he didn't know what might happen if he interrupted.

May you hear this chant
so our wish you may grant
on this special moonlit night.

Ingredients top grade have been evenly weighed,
and mashed to the desired texture.
They're now in the pot,
and not too hot,
but waiting the required temperature.

Titchietot paused just long enough to let Grumptious and Hipocritter know that they should be prepared for the smearing of the statues, and it reminded Helen of the first time she had watched a conductor instructing his orchestra.

Monte looked up again at the Pixity sky, and to his amazement there wasn't a cloud in sight. It was as if the moon could hear the chanting and had responded by clearing the heavens to be admired. And as the number one carried on singing the chant, Grumptious tilted the pot over so Hipocritter could scoop up the mixture onto what looked like a large spatula.

Moon do your stuff, not too much, just enough
to reverse the effect of ones plight.
And as we smear
this paste with no fear,
we beg you what's changed you put right.

Hipocritter worked as fast as he could to smear the concoction over the five statues that stood in a row before him, and was glad that Peter and Jake began

242

helping by using just their hands in order to cover them before Titchietot had finished singing the last verse.

> **Give thanks to the great,**
> **for the infected shall wake**
> **from a sleep that was as cold as stone.**
> **And return to a life of trouble and strife,**
> **in a world they insist they call home.**

The foul smelling concoction covered the statues and all the visitors waited. Through the sound of their own heart beats they listened carefully, in case the stone encasements of their former selves were encased in would start to crack.

Peter and Jake regretted instantly helping the two elders to cover the statues, as no matter where they walked the stench surrounded them everywhere they went.

The elders stood where they were, and everyone else wondered how long it would take for the recipe to take effect. 'Would they all have to wait there until the morning?' wondered Helen as she searched the elders eyes for clues, but there was no hint to be shown.

Monte was about to ask what would happen next as he knew he was becoming as impatient as the others, when there was a sound that could only remind him of when he was a young man, and heard one of the first passenger jet airliners take off from the airport he had visited with his grandparents. The sound grew louder, then louder, and he didn't think the sound was ever going to stop until, as if he had taken the needle from contacting the record, the din ceased completely.

The lack of noise gave them all a fright, just as the sudden sound of a noise would do exactly the same thing, and everyone who had never experienced a ritual before were as confused as each other.

Just then Trickster smiled and pointed to the sky as the moon started to shine as bright as the sun. Everyone did their best to shield their eyes from the bright light in the sky but at the same time didn't want to miss the spectacle as the moons rays landed directly on to the statues. White at first, then pink, then red, then blue green rays came from the sky, and they all stood back a little as a faint crackling sound came from the statues.

'Is it working Trickster?' asked Jake.

'Yes Jake, well I think so, I have only ever seen this done once before!' he said without taking his eyes off the statues that were now radiating light on their own.

The brilliant moon slowly went back to its original brightness and was then covered by clouds as it had been only ten minutes ago. All eyes and ears were on the statues to see if they could yet see any change or hear anything that would tell them that the recipe had in fact worked.

Helen and her Granddad watched to see if there was any colour emerging from any of the statues, and the boys kept their eyes on the female statue in particular, and they put their hands together as if to pray and said over and over again . . .

'Please please please let it be mummy!' prayed Peter.

'Please please please let it be mam!' prayed Jake.

Then Titchietot said something that they didn't want to hear right then.

'Very good.' he said, 'And now we wait! Marcus? May we go back to your house to refresh ourselves?'

'Wait?' said Helen, 'How long? I want to be here when they awake!' she said, 'My parents could be right before my eyes and I want to be here when they finally open theirs! I'm staying!' she said, and she reminded herself of how Jake used to be before he had matured since his arrival.

'Very well Helen,' said Titchietot, 'But it can be quite some time for some to emerge, it all depends on how long they have been cast!'

'I don't care, I have to be here!' she said, and Titchietot knew he was in a losing battle.

'I'll stay with you!' said Monte.

'So will I!' said Jake.

'And me!' said Peter.

Trickster then walked over to Helen and placed his arm around her shoulder. He didn't say anything, but everyone knew that he was going to wait with them also.

'So be it!' said Titchietot, and he sat on the highest place around and got himself comfortable for what could be a very long wait.

Bumbad and Hipocritter later returned from a short walk to find more firewood to keep them warm during the night, and as they placed the dead twigs and dried out bramble onto the small fire in which they used to brew the antidote, Trickster remembered a question he had for Titchietot that he was going to ask that afternoon.

'Sir?' he asked.

'Yes old friend, what is it?'

'Why wasn't I told that after one hundred and twenty years I could leave of my own free will?' he asked, and the others were also curious.

Titchietot didn't say anything straight away, and it was number two that finally answered his question.

'Trickster dear boy.' said Jobberbob. 'Whilst trying to increase the population of Pixity, why *would* we have told you that?'

'But I asked on another two occasions, and was refused profusely!' said Trickster.

'But those two requests were too early my friend, You have never once asked since you got to the one hundred and twentieth year! If you had, we could not have lied to you. We would have granted your wish instantly!'

'But I was coming to see you all in a couple of days time to ask!' argued Trickster.

'Yes, and we would have said yes!' said Jobberbob, and Trickster just said . . .

'Oh!'

Trickster was walking around for a while dreaming about his future and to stretch his legs, and as he went by the first statue, he was sure he heard a creaking noise coming from within. He stopped, put his right hand to his right ear and formed a cup shape with his hand. 'Must have imagined it!' he thought, and was about to turn to return to the others when he heard what sounded like a plate smashing on the floor. Before he could see what it was, he heard the same again, but this time he saw where the sound had came from. Slowly but surely the outer casing of stone was falling off one of the statues, and underneath he could see flesh, flesh of a human he knew instantly, and he called for the others to join him.

Peter and Jake were there first, but were only interested in watching the only female statue there was for obvious reasons, and when that statue started to shed its outer casing of stone, Jake remembered the torch he had in his pocket. He took it out, switched it on, and shone it towards the face of the statue that he and Peter were staring at.

'No!' shouted Grumptious, and Jake got a fright as he was standing right next to number four.

Grumptious took the torch from Jake and switched it off.

'Hey you!' shouted Jake, and Grumptious gave him the torch back.

'Remember young Jake, This life has not seen the light of day for a very long time! The eyes will be very sensitive, so no torch eh?' said Grumptious and smiled at him to let him know he was not telling him off.

'Understood sir, thank you!' said Jake, and stood closer to the statue to watch the flakes of stone fall from the statues face.

Monte, Helen, Peter and Jake, stood and stared at the man that stood motionless before them, waiting to see any sign of life. There was none, but were asked to stay out of the way as Hipocritter and Bumbad lay fresh straw thickly around all the statues. They didn't have to ask why, as the first statue that was smeared with the antidote collapsed in a heap into the freshly laid straw. Nobody panicked as they realized why the straw was placed where it was, and the former self of the first statue started breathing.

Helen ran over to see if it was the statue she had earlier thought may have been her father. 'The jaw line,' she thought, 'the normal clothes!' she thought, and she stayed with the person who had just been given the gift of life once more, and wondered after all these years if she would be finally talking to her father again.

Monte rushed over and joined her, and as they both knelt down beside the first of the statues to be reborn, they saw his eyes open. The look of bewilderment in his eyes told the elders that he was definitely confused as he looked around himself, and that to them, was good news. He rubbed the back of his neck while stretching out as hard as he could, and as he tried to get up, he was quickly stopped by Titchietot as he ran over to him.

'Stay still dear boy.' he whispered, 'You're going to be fine. Just rest, and your senses will come back to you in a short while. What is your name? And do you know where you are?' he asked, and by that time, all had gathered around to hear what he had to say.

The man looked around again and was obviously confused as to why he was back inside the gate. The last thing he knew was that he was hiding so he wouldn't be spotted by a human, but as he saw everyone around him that were the same size as himself, he sighed and lay back down as he thought he hadn't been caught.

'I'm Buckranch, and I was hiding!' he said, and swallowed hard.

'What from?' asked Peter.

'Erm . . .' he tried to remember, 'I think it was a badger, or something like that!'

'And where were you hiding?' asked Jake.

'In some tall grass. I was looking for some fern for the recipe.'

'This one must be the one we found at the edge of the moors. The last one we found!' whispered Jake to Helen.

'That's what I was going to say!' said Peter, and he tutted once more.

Titchietot nodded to the other elders, and as they came closer, they got him to his feet and stood by him until he woke a little more. He was then taken to a bench nearby and Trickster sat with him.

A few minutes later, the statue that they had to balance carefully as it was in an awkward position had shed nearly all of the outer casting, and was slowly collapsing as more of the stone was falling off it. Bumbad and Hipocritter saw what was happening and they rushed to his side and gently lay him on his side.

Again, the statue who was next to be reborn started breathing, and they all rushed over to give whatever aide they could. As the man's eyes opened, he too looked around as if he didn't understand why he was where he was.

Titchietot once again approached the reborn and asked the same questions.

'Stay still dear boy,' he whispered, 'you're going to be fine. Just rest and your senses will come back to you in a short while!'

The man nodded slightly to show that he understood, and Titchietot repeated his line of questioning.

'What is your name? And do you know where you are?' he asked, but there was an interruption before the man could answer.

'Granddad, what's the matter? Are you all right?' asked Helen, and she worried more about his health as he didn't reply. His breathing was becoming faster and she checked his pulse. 'Granddad, your heart is racing, what is it?' she asked, and Monte stared at the young man that sat before him.

'Edward? Is that you?' he asked, and Helen's head spun to look at the man who was laying on his side.

The man stared into the eyes of the old man that knelt in front of him and he searched his own feelings as he knew that he knew him. From where and when he wasn't exactly sure yet, but he knew if he stared long enough, the senses he had would eventually reveal who the man was. He looked at the woman who was staring back at him, but only the likeness of his wife told him that he should know her, but as yet, nothing and no recognition came to mind.

'Ask me that again old man.' he asked, and when Helen asked him her question, two and two had became four, and he remembered that he was desperately trying to find the riddle before his time had run out.

'Daddy?' Helen smiled, and the tears fell from her eyes without the sound of crying.

'Helen?' Edward half whispered, and he looked at the old man. 'Dad?'

Monte held his arms out, and Edward still wasn't sure what had happened to him. He knew his time had run out, but he had no idea when. When he stared more at the two that sat before him, he guessed that it had been a very long time, and he threw himself towards his father and daughter.

'Am I home yet dad?' he whispered.

'No son,' he answered, 'not quite yet, but it won't be long now!' and then Edward jumped as he realized his wife was not with him. 'Winifred!' he shrieked.

'Daddy, it's ok, everything is under control, mummy will be with you soon,' said Helen, 'I hope!' she said under her breath, but her father heard what she had said.

'Hope? What do you mean hope?' said Edward, and his father had to quickly explain to stop him from panicking.

Edward sat and listened to every word his father was saying, but not all of what he was saying was being acknowledged, as his daughter now looked the same age as himself, and his father looked more like his *own* granddad that he had never seen since he was the same age as his daughter was when he last seen her.

Then Edward wept as his father explained that his grandmother had now passed on and that he was now living alone in the house that they all grew up in. He asked Helen where *she* lived now if not with her granddad, and when she told him she worked now at the old school just outside the maze, he then worked out how it came to be that they were all together again.

'But why are we still on the inside of the gate?' he asked, and as he looked around himself, he noticed that one of the people he recognised from when he first came here, was rushing towards a statue that had just collapsed into a pile of straw.

Marcus had just caught the only lady statue in time as she was about to fall hard on a rock that was not cleared like it should have been.

'Bumbad!' shouted Marcus, 'Didn't you see the rock?' he asked.

'Sorry Marcus,' he said as he dipped his head, 'It's so dark! Hipocritter missed it as well though!' he said as to suggest it wasn't his entire fault.

Marcus shook his head at Hipocritter and carried on with what he was doing.

Helen and Monte helped Edward to his feet, and they went as quick as they could to the woman who lay in the straw breathing heavily. Edward wiped away the remaining stone casing that was still covering part of her face, and when it was all gone, Helen got as close as she could and said softly in her ear . . .

'Mummy, wake up Mummy, I've found you at last.' she said, and the four were reunited once again.

Peter and Jake slowly walked over, and Helen could see that they too had been crying, as Peters eyes were all red, and Jake was quickly wiping his tears away as not to be seen. To him, being the hero of the hour and the chosen one in all the same day, showing your weaknesses, didn't go with the job title.

'Peter, Jake, I'm so sorry! I didn't think. Come here!' she said to them, and they went to her to receive a warm motherly cuddle. 'We will find your mother boys, I promise, and none of us will stop until you do ok?' she said, but Peter pulled away from the embrace he was receiving and Helen thought she had hurt him even more.

'Helen,' he said and tried to explain, 'These aren't just tears for *our* mother, these are also because it's so good to see *you* so happy! I know that Jake and myself will also feel that good when we find our own!' and he returned to her hoping to embrace again as it really *did* feel what he thought a motherly cuddle would feel like.

As Marcus and the elders were seeing to the last two reborns, Peter and Jake weren't interested to see who they were. So they sat with Monte, Helen,

Edward and Winifred, who were doing nothing much more than cuddling, crying, and staring at each other. Then Jake felt he had to interrupt as there was lots of planning to do.

'I hate to break this up,' he said in a soft tone, 'but can we get going now? There is lots to plan, and I'd like to time it so we can see dad before we return!'

Helen, no matter how hard it was to do, tried to peel herself from her mother and father, as she knew their mission was not over yet. She remembered saying to the boys only a moment ago that she had promised that they wouldn't stop until they had found their mother, and had a thought.

'I've been thinking boys.' she said, 'Now that we've found my father, the chances of getting the two larger statues to the gate has just become much easier!'

The boys knew that she was right, and Jake knew just the person to make sure they could succeed.

'I'll get dad to help!' he said and smiled, but Peter was a bit hesitant about the idea.

'I don't think we should get daddy involved Jake.' he said. 'He'll think we're all mad when we ask him!'

'Trust me Peter!' and he winked to Peter as he had a secret to tell him later on.

Peter knew that Jakes new mind wasn't going to disappoint him, so he reluctantly agreed to allow Jake to go ahead with whatever idea it was that he had.

CHAPTER TWENTY FOUR

So what happened?

Monte opened the door of his house and walked straight into the kitchen to boil the kettle. Helen guided her mother and father into the sitting room with Peter and Jake following. Edward and Winifred were still a bit slow on their feet after their long hibernation, and they walked with caution in their step. They stared at the modern furniture and gadgets around them, but were still too tired to ask all the questions that they had, then they smiled as granddad came through with a pot of tea.

'Oh, thank you dad!' said Edward, and Monte paused for a moment as he hadn't heard himself called by that name for such a long time, and he had missed it. 'Pixity tea isn't a patch on our own!' he said, and Winifred put a few more lumps of sugar in her own cup as she felt she needed more energy than ever.

'How does it taste daddy?' asked Helen, 'It's been a long time since you had a fine brew isn't it?'

'Well actually Helen,' he reminded her, 'to us it's only been a couple of days!'

Helen just smiled and nodded, as she was working out how long they had been in Pixity, and she now thought she knew what must have happened all those years ago.

'Daddy?' asked Helen, 'You must have been tricked into becoming a newcomer, am I right?' and it was her mother that answered.

'After your father and I, Helen,' she said, and she took another quick sip of her tea, 'had discovered that place, we had been introduced to some of the nicest people we had ever met. Then this one time we visited, we were taking a stroll down the side of this lovely little river we had come across, when we saw two pixies splashing about and having so much fun that we decided to join in with them. They were singing a song that I thought was so enchanting, and then both your father and myself were soon singing along with them and having a good time ourselves. When the time came to leave, we whistled the tune backwards like usual, and headed back to the guest house. Your father remembered that he had left something on the side of the river, so we headed straight back and ended up staying there over night, as we ended up meeting the one who knew granddad a long time ago!'

'Marcus!' said Peter.

'Why yes, do you know him?' asked Winifred.

'Yes,' said Jake, 'he's the one who wrote the riddles I expect you came across!'

'Yes, It was through Marcus we learned that there was a recipe to turn statues to their former selves!'

'We learned that too!' said Peter.

Monte was listening to everything that was being said, and he had a few questions of his own he was curious about.

'At what point did you realize that there was something wrong with the place?' he asked, and then it was Edward that took over from then on.

'We then met some pixie called Trickster, and he said that he recognised our names. He didn't tell us anything else, apart from that Marcus would explain everything to us if we asked. So we did.'

'And what did you learn?' asked Helen.

'He told us to leave!' said Edward plainly, and everyone apart from Edward and Winifred knew why, 'That is when we learned about having only one hour in our own world! As soon as we knew that, it was a mad rush to find the recipe he told us about. I don't remember much after that, but what I do remember, is that your mother and I became separated, and I did everything I could to get back to her.

'And you ran out of time before you found her then,' asked Jake, 'as you wouldn't have turned into a statue as you climbed up onto that shelf?' he asked, and Edward wondered how this young man knew as much as he did.

'How do you know this?' he asked in bewilderment.

'It was me that found you!' he said, and Peter's eyes widened.

No it wasn't!' he protested, 'It was me! It was me that found the statue that was trying to climb up on to the shelf!'

'Ok Peter, I'm sorry!' said Jake, and they all waited further for what Edward had to say.

Peter explained how he had spotted Edwards statue that was hanging of the side of a cellar shelf while they were exploring their new surroundings, and Edward was still trying to work out his mathematics as he still felt he had only been absent for a couple of days.

'Daddy?' asked Helen, 'I am now twenty seven! You and mummy have been gone for twenty five years!' she said, and her father gave a large sigh, as if he knew deep down what had really happened to himself and Winifred.

'Helen!' he said, 'I, and your mummy, have missed you for two days! And believe me, *that* is long enough! So please be patient, as it is hard to comprehend just now how long we have actually been away. Do you understand honey?'

And as soon as Helen heard those words, she was soon at her parents sides, trying to give all the kisses and cuddles she would have given them over the numerous amounts of years that she had missed.

Jake was still thinking hard as there were still a lot of questions whizzing around in his head, but Peter beat him to it, as his own mind was becoming once again how it was before they entered Pixity.

'Winifred?' asked Peter, 'It looked like you were about to jump off a bedside cabinet when we found you, what was going on there? It was obviously too high, you would have hurt yourself!'

'Is that where I was? I can't remember.' she said. 'All I know is that I had to find Edward! I had to find him because he knew the way through the maze.'

'Well we've found each other now Winifred, and we're never going to be apart ever again, do you hear me?' he asked as he looked into her eyes, and she smiled back at him believing every word she had just heard.

'Winifred?' asked Peter again, 'Do you happen to know who the two large statues in the garden are?'

Jake screwed his face up and folded his arms.

'That's what I was going to ask!' Jake moaned, and he gave an almighty tut.

Helen and Monte laughed as they were glad that everything was becoming as normal as it was before.

'It's nice to see you two as you were!' said Helen, and Jake nearly gave another tut, but decided not to as he would have proved them to be right.

'It's funny you should mention that!' said Winifred, and the boys attention was fixed on what she had to say. 'As we came out of the maze a short time ago, I was sure that the head was facing us, and as we passed I turned to look again, and I'm sure it was still facing me! I know it sounds silly, but it was as if the head was watching me!'

'Which one?' asked Jake.

'He means which statue!' said Peter, and he rolled his eyes at Jake.

'Oh, I see,' she giggled, 'I thought he meant which head! Erm . . . It was the lady one, why?' she asked.

Monte took over at that point as he could see that the boys were becoming agitated, and he knew they were eager to get back and find a way of getting the two larger statues to the gate.

'We have reason to believe that the female of the two statues could well be their mother!' he said, and as soon as Winifred heard the words of her father in-law, she was as anxious as Peter and Jake were to find a way of getting the statues to the entrance of Pixity.

Edward stood, slowly but adamant about doing something about it as soon as possible, as they knew how anxious *they* were to get back to their loved ones, and he insisted that there was no more time to lose.

'Our family is whole again, thanks to you two boys,' he said, 'And we have no excuse to relax until you too are reunited with your mother!'

Peter and Jake couldn't control themselves, but this time it wasn't the thought of another adventure, all they could think of was reuniting themselves with their mother, and then giving their father the biggest surprise ever. 'If father only knew what we know now!' thought Peter, as he knew that father always thought that mummy had just walked away and left them all to cope on their own without her.

'Helen,' asked her granddad, 'how long have we got before midnight in Pixity?'

Helen looked at her watch, and after doing some quick sums in her head, revealed the length of time they had to get the two statues to the entrance of the gate.

'Let me see!' she said, 'Five hours in their time is ten minutes in ours, so, we've been back an hour in our time . . . .' she guessed, 'That will still leave us . . . forty minutes, I think!' she said and smiled, but the smile didn't last long as there was so much to do in the short time that they had.

'Dad? Have you got anything with wheels that will carry something heavy?' asked Edward, and he tried to hurry his father for an answer.

'Er, wait erm, yes! I've got an old trolley that we don't use for removals any more, I knew it would come in handy!' he said, and went away instantly as to not lose any more time.

'We could still use another person to help lift these statues onto the trolley though!' said Edward as his father left the room, and Jake repeated his idea about asking their father.

'Jake!' said Peter, 'I really don't think we should let father know what we're doing! It might build his hopes up, as well as our own by the way about finding mummy!'

'Like I said Peter, we'll just go straight up and ask him!'

When Jake used them words for the second time, he remembered when he was told about how they got the new recipe from the mines, and he wondered at which point Jake was going to use the same potion on their own father, and did it work in this land?

Monte shouted from the front of his house for the others to hurry, and as they all went outside, Monte was standing there with the trolley in question reminding them all about the lack of time.

He had it all planned. Helen and Peter were to look for more fern and clover and meet them in twenty five minutes at the statues, and Jake was to go and 'ask' his father to help. Edward and Winifred were to accompany the trolley and himself to the entrance of the maze and wait for everything needed for the ritual that night.

'Come on, we all know our tasks, lets get with it!'

And as soon as they heard the words, they all split to the direction of their task.

CHAPTER TWENTY FIVE

The final mission

As Jake ran around the final bend in their new driveway he was relieved to see that his fathers car was parked up outside the old oak door. He wondered how he was going to do what he intended to do, and he tried his best to think back about how Trickster told him how he did it.

The door wasn't unlocked so he walked straight in.

'Dad?' he shouted, 'Dad, it's me! where are you?' he asked, but there was no answer.

Jake walked to the kitchen, and was surprised to see his father listening to a personal cassette player and dancing about as if he was in the best mood ever.

'At least he's in a good mood!' Jake thought, and he approached his father whilst trying not to give him a fright.

He tugged at his fathers sweater and waited for him to turn, and when he did, His father dropped the omelette that he was frying onto the floor that he was about to flip over.

'Jake! You gave me such a fright!' he said, and he bent down to pick up the snack that was now destined for the waste bin. 'Are you on your own? Where are Peter and Helen?' he asked, and he picked up a packet of crisps he was saving for afters.

'Hi dad by the way, they're just around the back, I'm sorry I gave you a fright!'

'It's ok son, I got back a bit early and thought I'd make myself a snack to save Helen the bother. Busy Day?' he asked, and Jake thought, 'I'll say!'

'They're around the back exploring, and I just needed a glass of water.' was the only thing that came into his head.

'Oh, well help yourself Jake, here's a glass.'

Jake knew that their time was running out, and he seized the moment to put his plan into action.

'Dad?' he asked, 'This glass is chipped, look!' he said, and his father bent over to study the glass he had just given Jake.

Jake grabbed a handful of the crushed Forgetmewil that he had been working on from his pocket and he timed it for when his father was breathing in, then he blew the dust from his hand into the face of the last person in the world he would want to trick.

Brian sneezed as the dust entered his sinus and he was about to ask Jake what he thought he was up to, when he stood straight, stared straight ahead and said nothing.

'That was easy enough!' thought Jake, and he instructed his father on what he was do do next.

'Yes!' his father simply said, and it wasn't long before Jake and his father were standing at the rear of the house waiting for Helen and Peter to join them.

As Jake and his father sat next to the two large statues, Jake reached up to touch the hand of the statue that he was now convinced was his mother, and he talked quietly to her. He explained to her that she had nothing to worry about, and that they would all be together as a whole family again.

Just then, Jake saw Monte, Edward and Winifred come around the side of the house with the trolley, and he wondered where Helen and Peter were.

'Is Helen and Peter not with you?' he asked.

'No!' shouted Monte, 'They'll be here soon, don't you worry!' and right on queue, Peter and Helen came running around the corner with bags full of the fern that they needed.

'Ah good,' said Monte, 'you found lots I see!'

'Yes,' said Peter, 'we thought we'd better get as much as we could find as these statues are much bigger than the others!'

'Good thinking!' said Jake, then he noticed Peter staring at him with a cross expression, and Jake knew why.

'You used the powder on daddy?' he said in horror.

'Yes, I had to! How else are we to get the statues to the gate?' said Jake in his own defence.

'He's right Peter,' said Monte, 'my old legs can't help much these days, and I expect they will weigh quite a bit!'

'I suppose so,' admitted Peter, 'but I hope he's going to be all right Jake, and not end up like that guard!'

Jakes head lowered as he forgot about the guard, and he quickly changed the subject by asking his father to help them get the statues onto the trolley.

Edward and Brian stood either side of the female statue first and they gently tilted her over while Monte placed the trolley directly in front.

'Easy does it.' said Edward as they laid the statue on her back, and without resting, went straight to the other as there was no time to lose.

'Wait!' shouted Peter, and they all wondered what they had forgotten.

'What is it Peter?' asked Jake.

'The clover!' he said, and they quickly gathered as much as they could.

With the two statues safely tied to Monte's trolley, they slowly started to head towards the gate. Everyone helped to push the heavily weighed down trolley with its precious cargo and they all sighed with relief as they had finally made it to the little green gate.

Peter whistled the tune that was now permanently in his memory, and as the creaking sound began, Titchietot was already there, urging them to hurry as in their land it was nearing midnight. But then he looked closely at the two large statues that were lying on their backs on the trolley.

'What's wrong sir?' asked Trickster who was directly behind him, and he looked to see what it was that Titchietot was staring at, and then he saw who it was.

'Do you recognise him Trickster?' asked Titchietot.

'I'll say I do sir!' he snarled, 'That is the person, er vermin,' he said as Titchietot was looking at him, 'who changed our fresh water into salt water!'

'Correct!' said Titchietot. 'Now this *does* cause problems!'

'Problems?' asked Helen, 'What do you mean? We *are* still going ahead with the ritual aren't we?' she panicked.

'We honour our promise miss,' said Titchietot, 'but we totally and utterly refuse to help the male of these two. He is trouble of the worst kind, and we must insist that you to keep him as an ornament in the school's gardens!'

'Very well,' said Monte, 'now can we hurry and get the woman through the gate?'

'Certainly Monte,' said Titchietot, and he helped as much as he could.

Bumbad and Hipocritter were already getting started on the fire while Grumptious and Jobberbob were placing the fern and clover into the large cooking pot. Peter and Jake were helping by laying lots of clean straw around what they hoped would soon be their mother. Monte once again looked to the skies and all he could see were clouds, but this didn't worry him as he remembered how the moon cleared the skies the night before.

Then once again, Titchietot stood on the highest ground in the area and pulled out the new song that Jobberbob had quickly written for the occasion.

'The ritual song number thirty five!'

he announced, and he secretly kept his fingers crossed behind his back hoping it wasn't as silly as the last verse he had read out.

Our moon we invite on this glorious night
to hear our song once again.
To help these young men
who are still only ten,
cast off their suffering and pain.

Peter and Jake were just about to burst when Jobberbob got their age wrong, but Helen quickly hushed them by giving them a hard look.

> *To help us once more is all we ask for,*
> *so our friends once again can smile.*
> *A daughter a mother,*
> *are like no other,*
> *that can make ones life so worthwhile.*

Titchietot wiped away a tear as he nodded to Grumptious and Jobberbob to start spreading the mixture over the statue, and he remembered his own mother who he had missed deeply since she sadly passed on before he discovered the land that could have saved her. He cleared his throat, then tried his best to carry on with the ritual song.

Helen and Monte also hurt as they listened carefully to the words that were being spoken, and although Brian was present, being under the spell of Forgetmewil meant that all *he* was waiting for was his next instruction.

'Er hum.' Titchietot coughed and then swallowed hard . . .

> *As we begin to smear this thin veneer,*
> *upon the one who's been cast.*
> *Please send us your rays*
> *to end the days*
> *of this mothers dilemma at last.*

Just like the last time, the colourful rays shone down upon the statue, and they all marvelled at the array of soft colours that covered the statue. The light started to come from the statue as they had seen before, and the boys went over to watch for signs of bits falling off.

The light was still radiating from the statue, and still nothing else was happening, but Titchietot carried on with the last verse all the same.

We again say please to put them at ease,
and a family can again be united.
To be away for so long
is definitely wrong,
and your subjects would be so delighted.

Titchietot stopped and was about to fold the piece of paper up, when Jobberbob urged him to carry on.

'Sir! sir!' he whispered loudly, and Titchietot wondered what he wanted. 'There's more sir!' he said, 'I wrote one last verse as an extra plea!' he said, and Titchietot noticed that at the bottom of the sheet of paper was written P.T.O. and he tutted whilst rolling his eyes at him.

Once again Titchietot stood and read the final verse on the reverse of the sheet of paper.

'Er hum,' he coughed again to grab everyone's attention.

To beg once more would be hard to ignore,
but we must admit to being adamant.
These boys taught us trust,
an ingredient that's a must,
to ensure our way, that's important.

As Titchietot sang the last verse, The moon shone as brightly as the last time, and everyone thought that the last verse must have been the one that had done the trick.

As the rays beamed clearer, and the statue shone brighter, they all gathered and waited for the outer casing to start to fall off, but it didn't.

Peter looked at Jake, and Jake looked at Helen, but no-one knew what to say. They all looked at Titchietot who was looking at the rest of the elders, but still no-one had an explanation for what was happening, or for a lack of what was happening.

The elders gathered away from the visitors, and they discussed and mumbled at a volume to which only *they* could hear, The others wanted to know what was going on, and Jake even thought of reminding them that it was rude to whisper, when Titchietot finally returned to them.

'There is good news, and bad news!' he said, and this time Jake didn't want to hear any bad news so he kept quiet and listened carefully. 'The good news,' Titchietot carried on, 'Is that we can still do this!' and there was such a big sigh of relief, until they heard the bad news.

'What is it?' asked Monte, and Titchietot tried to find the right way of saying what he had to say.

'There is only *one* other way we can do this!' he said seriously, 'But it comes at a price!'

Monte thought he knew what the price was, and when he remembered there was no such thing as money in Pixity, he was then sure that his thoughts were correct.

Titchietot shook his head, as this wasn't how he wanted to repay the deed, but from all of the experience that he had in that land, he knew that there really was only one other way, and he asked the visitors one more thing.

'Peter, Jake, Helen, Monte, and the two reborns,' he said as he couldn't remember their names, Please return to your homeland for now.' he said, and the boys burst into tears as the thought of not seeing their mother that night was more heartbreaking than it would have been to lose her in the first place they thought, and they were quickly comforted by Helen and Winifred.

'Please,' said Monte, 'Lets do as they ask and I promise we'll return in the morning. Nobody has slept properly for days, and I'm sure we can all think more clearly on fresh minds.'

Reluctantly they all agreed, and they headed for the boys new home as it was the only place big enough for them all to sit, think, and rest until the morning.

As Helen opened the front door, Jake suddenly had the best idea, and he asked Edward to help him take father up the stairs to his study.

'Of course Jake, but why?' he asked.

'Because he is still under the influence of Forgetmewil, and I haven't got a clue to how long it's going to last in our world!' he explained, and Edward caught on straight away.

Jake and Edward put Brian in his armchair that was next to the old gramophone and Jake placed the headphones around his neck.

'I see what you're doing Jake,' said Edward, 'but for added effect!' he said, and Jake didn't know what he had meant, until he saw Edward empty the last drops of whiskey from one of the bottles that Brian had found in the cellar and place it on the cabinet next to the chair.

Jake smiled and he got hold of an empty glass, then placed it in the grip of his fathers hand who was about to be duped beyond belief, and they both joined the others who were gathered around the kitchen table.

They talked and talked until they could talk no more, and Peter was the first to fall asleep while sitting on Helens knee.

Monte got out of his chair as he decided that 'a bit of fresh air is what he needed right then', then he told everyone he'd see them soon and headed for the door.

Jake announced that he was going to bed and he asked Helen to tuck him in, so Helen stood whilst trying not to wake Peter and followed Jake up the stairs to their bedroom. She placed Peter in his own room, then through the adjoining door to Jakes room she went to tuck Jake in. She sat on the bottom of the bed, and she could tell that she wouldn't have to stay there long as Jakes eyes were already half closed.

'Helen?' Jake asked, 'Do you think we'll ever see our mother?'

Helen didn't quite know what to say as she didn't want to build their hopes up any more than she had already, and she regretted telling them anything in the first place.

'I don't know Jake,' she said, 'I really don't know.'

'Oh,' Jake said softly, and then he yawned. 'Goodnight Helen.'

'Goodnight Jake.' said Helen.

Before going back down to the kitchen, Helen popped her head around Peters door to check he was ok. He was snoring loudly, and soon so was Jake. She smiled at the two boys and closed the door.

Edward and Winifred were standing next to the table enjoying a warm cuddle when Helen entered, and she still found it hard to believe that these two people were in fact her parents that she had searched for for most of her life. She watched them for a moment or two before they noticed she had returned, and they both stood with their arms out for her to join them.

'Mummy? Daddy?' Is it really you?' she asked, even though she knew it *was* them.

'Helen my sweet,' said her father. 'You've turned out exactly as your mother and I expected. You're beautiful, and intelligent and . . .'

'Please daddy,' Helen blushed, 'you're embarrassing me!' and she couldn't hide her smile.

'Helen, my Beautiful daughter,' said her mother. 'Come, hold me close.' she said, and held her arms out even more.

Helen ran to their side, and the three of them held each other tight. The tears were falling and they didn't want to let go in case all of this had just been a dream.

'Why don't you both try to sleep, I'll give you my room. Come,' she said, and she took them both by the hand and led them up the stairs to the room she had only used a few times herself.

Helen sat by the bed that her mother and father were lying together in, and she stayed there until they were fast asleep, and as she crept out of the room, she looked into Brian's study to see if he was ok. He was still sat in his chair with the empty glass in his hand, and she didn't know if that was good or bad. 'Is he still asleep? Or had he woke and finished the bottle?'

she thought, and decided to leave him there until the morning when they had all rested properly.

Helen sat in the living room with the television switched on but with the volume down, as she was waiting for her granddad to return from his walk. But the last twenty four hours for her had felt like seventy two, and she could no longer stay awake for his return.

CHAPTER TWENTY SIX

Tricksters return

Helen jumped as she thought she had heard something, and she glanced at the old clock on the wall of the living room. It read twelve twenty five, and at first she thought that they had all overslept, but when she saw that the only light in the room was coming from the television set, she knew that she had only been asleep for a few hours. She sat silent and listened harder to see if the sound would repeat, and after a few seconds the front door bell rang twice in a row.

'That can't be the door bell at this time of night!' she thought, but still she had to get out of her chair and go to check, and as she passed the bottom of the stairs in the hallway, she was greeted by both Peter and Jake who were rubbing the sleep from their eyes.

Helen looked puzzlingly at the boys and she asked them who it could have been at this hour.

'Search me!' said Peter, and Jake just shrugged his shoulders.

Helen approached the front door and before opening it, she realized that she had forgotten that granddad was out for a walk. But she remembered that she had left the door unlocked so that he could let himself back in, and that it had been far too long since granddad had been gone anyway, so she knelt on one knee and

275

opened the letter box. There was a man standing there and he had a huge grin on his face. Helen thought she recognised him but it didn't come to her immediately to who it was.

'Who is it?' she asked.

'It is I Helen,' he said, and when Helen heard the voice she realized that she knew the face that went with it.

Helen opened the door, and she was amazed at what she saw. She invited Trickster in and closed the door behind him.

'Trickster, what are you doing here?' she asked, and before he could answer, she had another question for him. 'How long have you got left? I mean, you might turn into stone like the others if you are not care . . .'

'Fear not Helen!' a tall Trickster interrupted, 'For I have all the time in the world! And Yes, I mean this world!' he said with a smug look about him.

At first, Helen didn't know what he had meant, but the boys did!

'Do you mean . . . . you are free?' asked Jake.

Trickster said nothing at first, then Peter with *his* newly found knowledge said . . .

'You are aren't you? You've done your time of one hundred and twenty years, and they've let you go!' said Peter smiling as he knew he was right.

'Why yes Jake.' he said. 'You're a smart young man!' and Peter shook his head and never said anything while Jake held his laughter in.

Jake knew that the time had returned that when Peter was once again the smarter of them both, and he didn't know if he was jealous, or relieved that the pressures of being the smarter one of the two had gone, but there were more important things to think about he thought, and he followed Helen, Trickster and Peter into the kitchen.

The kettle was once again put on to boil, and Trickster was being bombarded with questions. He didn't mind, as being outside the confinement of Pixity without having to worry about how long he had was the best feeling he had had in many a year. Then Helen remembered something she had wanted to ask

'Trickster?' she asked.

'Yes Helen?' he asked.

'Did you have any relatives in Little Thornton when you enlisted in Pixity?'

Trickster understood the question, but there was something wrong with what she asked.

'First of all Helen,' he said, 'I too was tricked into saying the vows, I never left this world deliberately!' he said, and the others noticed how serious he was becoming. 'I would never have left of my own accord, because of my two nephews!'

'Your two nephews?' asked the boys at the same time.

'Yes,' he carried on, 'my brother, at the time was a widower, and after he passed on also, I took it upon myself to raise the boys myself as well as I could!'

'So where are they now?' asked Jake.

'Oh, they'll have been gone for years now Peter, don't forget that I am in my one hundred and fifty second year now!' he said and giggled a little to hide his embarrassment.

'Is that in our years, or in Pixity years?' asked Peter, and Jake remembered that question being one of the questions he also wanted the answer to while he had his new found intelligence.

'Only Pixiborns count their years in Pixity time, but us newcomers still measure their years in the land that they were born, so yes, I am one hundred and fifty two in your years!'

'But Trickster,' said Helen. all I need to know is your full name and birthday, and we can find out what has happened to your family since you've been gone by the click of a mouse!'

'My my,' said Trickster, 'There are some funny sayings in the world today!'

And Helen forgot that she was talking to a man that didn't know about all of the fancy gadgets that were around today.

'I'm sorry, I forget.' she said. 'What is your real name Trickster?'

Trickster didn't want to reveal his true name at first as he never did like it very much, but did so in the end as he really wanted to know if there *were* any relatives he might want to see.

'My name is . . . Bartholomew . . . Winston . . . Brannigan!' he said, and he noticed the looks on the others faces. 'What?' he asked.

'Nothing, nothing,' said Jake, it's just, Monty and Marcus knew a Brannigan once!'

'Did they?' he asked, 'But they never said.'

'Well they wouldn't have Trickster, unless you told them your real name at any point.' said Helen, and she wondered if they really could have been related at all.

'No,' said Trickster, 'I don't suppose I ever did!'

'So what do we call you now? I'm used to calling you Trickster!' said Jake.

'Trickster will do fine everyone!' he said as he was so used to being called that for the last one hundred and twenty years.

They chatted for almost an hour when Helen realized that she had forgotten all about her granddad. Earlier she assumed he had went home to rest, but with everything that was going on she had forgot to check, and she stood as she had the most awful feeling.

'Helen, what is it?' asked Peter.

'Are you alright Helen?' asked Jake.

'Granddad!' she whispered, and as Peter and Jake jumped up to go looking, Trickster slapped his own forehead with the palm of his hand, and the others stared at him.

'I almost forgot Helen!' he said. 'As I was leaving the maze, Monte was on his way in!'

'What?' Helen shrieked. 'Why?'

'He said he had something to sort out and that he would see you all soon. He told me to tell you not to worry about him, then he continued to enter the maze! I'm sorry I forgot, I'm just so happy to be out.'

'Something to sort out? What?' asked a now concerned Helen.

'I don't know, but I don't mind telling you, he didn't look too well!'

Helen slumped back into her chair and tried to be calm, but it was no good as her granddad was the only family she had known up until now, and after talking more with Trickster she decided that to go into the maze tonight would be pointless.

Helen left the front door unlocked for granddad to return as herself and the boys tried to rest. Peter and Jake returned to their rooms and the sound of snoring soon filled the upstairs hallway once more. Trickster lay down in the living room next to where Helen was, and although everyone else had fallen asleep, Trickster kept an ear open for the front door opening

CHAPTER TWENTY SEVEN

It's for the best

Brian tried hard to get up from the awkward position he had found himself in, and he ached from his head to his toes. He tried to stretch but it hurt too much, and as his eyes began to focus, he noticed the empty bottle of old single malt on the table next to him and the empty glass in his right hand.

'Oh my head!' he said to himself as he did his best to sit up straight, but the headphone lead was stretched around his neck and pulling him backwards.

He tried to remember what it was he was doing last, but his heartbeat was so loud inside his brain that it overpowered his concentration, so he took the headphones off and tried to stand. 'I can't remember drinking all of that last night' he thought, and he made his way along the landing to the top of the stairs.

Brian concentrated harder so he could make his way to the kitchen for a drink, as his balance wasn't at all that good, and he slowly started to descend the staircase one step at a time. 'There, made it!' he thought, and he rushed to the kitchen to quench a thirst he had never experienced before.

The kitchen light was on and he assumed it was himself that had left it that way, but somehow he knew it wasn't the old malt that had made him feel as he did.

He walked over to the sink and took a glass from the draining board. He let the cold water run for a short time until it was icy cold, then he filled the glass to the brim.

A drink of water had 'never tasted so good,' he thought and he went to sit at the kitchen table.

As he sat there trying to remember the night before, he heard footsteps from the hallway. He turned expecting to see Helen, Peter or Jake, but was shocked to see who it was.

'Who are you?' he asked as he squinted his eyes, but as that person got nearer, he realized who it was.

'Hello,' said the late visitor.

'You?' said Brian, and he had to look closer. 'You are the removal man we hired when we moved in! What are you doing here at this late hour? And how did you get in?'

'I'm sorry sir,' said Monte, 'I don't have much time to explain, so please listen carefully!' and he sat on the opposite side of the table to Brian.

Brian was confused to why he was sitting at the kitchen table at a silly hour with someone he had only seen once before, and he put it down to the age old drink that he was never going to sample ever again.

'Well, go on then,' said Brian, 'I'm dying to hear this!' he said, and gave a false laugh to show this old man that he already thought that what he was about to say was a load of old rubbish, but before Monte could explain, another joined them at the table.

'Granddad?' asked a tearful Helen, 'What exactly did you mean by 'I haven't got much time?'

Brian looked at the old man, then at Helen, and back at the old man.

'Granddad?' asked Brian, and he tried to stand as quick as he could without giving himself an even worse headache. 'Now what's going on?' he asked in a stern voice, 'First of all, you,' he said and looked at Monte, 'were trying to tell my boys a load of nonsense about a magical place, and then trying to scare them about this place being some sort of a school for naughty children, and you're trying to tell me that it's just a coincidence that you, Helen, just happen to apply for the job here? Now what is going on?' he asked, and he wouldn't sit down until he had an explanation.

'I'm sorry Brian,' pleaded Helen, 'but we'll come back to that I promise!' and then her attentions were directed at her granddad once again.

Brian was stunned by what he had just said was being ignored, but he listened to what Helen and her granddad had to say, as it must have been very important for Helen to ignore him like that.

'Granddad?' she asked, 'Why?'

Monte knew that his granddaughter knew that he had taken the vows, so he did his best to explain in the short time he had left.

'Helen, I've been ill for a long time now, but I've never had the courage to tell you.'

'Ill? What do you mean granddad? I can take care of you, there was no need to go and do that!' she said, and she couldn't stop her emotions.

'I would have loved that Helen, you know I would. But I only had a short time left!'

Helen was putting one and one together, and she didn't interrupt her granddad again.

'You have just found your mother and father Helen, and I've just found my son and daughter in-law. I want

283

to get to know them again, can you understand that?' he asked and smiled.

Helen slowly nodded as she began to realize that he probably *was* doing the right thing, even if it did mean that they could only visit him in Pixity.

'So are you alright now?' she asked through the tears.

'Yes Helen!' he simply said and he went to her to comfort her.

'Er, excuse me!' said an agitated Brian, 'Does anyone mind explaining all this to *me*?' and both Monte and Helen tried to tell the story as thorough and simple as they possibly could.

Brian listened carefully, but most of what he had heard he dismissed as it all seemed 'too ridiculous' he thought, but some of what he had heard, gave him lots of thought about what had happened when he and his wife spent time there nearly nine years ago. 'Is that where Olivia had gone missing?' he thought, and as his mind raced, he could think of another twenty questions for Monte and Helen, but Helen jumped as she had an important question for her granddad.

'Granddad?' she asked.

'Yes dear, what is it?'

'How much time do you have left?'

Monte shouted . . . 'I'll see you all soon, I promise!' and he ran like he used to as a teenager down the hallway and out the front door.

Brian sat shaking his head trying to take it all in, and his mind was only on one thing.

'Is Olivia there?' he asked softly through glazed eyes.

Helen really didn't know what to say. They hadn't told Brian about the part when the ritual hadn't worked with the larger statue, and neither did she tell him about the one other way they could have made it work.

Then Helen stopped everything she was doing, she even stopped breathing as she realized that being ill wasn't the only reason why her granddad did what he did.

'Are you ok?' asked Brian.

'Yes, I'm ok.' Helen smiled, 'And so will you be!' she thought.

CHAPTER TWENTY EIGHT

The truth is out

Brian couldn't rest at all as the nights findings kept his mind working overtime, and he went over all the things he had heard over and over again to see if he could make any loose ends meet.

'If this Monte chap is Helens Grandfather, then Helen must have known about this place in the maze too,' he thought, 'and that is why Helen must have applied for the nanny job. She must have thought there would be clues inside this place, and never before been able to search thoroughly like she can now!' he concluded. 'Helen has found her parents, Monte has found his son, and they were supposedly in this magical land within the maze. So, is Olivia still in that land they say is real?' and as soon as he thought that, Brian was thinking of a way to get to this land and search for the love he had lost over ten years ago.

The prospect of being a proper family again after so long wasn't the only reason Brian was full of joy, it also meant to him that Olivia *didn't* leave him for anyone else, and it was just a simple case of her being tricked into staying somewhere where she didn't want to stay. 'But if they are able to leave for an hour at a time,' he thought, 'then why didn't she at least try to let me know?'

Brian boiled the kettle for the third time that night and he sat at the kitchen table with a coffee and a slice of toast. He heard a thunderous roar coming down the stairs and he knew there was a race on.

'I won!' said Jake as he did his victory ritual dance.

'Hello boys!' said their father, 'What are you two doing up? It's four o'clock in the morning!'

'We couldn't sleep daddy!' said Peter breathing heavily.

'Why are *you* up this early as well dad?' asked Jake, and he hoped that he couldn't remember the concoction he had blew into his fathers face the day before.

'I think you know why, don't you boys?' he said, and Jake thought he was about to receive the biggest telling off he had ever had.

'Know what daddy?' asked Peter, and wondered what it was that daddy had found out.

'How is Trickster these days?' asked their father, and Peter and Jake were shocked at what they heard their father ask. 'You've been busy I hear.' he said, and still Peter and Jake were at a loss for words.

Just then, Helen entered the kitchen and she put her arms around the boys shoulders.

'It's ok boys,' she whispered, 'Your father knows everything, there's nothing to fear.'

Peter and Jake ran to their father and flung their arms around him. They were so glad there was to be no more secrecy and that they could finally talk to *him* too about the land they had visited.

'It's alright boys, everything going to be alright.' he said, but Jake had something to say.

'But it's not going to be alright dad!' he said in one of his bad moods.

'Why Jake, what's the matter?' and Helen hoped he wasn't going to tell him about the ritual not working with the larger statue.

'We still couldn't bring mother home though!' he said and started to sniffle.

'We'll find her son, I promise!' he said.

'Does that mean you are coming with us to Pixity daddy?' asked an excited Peter, but before he had a chance to answer, they heard someone close the front door and walk into the house.

'Granddad!' said Helen and she raced to the bottom of the staircase.

'I quite like that old man now!' said father, 'He has given us all new hope of finding mummy!'

'I know daddy,' said Peter, 'But what do you mean 'like him now'? Does that mean you've seen him recently?'

'Yes,' he said, and the boys wondered how recent it was. 'Monte paid us a visit earlier, but he couldn't stay for long as he had to get back to Pixity.'

'What do you mean by 'back to Pixity' dad?' asked Jake, and he was now as confused as ever.

'He said he didn't have much time left and he ran out the house as if he was in his twenties again.

Peter knew what Monte must have done, and thought, *'That* must have been what Titchietot meant by there is another way, but it comes at a price!' But then Helen came back to the kitchen and stood in the doorway.

'Where's Monte?' asked Brian.

'It wasn't him.' she answered, and she pretended to be sad.

'Then who was it?' asked Jake.

Helen smiled at them all and moved to the side. They all could see that there *was* someone at the door as this person emerged from behind Helen, and only one of them recognised who it was immediately.

'Peter? Jake?' she asked, and then she looked at their father. 'Brian?'

Brian stood with his mouth open and a tear fell from the corned of his eye and dripped down his whitened cheek onto the floor.

'Olivia?'

Epilogue

Six months later

Despite the boys mother returning, Helen was kept on as their nanny. Not just because she played a major role in bringing their family back together and that they now lived in a larger house, but Olivia had took a long time to come to terms with losing ten years of her life, and had become dependant on Helen with her everyday chores. Besides that, Peter and Jake wouldn't allow her to leave, much to the liking of Brian who thought of Helen now as a member of their own family.

Monte was now enjoying his health and living in a tiny little cottage on the outskirts of Pixity. He worked for their postal service which kept him not too busy, but busy enough for him to feel needed by the community in which he now resided. He looked forward to the visits from Edward, Winifred, Helen and the boys every five weeks, and wished it had been more often, but with the time difference between their two worlds, he didn't expect to see them more often than that as after all, one week in 'the real world' was more than a whole month in Pixity.

Edward and Winifred now lived in Monte's old house and at first, Peter and Jake would visit to show them how to use the likes of the microwave, the modern TV, the modern Hi-Fi, and other things like mobile phones and computers. Edward had taken over his fathers old job at the removal firm, while Winifred found herself some work in the kitchens at the boys new school. They didn't make a fortune, but they earned enough to get by in the modern world that they now lived in.

Trickster spent most of his time at Peter and Jakes house as he was researching his family history back to when he had left one hundred and twenty years ago, and most nights he would end up staying there as looking up his family tree wasn't the only thing he found interesting. Just the fact that he was watching moving pictures as clear as reality was enough for him to become addicted to the machine, and he used it to learn about all the new ways of his now modern life.

Unlike the others, Trickster did his own thing on the days that the others visited his old land, and he liked to sit in the garden with a book to read and a Thermos flask filled with the taste of the tea that he had truly missed. He didn't want to remember that place, not because he didn't have any good memories about the place, but because he could now enjoy growing old and not have to check his timepiece every five minutes.

Even Marcus visited Trickster every now and then, but those times were times when Trickster had to venture into the maze to the clearing in the center in order to give himself and Marcus maximum time, and Trickster hated the fact that he had to exit the maze on his own sometimes. He would walk with a quickened pace back to the entrance in case he heard giggling, or the route would change before he had got out, but that never did happen. It was as if those that resided within were leaving him alone, for whatever purpose he didn't know but he was grateful.

Trickster was sitting in the garden one day when the others were going about their daily routine, when he heard a commotion going on at the front of the house.

Trickster finished what was left of his tea and headed to where the sound of the commotion was coming from, and as he turned the last corner, he saw that there was a post van parked outside the door. As he walked to the door, he noticed Olivia, Peter and Helen jumping about excitedly.

'What's all this about?' he asked, but no-one answered him and he tried to see what it was the postman had delivered.

From the back of the van came a large parcel, and the postman struggled to get it into the house. Then Trickster heard Olivia shouting.

'Darling! Darling it's arrived!'

'What's arrived?' thought Trickster as he joined them in the house.

Brian came running down the stairs with a smile on his face and he took a small penknife from his pocket and carefully cut along the seams of the large cardboard box. He opened it carefully, put his hand inside and pulled out a book.

'A book?' thought Trickster, 'What's so special about that?' he wondered, but when the book came out into full view, Trickster then knew what all the fuss was about.

The book was Brian's first story book about a land called Pixity, and it had a picture on the front of it that Trickster recognised instantly.

'That's me!' shouted Trickster, and he insisted on being one of the first to hold it. He read the title and was all overcome with emotion. 'Beyond the maze, by Brian Stokes'.

'Surprise!' sang Brian to Trickster, as he had never told of his intentions to immortalise him in a story book, and the newest ex Pixity inhabitant was so overjoyed that he took the book and headed for his seat in the garden to read it from start to finish.

'Er, not so fast Trickster!' shouted Jake who was running down the stairs, and Trickster stopped. He kept forgetting that money was used in his new world and he immediately apologised. He put his hand in his pocket and searched for some change when Jake stopped him again.

'It's not about money, silly!' he said, and Trickster wondered if he had done something wrong.

'Then what is it Peter?' he asked, and Jake gave the largest tut he could do.

'It's Jake! But anyway,' he continued, 'I've found a relative of yours!'

'A relative?' asked Trickster, and it made him completely forget about the book. 'What's this persons name?' he asked with all of his attention.

Jake looked at Peter to see his reaction when he would announce the name that he knew he would recognise, and Jake cleared his throat. 'His name is . . .'

'His?' asked Trickster.

'Yes, *his* name is . . . Brandon Bartholomew Brannigan!'

Trickster smiled uncontrollably as he thought that with this person having an almost identical name, *must* be a relative of his, and he was eager to hear more.

'Wait wait Trickster, don't be too overjoyed!' said Jake, and both Peter and Helen thought they knew why.

'Your name is Brannigan, right?'

'Er . . . Yes, why?' asked a nervous Trickster.

'Well, er . . . He was the certain father of a Brannigan that Marcus and Monte had the 'not so pleasurable' experience of knowing during their stay here some summers ago,'

'Ok.' said Trickster softly as he had the feeling that what was about to come out was probably going to shock him.

'Well it turns out Trickster, that this Brannigan, the father that is, is the one you turned away at the gate, and we all know why and where he is. Don't we?'

'Oh dear!' Trickster simply said.

'Dare I ask you all for one final mission?' he asked.

The end.